SAPPHIC INK

TATTOOED BRIDE

TESS SHELLEY

FOREWORD

In the enchanting pages of "Sapphic Ink," a small town WLW romance that will steal your heart, Celine embarks on a courageous quest to chase her dreams. But when fate reunites her with a love she never expected, their conflicting ambitions threaten to tear them apart. Can they find a way to harmonize their lesbian passions and create a future that fulfills their deepest longings? Discover a tale of boundless love and transformative self-discovery. Prepare to be captivated as tattoo artist femme Celine, and cinnamon roll butch Jemima, embark on an extraordinary adventure where the beauty of their shared ff love unfolds in ways beyond imagination. Get ready to fall in love.

Sometimes, sweet, sometimes spicy, Tess Shelley invites you to experience the heartfelt joy of small-town romance and sapphic love. Set against charming backdrops, her lesbian stories where women love women will capture your heart and transport you to worlds where love knows no bounds. Join her endearing characters as they navigate the delicate dance of compromise and self discovery.

With a skillful blend of passion, emotion, and heartfelt storytelling, Tess Shelley takes readers on extraordinary journeys of love and personal growth. From the sweetness of small-town romances to the triumph of love against the odds, her narratives leave a lasting impression, leaving you eagerly turning each page.

CHAPTER 1

*C*eline Montgomery was the embodiment of artistic passion, her striking features amplified by the intensity that shone in her eyes. In her late 20s, she had made a name for herself as one of the city's most sought-after tattoo artists. Her blonde hair was often pulled back into a messy bun, revealing the delicate curve of her neck adorned with an intricate ink design – a testimony to her own skills. Celine's smile had the power to light up a room, but it was her unwavering dedication to her art that truly set her apart.

The tattoo parlor buzzed with life, both metaphorically and literally. The hum of tattoo machines melded with the murmur of voices, creating a symphony of creative energy. The scent of ink filled the air, mingling with the more subtle notes of disinfectant, reminding visitors of the sterile environment beneath the parlor's edgy exterior.

"Hey Celine, you've got a walk-in," a voice called out from the front desk. She glanced up from her workspace, brushing a stray lock of hair behind her ear.

"Thanks, I'll be right there," she replied, carefully capping the inkwell on her station before rising to greet the new client.

As she approached the waiting area, the corners of her mouth lifted into a warm smile, welcoming the young woman who nervously fiddled with the strap of her purse. Despite the bustling atmosphere around her, Celine's focus remained solely on the person in front of her, her genuine interest in their story evident in the attentive tilt of her head.

"Hi, I'm Celine. What can I help you with today?" she asked, her soothing tone instantly putting the nervous client at ease.

Throughout the consultation, Celine's hands gestured gracefully as she spoke, revealing glimpses of the tattoos that danced along her wrists and forearms. She listened intently, nodding and offering gentle suggestions until the client's vision was crystal clear in her mind. It was this deep connection with her clients that truly set Celine apart, and it was something she cherished.

As the day wore on, Celine moved from one appointment to the next, her artistic talent shining through in each piece she created. With every completed tattoo, she felt a surge of satisfaction, knowing that she had played a small part in someone else's story. But as she wiped down her station at the end of the day, she couldn't help but feel a familiar pang of longing for a simpler life – one filled with quiet moments and rolling hills rather than buzzing machines and city lights.

"Another day in paradise, huh?" her coworker, Mike, joked as he walked by, snapping her out of her reverie.

"Something like that," she replied, forcing a smile as she glanced around the tattoo parlor one last time before grabbing her coat and heading home, her head filled with dreams of the open road and endless possibilities.

~

*A*s Celine dipped her needle into the inky blackness, she let out a contented sigh. The buzzing of the tattoo machine melded seamlessly with the low hum of conversation throughout the parlor. She looked up at her client – a young woman with vibrant red hair and a mischievous glint in her eye – and smiled reassuringly.

"Ready?" Celine asked, her voice warm and steady as she prepared to etch the intricate design onto the woman's shoulder.

"Absolutely," the woman replied, her excitement palpable.

Celine began the process, guiding the needle with precision and care as the ink slowly found its home on the woman's skin. As she worked, her mind wandered, her thoughts turning to the hills and open fields that filled her daydreams.

"Hey Celine, can you cover my shift tomorrow? I've got to go to some family thing," her coworker, Sarah, called out from a few stations over, pulling Celine back into the present moment.

"Sure, no problem," Celine responded, her thoughts still lingering on the serene countryside.

"Thanks! You're a lifesaver," Sarah grinned, blowing her a playful kiss before returning to her own client.

"Speaking of family things," another coworker, Jack, chimed in, "you ever think about moving back to your hometown, Celine? You know, settling down?"

Celine paused for a moment, considering the question. "Sometimes," she admitted, her voice barely audible over the hum of the machines. "But there's so much I love about the city, too."

"True, but don't you miss the peace and quiet?" Jack persisted, his tone teasing yet gentle.

"Of course I do," Celine confessed, her eyes wandering to the window where the busy streets outside contrasted sharply with the idyllic landscapes of her imagination. "But I've built a life here, and I can't just walk away from that."

"Who says you have to walk away?" Jack raised an eyebrow, a knowing grin spreading across his face. "You could always take your talents on the road – you know, bring your art to the people."

Celine laughed, shaking her head as she returned her focus to the tattoo at hand. "Maybe someday," she conceded, her heart swelling with the possibility.

As she continued to work, Celine found herself daydreaming of the countryside once more – the sway of the trees, the sweet scent of wildflowers, and the gentle crunch of leaves beneath her feet. With every stroke of her needle, she felt the pull of a simpler life grow stronger, and she couldn't help but wonder what might be waiting for her beyond the city limits.

"Done!" she announced finally, stepping back to admire her handiwork. The woman with the red hair beamed, her excitement mingling with Celine's own curiosity about the future.

"Thank you so much, Celine," the woman gushed, admiring her new tattoo in the mirror. "It's perfect."

"Always happy to help someone express themselves," Celine replied sincerely, feeling a warm sense of satisfaction wash over her.

"Good luck out there," the woman added, sensing Celine's dreams of adventure. "I'm sure you'll find everything you're looking for."

With a grateful smile, Celine nodded, her thoughts already drifting to where her heart longed to roam.

~

*D*ays later, Celine stood in front of her latest canvas – a blank sheet of skin waiting for her skilled hands to bring it to life. As she leaned over the table, focusing on the intricate design she was about to etch onto her client's forearm, she couldn't help but think about her conversation with her coworker.

"Imagine," she thought to herself, "a mobile tattoo business that allows me to explore the country and connect with people from all walks of life." The idea was both thrilling and terrifying, but she felt a fire ignite within her at the mere possibility.

"Alright, deep breath," Celine instructed her client

gently, her blue eyes sparkling with determination as she prepared to begin.

As the buzzing of the tattoo machine filled the air, Celine's thoughts drifted to the countryside once more. She envisioned rolling green hills dotted with wildflowers, towering oak trees casting dappled shadows on the ground, and a clear, star-filled sky that seemed to stretch into infinity. Her heart yearned for the peace and simplicity of such a place, away from the constant noise and chaos of the city.

"Hey, Celine?" her client called out, snapping her back to reality. "Could I get some water?"

"Of course," she replied, her cheeks flushing with embarrassment as she realized she had been lost in her daydreams. She quickly fetched a bottle of water and handed it to him, then returned to her work, her nimble fingers flying across his skin with practiced ease.

"Thanks," he mumbled, taking a sip before settling back into the chair.

"No problem," Celine responded, her mind already racing with plans and possibilities for her future. The more she mulled over the idea of hitting the open road, the more it seemed like an incredible opportunity – not only to explore the world beyond the city limits but also to grow as an artist and as a person.

"Taking my craft on the road would open up so many

doors," she mused, her heart pounding with excitement. "The freedom to go wherever I please, meeting new people, experiencing different cultures... it's like an endless source of inspiration."

"Hey, you okay?" her client asked, concern etched across his face as he noticed Celine's furrowed brow and distant gaze.

"Sorry," she apologized with a sheepish grin. "Just daydreaming a bit."

"About what?" he inquired, genuinely curious about the thoughts that had stolen her attention.

"About taking this show on the road," she confessed, her voice filled with equal parts wonder and determination. "Traveling around, sharing my art, and learning from others along the way."

"Sounds amazing," he replied, his eyes lighting up at the idea. "You should absolutely do it."

"Maybe I will," Celine agreed, her adventurous spirit shining through as she returned her focus to the task at hand. With every stroke of her needle, she felt more alive than ever before – and she knew that this was only the beginning.

*C*eline's fingers danced across her keyboard as she researched, brows furrowed in concentration. She was looking up the requirements for a mobile tattoo business, envisioning the possibilities of a life on the road. The screen illuminated her delicate features with a soft glow, reflecting off her blonde hair as it cascaded down her back.

"Hey, Celine," called out Marco, one of her colleagues as he approached her workstation. "What are you working on?"

"Research," she replied, briefly glancing up at him with sparkling eyes before refocusing on her screen. "I'm thinking of taking my tattoo business on the road, traveling and working from a mobile studio."

"Really?" Marco raised an eyebrow, leaning against her table. "That sounds like quite the adventure. What brought this on?"

"It's just something I've been daydreaming about," Celine admitted, her voice tinged with excitement. "Imagine the freedom of exploring new places and meeting new people while doing what I love. Plus, I've always wanted to experience the tranquility of the countryside."

"Wow," Marco said, genuinely impressed. "I can definitely see you doing that. You've got the talent and the drive to make it work."

"Thanks, Marco," she smiled, touched by his support. "There's still a lot to figure out, though. I need to get a suitable vehicle, gather all the necessary supplies, and make arrangements for my clients here in the city."

"Hey, don't worry about it," Marco reassured her, patting her shoulder. "We'll help you out however we can. Right, guys?"

"Absolutely!" chimed in Lucy, another coworker who had overheard the conversation. "We've got your back, Celine."

"Indeed," agreed their boss, Julia, joining the group. "Your success is our success. And if you ever need a pit stop, you're always welcome back here."

"Thank you all so much," Celine's eyes glistened with gratitude. "Your support means the world to me."

Over the next few days, Celine threw herself into planning her mobile tattoo business, her colleagues offering assistance whenever she needed it. She researched vehicles, made lists of supplies, and began reaching out to clients, informing them of her upcoming journey.

As Celine worked diligently on turning her dreams into reality, she couldn't help but feel a mixture of exhilaration and apprehension. She knew that leaving the city and her friends behind wouldn't be easy, but the promise of adventure and personal growth beckoned her forward. And as she looked around the bustling tattoo parlor, filled with laughter and camaraderie, she knew that no matter where life took her, this place would always hold a special place in her heart.

~

*C*eline's heart raced as she applied the final touches to the intricate tattoo on her client's arm, all too aware that each meticulous stroke brought her closer to the culmination of her life in the city. The buzz of the tattoo machine filled the air, punctuated by the lighthearted banter between her colleagues and their clients.

"Alright, all done!" Celine announced, beaming at her client. "Take a look."

"Wow, it's amazing," the woman gushed, admiring the vibrant colors and delicate lines in the mirror. "Thank you so much, Celine."

"You're very welcome," Celine replied, her excitement for the future mingling with bittersweet nostalgia. She cleaned up her workstation and headed to the break room, where she pulled out her phone, dialed a number, and waited for the call to connect.

"Hey, sis!" came the cheerful voice of her older sister, Isabelle. "What's up?"

"Isabelle, I have some news," Celine said, biting her lip. "I'm taking my tattoo business on the road. I've been dreaming of a simpler life, and I think this is my chance to find it."

"Really?" Isabelle sounded surprised but supportive. "That's quite the adventure you're embarking on. But knowing you, you'll make it work."

"Thanks, Izzy," Celine smiled, grateful for her sister's encouragement. "I've been planning and researching, and I feel ready. It won't be easy leaving everyone behind, but I can't shake the feeling that there's something more waiting for me out there."

"Trust your instincts, Celine," Isabelle advised. "You've always had a knack for making things happen. Just promise me you'll stay safe and in touch."

"Of course," Celine agreed, warmth spreading through her chest. "I love you, Izzy."

"Love you too, sis," Isabelle replied before they hung up.

Celine spent her final days in the city with a mixture of excitement and determination, working diligently to ensure that everything was in place for her new venture. She visited her favorite spots one last time, sharing laughter and memories with friends as she prepared for the next chapter of her life. Each night, she lay in bed, her thoughts brimming with visions of idyllic countrysides and the open road stretching out before her.

The day before her departure, Celine stood in her apartment, surrounded by packed boxes and the ghosts of memories past. She took a deep breath, feeling equal parts exhilarated and anxious, knowing that tomorrow would be the beginning of an entirely new journey—one filled with adventure, growth, and the pursuit of her dreams.

~

*T*he sun dipped below the horizon, painting the city in warm hues of orange and pink as Celine stepped into the tattoo parlor for one last time. A tinge of melancholy hung in the air as she took in the familiar sights—the worn leather chairs, the buzzing neon sign, and the walls adorned with intricate designs that brought life to countless stories.

"Hey," Celine called out to her fellow artists, Anna and Marco, who were absorbed in their work. "I just wanted to say thank you both for everything. It's been an amazing journey, hasn't it?"

Anna glanced up from her sketchbook, her eyes

brimming with emotion. "Celine, you're like a sister to us. We're going to miss having you around."

"Definitely," Marco chimed in as he wiped down his workstation. "But we're excited for you too. You've got guts, taking on the open road like that."

"Thanks," Celine replied, her throat tightening. "You two have been such a huge part of my life here, but I can't ignore this calling anymore. I need to find out what it is that I'm searching for—whether it's the art or the simpler life I've always dreamed of."

"Either way, the world better watch out for Celine Montgomery," Anna said, smiling through her tears. "You're destined for greatness no matter where you go."

"Remember to send us pictures of your mobile studio!" Marco reminded her. "And don't forget about us little people when you're living it up in the countryside."

Celine laughed, her heart swelling with gratitude. "Never. I promise."

With that, she gathered her belongings—a collection of sketches and mementos from her time at the parlor—and walked towards the door. As she turned the key in the lock for the final time, a wave of emotion washed over her. She was leaving behind a piece of herself, but in doing so, she was also opening the door to new beginnings.

"Take care, guys," Celine whispered, wiping away a

stray tear as she stepped into the fading twilight. The empty streets seemed to echo with the memories of her life in the city and the people she had met along the way.

As she climbed into her car, she felt the weight of her decision settling upon her shoulders. It was a delicate balance—her love for art and her desire for a simpler life. Yet, she knew deep down that this journey was necessary; it would lead her to the answers she sought.

With a final wave to her friends through the window, she turned the ignition and set off towards the open road. The city lights receded behind her, giving way to the vast expanse of darkness and possibility that lay ahead.

"Heres to adventure," Celine murmured to herself, her grip on the steering wheel steady and sure. "And finding my place in this world."

CHAPTER 2

The sun cast its golden rays over the picturesque town of Fountain Springs, bathing its cobblestone streets and quaint cottages in a warm glow. It was in this idyllic setting that Jemima Sullivan called home. A kind-hearted woman in her early 30s, Jemima was known by everyone in town for her warm personality and unwavering loyalty to those she cared about.

"Morning, Mrs. Thompson!" Jemima called out cheerfully as she strolled down Main Street, her dark hair ruffled by a gentle breeze. Her blue eyes sparkled with sincerity, a reflection of the pure heart that lay beneath a strong, rugged exterior.

"Good morning, Jemima!" Mrs. Thompson replied, beaming at her from her flower-adorned porch. "Beautiful day, isn't it?"

"Absolutely," Jemima agreed, taking a moment to appreciate the beauty surrounding her. Fountain Springs was truly a gem, with its lush gardens, friendly neighbors, and vibrant community spirit. The idyllic small-town atmosphere was one of the reasons why Jemima loved living there so dearly.

As she continued her walk along the tree-lined streets, Jemima couldn't help but marvel at the charm of Fountain Springs. It was like stepping into a painting – every detail meticulously crafted to create a harmonious blend of natural beauty and human touch. The air was filled with the sweet scent of blooming flowers and freshly baked goods wafting from the local bakery.

"Hey, Jemima!" called out Tom, the owner of the corner cafe, as he polished the windows. "Dropping by later for your usual?"

"Of course, Tom!" Jemima replied with a grin, her mind already savoring the taste of the perfectly brewed coffee that awaited her.

"See you then!" Tom waved, chuckling as he returned to his task.

As Jemima walked on, she couldn't help but feel grateful for the life she had built in Fountain Springs. The sense of belonging, the genuine connections she had formed with her neighbors, and the picturesque beauty that surrounded her all contributed to the contentment she felt deep within her soul.

Little did she know that her peaceful life was about to be shaken by the arrival of someone who would soon hold a special place in her heart – Celine. And as their story began to unfold, Jemima would find herself navigating complex emotions as friendship evolved into something more profound, challenging her very understanding of love.

~

*J*emima sat at her desk, scrolling through Celine's latest social media posts showcasing her exquisite tattoo artistry. Her unique style and intricate designs never failed to leave Jemima in awe. She felt a warmth in her chest, swelling with pride for her online friend who had turned her talent into a successful career.

"Wow, another masterpiece," she murmured under her breath, admiring the image of a delicate floral design that seemed to come to life on the client's skin. She could almost feel the texture of the petals as if they were real flowers.

"Hey, Jemima!" called out Linda, her coworker from

across the office. "Aren't you supposed to be working on that report?"

"Sorry, just taking a quick break," she sheepishly replied, quickly minimizing her screen. "I'll get back to it right now."

As Jemima refocused on her work, thoughts of Celine lingered in her mind. They had been exchanging messages for months now, sharing their passions, fears, and dreams. She had become an essential part of Jemima's life, even though they had never met in person. That was about to change very soon, however.

The anticipation bubbled within her like champagne in a glass, leaving her feeling giddy. Her heart raced as she imagined finally meeting Celine and getting to know the woman behind the beautiful artwork she so admired. She envisioned Celine's long blonde hair cascading down her shoulders, framing her radiant face. The thought alone sent shivers down her spine.

"Okay, pull yourself together, Jemima," she whispered to herself, shaking off the nerves. She couldn't help but think about how different things would be once Celine arrived in Fountain Springs. Would their friendship still feel as effortless and natural in person? Or would the dynamic change entirely?

"Only one way to find out," she told himself, determined to make the most of this opportunity. After all, life was too short to let fear hold her back.

"Jemima, you're grinning like a fool," Linda teased from across the room. "What are you so excited about?"

"Nothing," she said nonchalantly, though her face turned a shade of red that betrayed her true feelings. "Just thinking about something, that's all."

"Uh-huh," Linda replied, clearly not buying it. "Well, whatever it is, I hope it works out for you."

"Thanks, Linda," Jemima smiled, genuinely grateful for her well-wishes. She knew deep down that her connection with Celine was something special, and she couldn't wait to see where their friendship would lead them.

As the day drew to a close, Jemima couldn't contain her excitement any longer. She quickly finished up her work and rushed home to prepare for Celine's arrival. The anticipation danced in her veins as she gathered her thoughts, eager to finally connect with Celine in person and discover the depths of their friendship yet unexplored.

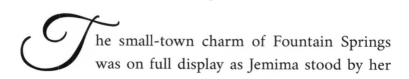

The small-town charm of Fountain Springs was on full display as Jemima stood by her front porch, anxiously awaiting Celine's arrival. The sun cast a warm, golden glow over the quaint houses and picturesque gardens that lined the quiet streets. The air was fragrant with the scent of blooming flowers and freshly mown grass, lending a sense of serenity to the idyllic scene.

"Come on, Jemima, relax," she muttered to herself, pacing back and forth in her nervous energy. She couldn't help but fidget with the hem of her blouse, smoothing it down every few seconds as if to iron out the creases in her anticipation. She glanced at her watch for what felt like the hundredth time, wondering if Celine was just running late or if something had gone wrong on her journey.

"Hey! You made it!" she called out, spotting Celine's SUV turning onto the street. Jemima's heart raced with excitement as the vehicle came to a stop in front of her house. As Celine stepped out of the car, Jemima found herself momentarily breathless, struck by Celine's radiant beauty.

"Wow..." she whispered under her breath, taking in the sight before her. Celine's blonde hair cascaded effortlessly around her shoulders, framing her stunning features in a way that was both ethereal and captivating. Her smile seemed to light up the entire street, causing a flutter deep within Jemima's chest.

"Jemima! It's so great to finally meet you in person!" Celine exclaimed, walking towards her with open arms. Her enthusiasm was contagious, and Jemima couldn't help but beam back at her as they embraced.

"Likewise, Celine. Welcome to Fountain Springs," she said warmly as she pulled away from the hug, her eyes roaming over Celine's face once more, still in awe of her presence. "I can't believe you're actually here."

"Me neither," Celine admitted, her voice laced with excitement and a hint of nervousness. "But I can already tell that this place is as charming as you described it."

"Wait until you see the rest of it," Jemima grinned, her eagerness to show Celine around evident in her sparkling blue eyes. As they stood there, chatting animatedly about Celine's journey and their plans for the coming days, Jemima couldn't help but marvel at how natural their connection felt.

"Here, let me help you with your bags," she offered, moving towards the SUV to retrieve Celine's luggage. As she hoisted the heavy suitcase from the trunk, she couldn't help but feel a sense of pride in being able to assist Celine, even in such a small way.

"Thanks, Jemima," Celine smiled gratefully, watching as Jemima carried her belongings towards the house. She followed closely behind, her eyes taking in Jemima well-toned phisique as well as the picturesque scene with wonder.

As they stepped inside and began to settle in, Jemima couldn't shake the feeling that something extraordinary was unfolding before her. It was as if the universe had conspired to bring them together, and she was more than willing to embrace whatever adventure lay ahead.

~

"*H*ey, Celine, would you like to join me for a walk around town tomorrow morning?" Jemima asked as they sat on the porch, enjoying the warm evening breeze and the sight of fireflies dancing in the dusk. "I'd love to show you some of my favorite spots."

"Absolutely!" Celine replied enthusiastically. "I can't wait to explore Fountain Springs with you."

Jemima's heart swelled at her excitement. She felt an incredible urge to share every aspect of her life with Celine, from the beauty of the surrounding nature to the mundane details of her daily routine. She wanted to know what brought Celine joy, what made her laugh, and what fueled her passion for art.

As they continued chatting into the night, Jemima

found himself captivated by Celine's stories about her life in the city and her adventures on the road. It was clear that she had experienced so much and yet still remained grounded and genuine. She couldn't help but wonder how many more layers there were to this fascinating woman.

"Tell me more about your artwork," she urged Celine, genuinely intrigued by her creative process. "How do you choose the designs for your tattoos?"

Celine smiled softly, her eyes lighting up as she delved into her artistic world. "Well, it's a mixture of things, really. Sometimes clients come to me with a specific idea or image, and I work with them to create something unique and meaningful. Other times, I'll sketch out a design based on a feeling or experience, and someone will connect with it."

Listening intently, Jemima marveled at Celine's ability to turn emotions into tangible art. She could tell that Celine poured her heart and soul into each piece, and it made Jemima appreciate her talent even more.

"Have you ever thought about getting a tattoo yourself?" Celine asked suddenly, catching Jemima off guard.

"Uh, I've never really considered it," Jemima admitted, rubbing the back of her neck sheepishly. "But who knows? Maybe one day I'll find something that speaks to me."

"Maybe indeed," Celine replied with a teasing grin, her eyes twinkling mischievously.

As they continued to talk late into the night, Jemima began to realize just how special their connection was. Despite having only met in person earlier that day, it felt as though they had known each other for years. She couldn't quite put her finger on it, but there was an undeniable magnetism between them that went beyond the boundaries of friendship.

~

The next day they met again. Strolling through the charming streets, Jemima eagerly pointed out her favorite spots – the cozy little bookstore with its well-worn armchairs, the vibrant farmers market bursting with fresh produce, and the serene park nestled by the river where she often went to clear her head.

"Wow, this place really is magical," Celine marveled, her eyes shining with wonder. "I can see why you love it so much."

Jemima smiled, feeling a strange warmth spread through her chest at Celine's words. "I'm just glad you like it too. Anything you need while you're here, you just let me know, okay? I want you to feel at home."

"Thank you, Jemima," Celine said softly, her gaze meeting hers with genuine appreciation. "I already feel so welcomed, and we've only just begun."

As they continued to explore the town, their conversation flowed effortlessly between them, laughter dancing in the air like a familiar melody. With each shared story and inside joke, Jemima found herself more and more captivated by Celine – not just as an artist, but as a person.

"Have you ever been to that little ice cream shop down by the pier?" Jemima asked, grinning as she wiped a stray drop of chocolate from the corner of Celine's mouth. "Their homemade flavors are amazing. You have to try it."

"Only if you join me," Celine replied, looking at Jemima's slender, muscular taught frame. "You look as if you work out and live on high protein body boulder food." Celine's eyes sparkling with mischief. "You look fabulous. I'd love to see my artwork adorning those biceps."

"Thank you, and, it's a deal—the ice cream that is." Jemima grinned. Her heart swelling with happiness as they continued on their adventure, hand in hand. And as they walked together through the picturesque town, she couldn't help but think that maybe, just maybe, Fountain Springs, know to insiders as safe and accepting for a growing lesbian community, had cast its spell on them both.

Jemima had never spoken to Celine about her sexual identity, and Celine had never spoken to her of hers. She was drawn to, and, liked Celine as a friend, and hadn't wished to risk losing that friendship by crossing an invisible line that Celine might not have been receptive to stepping over. She wanted Celine's friendship, with or without the possibility of it maturing to love.

Jemima did hope that perhaps Celine might have researched the town of Fountain Springs before coming, and thus have an inkling, without needing to be told, that it wasn't the mineral springs fountain the town was most famous for. Fountain Springs was known a a haven, of secluded bed and breakfasts, spa retreats, and wedding reception venues specialising in catering to sapphic love couples.

Of course, Jemima realised, that unless she revealed herself, how could Celine know. The friendship was too young, too fragile and precious to risk finding out how Celine might respond if she hinted at her feelings. No, best to say nothing, do nothing aside from what straight girlfriends might do—for new.

*T*he sun dipped below the horizon, casting an enchanting golden glow over Fountain Springs. Jemima and Celine strolled along the riverbank, listening to the gentle lapping of the water against the shore. The warmth of the setting sun painted their faces with a rosy hue, creating a picture-perfect moment in the small town's embrace.

"Your work never ceases to amaze me," Jemima said, breaking the comfortable silence between them. "I mean, I've always admired your talent, but seeing you create art in person... it's truly breathtaking."

"Thank you, Jemima," Celine replied, her cheeks flushing with pleasure at Jemima praise. She looked down at her sketchbook, filled with intricate designs inspired by the beauty of Fountain Springs. "There's just something about ink that brings out the best in me. I love the medium."

As they continued walking, Celine excitedly pointed out various spots that had captured her artistic imagination. Jemima couldn't help but share in her enthusiasm, watching her eyes light up with inspiration as she described the scenes playing out in her mind.

"Sometimes, I just want to climb to the highest peak and scream my joy to the world," Celine confessed, twirling around in a burst of unbridled energy. "I love the adventure of discovering new places and meeting new people. It makes me feel alive."

Jemima chuckled, completely captivated by her spirit. "Well, you certainly have a knack for embracing life," she said, marveling at the way Celine seemed to bring out the best in everyone and everything around her.

Yet, as they spent more time together, Jemima found herself increasingly drawn to Celine. Ste could no longer deny the magnetic pull between them - a connection that went far beyond friendship. Memories of shared laughter and heartfelt conversations played on a loop in her mind, leaving her both exhilarated and confused.

"Is everything okay, Jemima?" Celine asked, concern etched in her beautiful features. "You seem a bit... distracted."

"Uh, yeah," she stammered, trying to shake off the unsettling thoughts swirling in her head. "I'm fine. Just... thinking."

"About what?" Celine pressed gently, her curiosity piqued.

"Nothing important," Jemima replied evasively, unwilling to voice her inner turmoil. Instead, she forced a smile onto her face and gestured towards a cozy café nestled amongst the trees. "How about we grab some coffee and continue our adventure?"

"Sounds perfect," Celine agreed, her eyes brightening at the suggestion.

As they sipped their drinks and exchanged stories, Jemima couldn't help but wonder if she was on the precipice of something extraordinary. The thought both thrilled and terrified Jemima, leaving her with an unshakeable feeling that her life was about to change forever.

∼

*T*he sunlight filtered through the vibrant leaves of the oak tree, casting a warm glow over the small park where Jemima and Celine had decided to spend their afternoon. It seemed like the perfect spot for Celine to sketch her next tattoo design – a sprawling landscape inspired by the natural beauty of Fountain Springs.

"Jemima, you don't have to carry all my art supplies," Celine teased as they spread out her materials on a nearby picnic table. "I promise I won't break under the weight."

"Hey, it's no trouble at all," Jemima insisted, her eyes crinkling with amusement. "I'm just glad I can help in any way possible. Besides, I wouldn't want you to waste any energy on carrying things when you could be focusing on your art."

Celine grinned and shook her head, clearly touched by Jemima's unwavering support. As she began to sketch, Jemima found herself captivated by the fluid movements of Celine's hand, each stroke bringing the scene before them to life on the paper.

"Wow, Celine," she murmured, unable to contain her awe. "You truly have a gift."

"Thank you." Celine's cheeks tinted pink with a modest blush. "It means a lot coming from you – especially since you've been such an incredible friend and supporter from the very beginning."

"Of course," Jemima said, her chest swelling and small firm breasts heaving with pride. "I believe in you, Celine. I always have, and I always will."

As the hours slipped by, Jemima found herself becoming more and more entranced by Celine's artistic process. She watched as Celine dipped her brush into the palette, the vibrant colors mingling together to form something entirely new and unique – much like the friendship that had blossomed between them.

"Hey, Celine?" she ventured hesitantly, her heart pounding in her chest. "Have you ever thought about opening your own tattoo studio in a place like this? I know you love the city, and the idea of van life, but I think Fountain Springs would be the perfect setting for your art."

Celine looked up from her sketch, her eyes wide with surprise. "You know, Jemima, I hadn't considered it before, but... that's actually a really intriguing idea."

"Really?" Jemima asked, hope surging through her at Celine's response.

"Yeah," Celine confirmed, her expression thoughtful. "There's something incredibly appealing about the idea of creating art in such a serene and accepting environment – and having someone like you by my side to share in the experience would make it all the more special."

"Then let's do it," Jemima declared, thrilled by Celine's use of the work, accepting. Was Celine aware then, this town was a haven, a place where people such as herself, lesbians, were the norm? Jemima's heart raced in excitement at that possibility. "Whatever it takes, Celine, I'll be here to help you turn that dream into a reality."

As they continued to discuss the possibilities, Jemima felt a warmth spread through her – a sensation that went beyond simple friendship. It was a sense of deeper belonging and connection such as she had never experienced before – and it only seemed to grow stronger with each passing moment spent in Celine's presence.

~

*T*he sun was beginning to dip beneath the horizon, casting a golden glow over the picturesque streets of Fountain Springs. Jemima and Celine walked side by side, their laughter mingling with the soft rustle of leaves in the evening breeze. As they strolled through the town, Jemima couldn't help but steal glances at Celine, admiring the way her blonde hair shimmered in the fading light.

"Have you thought about where you'd like this tattoo studio to be?" Jemima asked, trying to keep her voice casual while her mind raced with anticipation.

Celine bit her lip, her eyes scanning the quaint store-fronts that lined Main Street. "I don't know yet, but I'm sure we'll find the perfect spot," she replied confidently.

"Did you have any specific ideas in mind for the design?" Jemima continued, eager to learn more about Celine's vision and how she could help bring it to life.

"Actually, yes," Celine said, her face lighting up with excitement. "I want it to feel warm and inviting, like an extension of my own home – a place where people can relax and feel comfortable being themselves."

Jemima nodded, imagining the cozy space Celine described, filled with her stunning artwork and the soft hum of happy conversations. It was a dream she wanted more than anything to help make a reality – not only for Celine but also for herself. The thought of sharing this adventure with Celine drove her forward, her heart swelling with affection for the incredible woman beside her.

"Whatever you need, Celine, I'm here to help," she affirmed, offering her a reassuring smile. "Together, we can make this dream come true."

"Thank you," Celine murmured, her eyes shining with gratitude. "You have no idea how much your support means to me."

As they reached the end of the street, their hands brushed against each other, sending a jolt of electricity through Jemima's body. She hesitated, debating whether to reach out and take Celine's hand in her own. But the moment passed, leaving her with a lingering sense of longing that she couldn't quite shake.

"Let's head back," Celine suggested, a gentle smile playing on her lips. "We have a lot to plan for tomorrow, after all."

"Right," Jemima agreed, trying to quell the butterflies in her stomach. "Tomorrow is a big day."

And as they walked back toward Jemima's home, the

soft glow of the setting sun casting long shadows on the ground, she couldn't help but wonder how her relationship with Celine would continue to evolve. Would their newfound partnership bring them even closer together? Or would it ultimately drive them apart? Only time would tell – and Jemima found himself more eager than ever to discover what lay ahead for them both.

CHAPTER 3

The late afternoon sun cast a golden hue on the charming brick facade of Anna Thompson's gallery, nestled among the quaint shops and cafes that lined Helen Springs' main street. With each step Celine took towards the entrance, she felt her heart race in anticipation. As she approached the glass door, Celine took a deep breath, steadying herself before pushing it open.

"Welcome, Celine!" Anna greeted her with a warm smile, her voice full of genuine enthusiasm. The gallery owner was an elegant woman, her dark hair swept into a stylish updo that framed her expressive eyes. Dressed in a navy blouse and crisp white trousers, she exuded sophistication.

"Thank you for having me, Anna," Celine replied,

trying to sound composed despite the butterflies fluttering in her stomach. She couldn't help but glance around the airy space, admiring the impressive array of artwork displayed on the pristine white walls. Each piece seemed to radiate its own unique energy, beckoning to be seen and appreciated.

"Your work is truly exceptional, Celine," Anna said, clasping her hands together as she regarded Celine with admiration. "I've been following your career for some time now, and I must say, I'm quite taken by your talent and versatility."

Celine felt her cheeks flush with warmth at the unexpected praise. "Thank you, Anna. That really means a lot coming from someone as esteemed as yourself." She hesitated for a moment, gathering the courage to voice her thoughts. "Honestly, I'm both excited and nervous about this meeting. This opportunity could potentially change everything for me."

Anna's gaze softened, her eyes brimming with understanding. "It's perfectly natural to feel that way, dear," she reassured Celine gently. "But I have no doubt that your art deserves to be showcased in the best possible light. And I genuinely believe that my gallery can provide that for you."

Celine nodded, her heart swelling with gratitude for this remarkable woman who saw something special in her work. She knew that the journey ahead would be filled with challenges and uncertainties, but with Anna's support, she felt ready to embrace the possibilities that awaited her.

"Thank you, Anna," Celine murmured, her voice barely above a whisper. "I can't express how much this opportunity means to me."

"Of course, my dear," Anna replied, her eyes twinkling with warmth and encouragement. "Now, let's discuss your art and what we can achieve together."

~

*C*eline glanced around the gallery, taking in the array of paintings and sculptures adorning its walls. The space was inviting and intimate, with natural light streaming through floor-to-ceiling windows that framed a picturesque view of Fountain Springs' charming main street.

"Your collection is truly impressive," Celine remarked, her eyes lingering on a particularly captivating abstract painting.

"Thank you," Anna replied, beaming with pride. "I've always been drawn to art that evokes strong emotions and sparks conversation."

The two women began to discuss Celine's work, as

they delved into the intricacies of different techniques she employed in her tattoo designs. "I find it fascinating how you're able to blend traditional styles with modern elements," Anna said, her interest evident in her thoughtful expression.

"I've always loved experimenting with various approaches," Celine responded, her voice full of enthusiasm. "Each piece tells a unique story, and I want to honor that by adapting my technique to fit its narrative. In some ways, it feels like I'm translating the essence of someone's experience onto their skin."

Anna nodded, clearly impressed by Celine's artistic philosophy. "That's a beautiful way to think about your craft, dear. And it's precisely why I believe your work would resonate with the patrons who frequent my gallery."

As they continued their conversation, Anna led Celine deeper into the gallery, describing her vision for the future. "Fountain Springs may be a small town, but it has a thriving arts community," she explained. "My goal is to create a space where artists like yourself can gain exposure and connect with audiences who appreciate the depth and nuance of your creations."

"Your passion for your gallery is so inspiring," Celine mused, her own excitement bubbling up inside her as she imagined her artwork displayed alongside the masterpieces surrounding them. "It's an honor to be considered for such a prestigious showcase."

"Believe me, Celine, the honor is all mine," Anna replied sincerely. "Your work has a magnetic quality that I believe will attract art enthusiasts from far and wide. And as your pieces gain recognition, I have no doubt that you'll find yourself at the forefront of the contemporary tattoo scene."

As Anna's words washed over her, Celine felt a renewed sense of purpose and determination. This was an opportunity she couldn't pass up, one that could catapult her career to new heights while allowing her to remain true to her love for the simplicity and charm of country life.

"Thank you, Anna," Celine whispered, feeling the weight of this momentous decision settle in her heart. "I'm truly grateful for your faith in my work, and I can't wait to see where this journey takes us."

~

Celine's gaze wandered over the intricate details of the paintings adorning the gallery walls, her eyes reflecting the vibrant colors that danced before her. The scent of fresh paint and aged wood intermingled in the air, creating an atmosphere of inspiration and longing.

"Anna," she began hesitantly, "I can't express how grateful I am for this opportunity. But I have to admit, I'm torn." She fidgeted with the hem of her blouse, feeling the soft fabric between her fingers. "You see, my mobile tattoo business has become such a big part of my life, and it's difficult to imagine letting go of that freedom."

Anna's eyes softened as she took in Celine's internal struggle, her own heart resonating with the young artist's dilemma. Stepping closer, she placed a reassuring hand on Celine's shoulder. "I understand your concerns, Celine. But consider this: being a part of the gallery showcase doesn't mean you have to give up your passion for your mobile business entirely."

Celine looked into Anna's warm, brown eyes, searching for answers. "But... how can I balance both?"

"By embracing the exposure and success that show-casing your work here can bring." Anna gestured towards the captivating pieces surrounding them. "Imagine the impact your unique style could have on the art world. Your talent is undeniable, and through the gallery, you'll be able to reach a wider audience than ever before."

As Celine listened, she felt the fluttering of excitement in her chest. Could it be possible to pursue the gallery showcase without sacrificing her love for the open road and the deep connections she forged through her mobile tattoo business?

"Think of the possibilities, Celine," Anna continued earnestly, her voice a soothing balm to Celine's uncertainty. "Your artwork displayed here, admired by countless people... It's a stepping stone to even greater opportunities, while still allowing you to maintain your adventurous spirit and independence."

Celine drew in a deep breath, her heart swelling with the weight of her decision. She stared intently at Anna, feeling the genuine support and encouragement radiating from the older woman.

"Alright," she whispered, determination lacing her voice. "I'll do it. I'll be part of the gallery showcase."

Anna's face broke into a radiant smile, and she squeezed Celine's shoulder gently. "You won't regret it, my dear. I have no doubt that this is just the beginning of an incredible journey for you."

Together, they stood amidst the awe-inspiring artwork, their hearts brimming with anticipation for the future that lay ahead. And as Celine contemplated the path before her, she knew that her life was about to change in ways she could never have imagined.

"Anna," Celine began, her voice soft and hesitant. "There's something I need to share with you. I've always been drawn to the simplicity and charm of country life. It's why I started my mobile tattoo business in the first place – to meet new people, explore different towns, and connect with others on a deeper level." She paused, her gaze drifting to the sunlit window, as if she could see the rolling hills and quaint villages that called to her heart.

"Traveling from town to town, I've found a sense of fulfillment and freedom that I haven't experienced anywhere else. The open road, the warm smiles of strangers, the stories shared over a cup of coffee in a cozy diner... That's what fuels my art and inspires me to create."

As Celine spoke, Anna listened attentively, her eyes never leaving Celine's face. She seemed to understand the magnetic pull between Celine's nomadic lifestyle and the stability of settling down in one place, particularly in a bustling city like Fountain Springs.

"Ah, Celine," Anna murmured, her voice full of warmth and empathy. "I can see how this is a difficult decision for you. On one hand, there's the opportunity to display your work in a gallery and gain more exposure. On the other hand, there's the love for your mobile tattoo business and the connections you've made along the way."

Celine nodded, biting her lip as she tried to suppress the whirlwind of emotions coursing through her. She knew that pursuing the gallery showcase would mean sacrificing some of the freedom she cherished so dearly, yet the potential rewards were too enticing to ignore.

"Your passion for the country life and your desire to explore its many wonders is truly inspiring, Celine," Anna continued gently. "But perhaps there is a way to merge both worlds – to seize this opportunity while still remaining true to your adventurous spirit and your love for the open road."

Celine glanced at Anna, her eyes filled with curiosity and hope. "Do you think it's possible, Anna? Can I really have both?"

"Only you can answer that question, my dear," Anna replied softly. "But I believe in you, and I know that whatever path you choose, you will find a way to make it work while staying true to yourself."

"Think of the gallery showcase as a catalyst, Celine," Anna suggested, her eyes sparkling with conviction. "Your work will be seen by a larger audience, people who appreciate art and understand its value. They might even be inspired to commission you for projects in their own small towns."

Celine's gaze drifted towards the colorful paintings adorning the gallery walls, her mind painting a vivid picture of her own creations on display. The thought sent a thrill of excitement down her spine, yet she couldn't shake the nagging feeling that she might be betraying her free-spirited nature.

"Maybe you're right, Anna," she conceded, tucking a lock of blonde hair behind her ear as she turned back to face the older woman. "Perhaps this is my chance to broaden my horizons while still staying true to myself and my love for adventure."

"Exactly," Anna agreed, a smile of encouragement playing on her lips. "You can always continue your mobile tattoo business, but this opportunity could open up new doors for you. It's not every day that an artist like yourself is given such a platform."

As Celine considered Anna's words, she started to see the possibilities unfold before her. The gallery show-case could act as a stepping stone, propelling her further into the world of art while still allowing her to maintain a connection to the country life she so cherished. Maybe, just maybe, she could have it all.

"Okay, I'll give it a shot," Celine decided, her heart swelling with determination. "I'll take this leap of faith and see where it leads me. Thank you, Anna, for believing in me."

Anna's smile widened, her eyes crinkling with genuine happiness. "You're welcome, Celine. I know you'll do great things, and I'll be here to support you every step of the way."

With newfound resolve, Celine felt the weight of her decision settle firmly on her shoulders. The path she was about to embark on would be challenging, but in her heart, she knew it was worth it. As she left the gallery, she couldn't help but feel a surge of excitement for the journey that lay ahead, ready to embrace the future with open arms and an open heart.

❧

"*A*nna, I can't thank you enough for this opportunity," Celine gushed, a warm smile lighting up her face as she grasped Anna's hands across the polished wooden table. "I've decided to accept your offer, and I'm ready to give this gallery showcase everything I've got."

"Excellent!" Anna beamed, her eyes twinkling with excitement. "I'm thrilled to have you on board, Celine. Now, let's dive into the details and make this event one for the history books."

Celine glanced around the gallery, taking in the elegant space filled with natural light from floor-to-ceiling windows. She could already imagine her artwork adorning the walls, captivating visitors and art enthusiasts alike. As her heart swelled with anticipation, she focused her attention back on Anna, eager to discuss the logistics.

"First things first, we need to set a date for the showcase," Anna said, pulling out a sleek planner from her leather bag. "I was thinking sometime in the next three months. Does that work for you?"

"Absolutely," Celine agreed, nodding enthusiastically. "That gives me enough time to finalize my pieces and prepare them for display."

"Perfect," Anna replied, penciling in the tentative dates. "Now, let's talk about your artwork. We'll need a strong selection of pieces that represent your unique style and tell a compelling story."

As their conversation flowed, Celine's mind raced with ideas for her collection, envisioning bold colors, intricate patterns, and the stories behind each piece coming together in harmony. The passion for her craft bubbled up inside her, fueling her determination to create something extraordinary.

"Promotion is key," Anna continued, tapping a manicured finger on the table. "We want to generate buzz for your showcase and attract a diverse audience. Press releases, social media campaigns, and targeted invitations will all play a role in ensuring the event's success."

Celine nodded, her thoughts shifting to the countless hours she'd spent cultivating her online presence and connecting with potential clients. She knew that leveraging her existing following would be crucial in promoting the showcase, and she welcomed the challenge of expanding her reach even further.

"Anna, I appreciate your guidance and expertise," Celine told her sincerely, her gaze locking with Anna's. "I promise you, this showcase will be unforgettable."

"I have no doubt, Celine," Anna replied, her confidence unwavering. "Together, we'll create something magical."

As they continued ironing out the details, Celine felt a renewed sense of purpose coursing through her veins, eager to embark on this new adventure. With Anna by her side, she knew that the sky was the limit, and she was determined to soar.

*C*eline stepped out of the gallery and into the warm sunlight, its golden rays casting a comforting glow on her face. She took a deep breath, soaking in the crisp, fresh air as she watched the breeze dance gently through the leaves of the nearby trees.

"Thank you, Anna," Celine murmured under her breath, her heart swelling with gratitude for this unforeseen opportunity.

As she walked down the quaint cobblestone street, her thoughts kept drifting back to the meeting with Anna. Images of vivid colors and intricate details filled her mind, each one representing a piece of her soul that would soon be on display for the world to see. The prospect both excited and terrified her.

"Can I really pull this off?" She wondered aloud, her voice barely above a whisper. But there was no time for doubt; she needed to focus on the task at hand, drawing inspiration from the world around her.

"Hey, Celine!" A familiar voice called out from across the street, pulling her from her reverie.

"Hi, Ben!" She responded, waving enthusiastically at the local baker who had become a fast friend during her stay. His cheerful demeanor and delicious pastries had quickly endeared him to her, and she couldn't help but smile as she jogged over to join her.

"Big plans for the day?" He asked, his eyes sparkling with curiosity.

"Actually, yes," she said, her excitement bubbling over. "I just met with Anna Thompson at the gallery, and she's offered me a showcase!"

"Wow, congratulations! That's amazing news!" Ben gushed, his own excitement for her evident. "You deserve it, Celine. Your work is incredible."

"Thank you so much, Ben," she replied, touched by his genuine enthusiasm. "It means a lot coming from someone who's seen my art up close."

As they walked together toward the town square, Celine felt a warmth spread through her chest – not only from the pride she took in her work but also from the knowledge that she had found a community that welcomed and appreciated her. She knew that Fountain Springs was special, and she felt blessed to be a part of it.

The conversation with Ben flowed effortlessly, and as they said their goodbyes, Celine couldn't help but reflect on how much her perspective had shifted. This gallery showcase wasn't just an opportunity to share her art; it was a chance to grow, to learn, and to become the artist she always knew she could be.

"Maybe this is what I've been searching for all along,"

she mused as she continued her stroll, feeling a renewed sense of purpose coursing through her veins. "A place where I can explore my passion, surrounded by people who understand and support me."

With newfound determination, Celine vowed to make the most of this opportunity, embracing the challenge and pouring her heart and soul into every piece she created. And as she looked around at the picturesque town that had quickly become her home away from home, she knew that she was exactly where she needed to be.

CHAPTER 4

*J*emima sat on the edge of her worn leather armchair, staring blankly at the dancing flames in the fireplace. The room was dimly lit, casting a warm glow across the walls adorned with framed photographs of cherished memories. She felt an odd mix of excitement and apprehension swirling in her chest.

She thought about Celine, her laughter, her eyes, the scent of her. Jemima's mind wandered through the easiness of their online conversations, the shared passion for art, and the undeniable pull she felt towards her when they finally met in person. Jemima fidgeted with a loose thread on her jeans, struggling to reconcile these emotions with the possibility of losing a dear friend if she were to revealed her true feelings.

"Hey! All set for movie night?" Angela's voice rang out as she entered the living room, a big bowl of popcorn cradled in her arms. Her dark curls bounced with each step, and her mischievous smile betrayed the excitement for their usual Friday night get-together. But as she looked up from the popcorn and caught sight of Jemima's distant gaze, her smile faltered.

"Jemima? Are you okay?" Angela asked, concern evident in her tone. She placed the popcorn on the coffee table and stood in front of Jemima, hands on her hips.

"Uh, yeah, Angie, I'm fine," Jemima mumbled unconvincingly, attempting a weak smile. "Just lost in thought, I guess."

Angela narrowed her eyes, not quite buying Jemima's explanation. She had known Jemima since they were kids, building forts in the woods and sharing dreams of grand adventures. She could read Jemima like a book, and she knew this wasn't just a passing daydream.

~

"Come on, Jemima. Spill it," Angela urged gently, sitting down next to her on the cozy couch. Her hazel eyes were warm yet piercing, as if she could already see the thoughts swirling in Jemima's mind.

Jemima shifted uncomfortably, her fingertips pressed against her temples, massaging them in a futile attempt to ease the tension building within. She let out a shaky breath and glanced over at Angela, who was patiently waiting with an encouraging nod.

"Angela... I don't know if I can explain it," she began hesitantly, her voice low and vulnerable. "It's just... Celine. She's been on my mind lately, and I can't seem to figure out what's going on in my heart."

"Ah, Celine," Angela mused, her gaze softening in understanding. "You two have become quite close, haven't you?"

"More than I ever expected," Jemima admitted, staring down at her hands. "But it's complicated. I'm feeling things I never thought I would for her, and I'm afraid of ruining our friendship if I let these emotions take over."

"Jemima, listen to me," Angela said earnestly, placing a reassuring hand on her shoulder. "It's okay to feel confused and scared when it comes to love. We've all been there, trust me." She chuckled lightly, a knowing glint in her eyes. "But sometimes, taking that risk is worth it. You'll never know unless you try, right?"

Jemima contemplated her words, her blue eyes

clouded with uncertainty but also a flicker of hope. As she looked into Angela's eyes, she knew she spoke from experience - the kind of experience only gained through trials and tribulations in matters of the heart.

"Maybe you're right," she sighed, offering Angela a small, grateful smile. "I won't know what could happen with Celine unless I confront these feelings. And who knows? Maybe she's feeling the same way."

"Exactly," Angela beamed, her mischievous grin returning. "Now, let's enjoy our movie night, and tomorrow, you can figure out how to have that conversation with Celine."

As the opening credits of their chosen film began to roll, Jemima found herself grateful for Angela's unwavering support. While the uncertainty of her emotions still lingered, she knew that she had the strength to face them - and whatever outcome awaited him with Celine.

～

The sun dipped low in the sky, casting an amber glow through the living room windows. With every passing second, the golden rays seemed to intensify the quiet turmoil brewing within Jemima. Her fingers drummed nervously on her knee as she tried to process everything Angela had said.

"Jemima" Angela began gently, leaning forward and fixing her with a warm, understanding gaze. "It's completely normal to feel conflicted when it comes to matters of the heart. You're not alone in this."

She sighed, unable to shake the gnawing anxiety that clung to her chest. "But what if I tell Celine how I feel, and she doesn't feel the same way? What if it ruins our friendship?"

Angela leaned back into the couch cushions, her dark curls spilling over her shoulders as she considered Jemima's concerns. The movie continued to play, but the characters' quips and antics went unnoticed, their laughter drowned out by the weight of Jemima's thoughts.

"Jemima," she said finally, her voice steady and reassuring. "You have to trust that your friendship is strong enough to withstand something like this. If you both value each other, then you'll find a way to navigate these feelings together."

Jemima's blue eyes searched hers for any hint of doubt or hesitation, but all she found was unwavering conviction. It was as if Angela's confidence had seeped into the very air around them, wrapping Jemima in a comforting embrace.

"Maybe you're right," Jemima murmured, her voice

barely audible above the sounds of the movie. "I just... I don't want to lose her, Angie."

"Then be honest with her. Talk to her, listen to her, and let her know how much she means to you," Angela advised, her tone softening. "And remember that whatever happens, you've got people who care about you – like me."

"Thanks, Angie," Jemima whispered, feeling the tension in her chest begin to dissipate. As they turned their attention back to the movie, Jemima couldn't help but feel a renewed sense of determination taking root within her. It was time to face her fears and have an honest conversation with Celine about her true feelings. And whatever the outcome, she knew that she had the support of other friends.

~

*W*ith the late afternoon sun casting a warm golden glow on the living room, Jemima sat there, her fingers tapping anxiously on her knee once again. Angela's words echoed in her head, encouraging her to be honest with Celine and take a chance on love. She felt a whirlwind of emotions - fear, excitement, and a glimmer of hope.

"Jemima," Angela said gently, her dark curls bouncing as she tilted her head, "honesty is crucial in any relationship. Trust me, I've learned that the hard way." Her mischievous smile made a brief appearance, softening the serious mood.

"Really? How?" Jemima asked, genuinely curious to hear more about Angela's experiences.

Angela leaned back against the couch, her eyes distant as she recalled her past. "Well, there was this guy named Mark. We were friends for years, but I never had the courage to tell him how I truly felt. Eventually, he moved away, and we lost touch. I always regretted not telling him, even if it meant risking our friendship."

Jemima furrowed her brow, pondering her words. The thought of losing Celine due to her own hesitation sent a shiver down her spine. She glanced at Angela, who continued.

"Then there was Peter. We worked together and had great chemistry, but we kept things professional, never venturing beyond the boundaries of our workplace relationship. It wasn't until he got a job offer in another city that I realized how much I cared for him. So I took a leap of faith, confessed my feelings, and to my surprise, he felt the same way."

"Wow! So it was you who made the first move." Jemima's heart raced at the idea of taking such a risk, not knowing if Celine was even interested.

"Taking chances in love can be terrifying, but it can also lead to the most rewarding relationships," Angela said earnestly, her brown eyes locking onto Jemima's. "You'll never know if you don't try, and I believe Celine deserves your honesty."

Jemima took a deep breath, soaking in Angela's words. She was right - she owed it to both Celine and herself to be honest about her feelings. She couldn't let fear dictate the trajectory of their relationship, no matter how daunting the prospect of vulnerability seemed.

"Thank you, Angie," Jemima murmured, feeling a newfound sense of resolve. "I appreciate your insight. I don't want to live with regrets, so I'll give it a shot." Her blue eyes shone with determination as she finally made up her mind.

"Good," Angela smiled warmly, leaning over to give her a friendly hug. "Just remember to be patient and understanding with Celine. Open communication is key. And no matter what happens, I'm here for you."

As they parted from their embrace, the weight on Jemima's shoulders felt lighter. With Angela's support, she found the courage to face her fears and take a chance on love. And whatever the outcome, she knew that she had the unwavering support of those who cared for him most.

~

The sun dipped low in the sky, casting warm hues of orange and pink that were reflected in Jemima's eyes as she gazed out the living room window. She stood there, her hands in her pockets, her thoughts a whirlwind of emotion. Angela's words still echoed in her mind, urging her to confront her feelings for Celine. And yet, there was something terrifying about laying her heart bare.

"Jemima," Angela said gently, her tone both understanding and firm. "You've been standing there for ages, deep in thought. It's time to make a decision."

She sighed, nodding slowly. "I know, Angie. I just, … what if Celine in straight and the thought of—the thought of me and her—repulses her? Yet, I don't want to live with regrets, you know? I need to follow your advice." The resolve in her voice was palpable, even as doubt continued to gnaw at the edges of her mind.

"Good." Angela's lips curved into an encouraging smile. "Now, let's focus on what you're going to say to her. Be honest and open, but also... be gentle. Remember, she might not be ready for this conversation."

Jemima took a deep breath, feeling the weight of her words. She knew that approaching Celine required care, and the last thing she wanted was to push her away.

"Thanks, Angela," she said sincerely, offering her a grateful smile. "Your support means the world to me."

"You're welcome, Jemima," Angela replied warmly, her eyes shining with affection. "Just remember that I'm here for you, no matter how this unfolds."

Her reassurance brought a sense of relief over Jemima, and with it came a newfound determination. Her heart raced in anticipation, excitement mingling with anxiety as she prepared to face Celine and reveal her true feelings.

"Alright," Jemima said, her voice steady. "I'll talk to her tonight, after I close up the shop. That should give us enough privacy to have this conversation." She clenched her fists, taking a small measure of comfort in the strength she found there.

"Great," Angela beamed. "You've got this, Jemima. And remember, whatever happens, you're not alone."

That night, as the sun dipped below the horizon and shadows stretched across the small town, Jemima made her way toward the shop with a newfound purpose. Her heart swelled with gratitude for Angela's unwavering support, and she knew that, no matter what the outcome, she was ready to take a chance on love. No more regrets, no more hiding behind fear. It was time to let the truth set her free.

"Jemima," Angela's voice cut through the air, pulling

her from her thoughts. "Before you go, I just want to remind you to be patient and understanding with Celine."

Jemima looked at Angela, Jemima eyes searching hers for a moment before nodding in agreement. "You're right, open communication is important." Her hands moved to adjust the collar of her blouse, betraying her nerves.

"Exactly," Angela replied, stepping closer and placing a reassuring hand on Jemima shoulder. "And don't forget to really listen to her, too. Sometimes we get so wrapped up in what we want to say that we forget to pay attention to the other person's needs and feelings."

"I'll keep that in mind." Jemima took a deep breath, feeling the weight of the impending conversation settling on her chest like a heavy stone. She could feel the warmth of Angela's touch seeping into her skin, grounding her in the present moment.

"Good luck tonight," Angela said as she stepped back, giving Jemima room to breathe. "Just remember to be honest and true to yourself, okay?"

"Okay," she whispered, her voice barely audible. She closed her eyes for a brief moment, collecting herself before meeting Angela's gaze once more. "Thank you, Angela. For everything."

"You're welcome," she replied softly, her smile filled with genuine affection. "Now, go get 'em, tiger."

With a final deep breath, Jemima turned and walked toward her shop, her steps growing more resolute with each stride. As the distance between Jemima and Angela grew, she felt a strange mix of fear, excitement, and resolve coursing through her veins. This was it – the moment of truth.

Celine's laughter echoed through the quiet shop as Jemima approached, her familiar lilting voice causing her heart to swell. She paused just outside the door, taking a moment to appreciate the sight of her, bathed in the warm glow of the setting sun. Her blonde hair shimmered like gold as she tilted her head back, eyes crinkling with mirth.

"Alright," Jemima murmured to himself, steeling her resolve. "Let's do this.

As she pushed open the door and stepped inside, Celine's laughter subsided, and her gaze met Jemima's – a mixture of surprise and curiosity lighting up her beautiful features. The air between them seemed to crackle with anticipation, but there was no turning back now.

"Hey, Celine," Jemima began, her voice steady despite the pounding in her chest. "There's something I need to talk to you about. Can we sit down for a moment?" Jemima inhaled deeply, reminding herself to be patient, understanding, and open. This was her chance to lay everything on the line, and she wasn't about to let fear hold her back any longer.

"Sure, Jemima, but can we chat tomorrow night?" Celine blurted out quickly. "If it's okay with you, I'll head off now and work on some sketches. I got a call from the owner of Dawson's Ink, a tattoo shop in a neighboring town. He wants to see me tomorrow. I'd like to be prepared with some new examples of my work to show him."

"Why that's wonderful." Jemima hid her disappointment. "Frank Dawson buys all his designs, so maybe you'll have a good customer." Jemima pulled two ledger books out from under the counter. "I'll be fine. I'll tidy up the tools out the back and square the account books so you can have my place to yourself to focus on your art."

"You are so understanding." Celine leaned in and left a peck on Jemima's face as she rushed past her and out the door.

Jemima's heart sank as Celine's words sunk in. She had built up the courage to finally share her feelings, only to be brushed aside in favor of Celine's own pursuits. The disappointment weighed heavily on her, threatening to overwhelm the fragile hope she had carried into the conversation. She watched as Celine hurriedly left, the sting of the brief kiss lingering on her cheek.

As the door closed behind Celine, Jemima fought to hold back the tears that welled up in her eyes. She couldn't help but feel a pang of betrayal mixed with the ache of unrequited love. The untouched account books blurred before her, their neat rows and columns becoming a painful reminder of the distance between her and Celine.

With a heavy sigh, Jemima wiped away a stray tear and straightened her posture. She wouldn't let this setback deter her. She had been patient for so long, but now it was time to face the truth. Celine's priorities lay elsewhere, and perhaps it was time for Jemima to find her own path as well.

Gathering her strength, she closed the account books with a resolute snap. The sound echoed in the empty room, a symbol of her determination to move forward. Jemima squared her shoulders and whispered to herself, "I deserve someone who will prioritize me too."

And with that, Jemima took her first steps toward a future where her own dreams took center stage, determined to leave behind the unrequited love that had held her back for far too long.

CHAPTER 5

The sun cast a warm glow on Celine's cheeks as she pulled into the quaint town where Frank Dawson's tattoo parlor awaited her. A subtle tension coursed through her body, leaving her fingertips tingling with anticipation. It wasn't every day that she ventured into new territory to face off against potential competition. She hoped they might be friends, and maybe she could sell him some of her tattoo designs.

"Alright, Celine, you've got this," she whispered to herself, adjusting the rearview mirror to check her appearance one more time. Her blonde hair was pulled back in a loose ponytail, strands framing her beautiful features. She took a deep breath and stepped out of her car, feeling the crunch of gravel beneath her boots as she made her way toward the tattoo parlor.

The moment she pushed open the door, the scent of ink and sterilizing solution greeted her like an old friend. She found herself enveloped by the edgy decor of the parlor – dark walls adorned with vibrant framed artwork, neon signs casting an eerie glow over the space. Tattoo designs covered every inch of the walls, showcasing the range of styles and creativity the artists had mastered.

"Welcome to Dawson's Ink," said a voice from behind the counter. Celine glanced up to see a young woman with a pixie cut and a septum piercing, offering her a friendly smile. "What can I do for you today?"

"Hi there!" Celine replied brightly, her nerves momentarily subsiding. "I'm actually looking for Frank Dawson. Is he around?"

"Sure thing! Just give me a sec," the girl replied as she disappeared through a doorway.

Celine took the opportunity to survey the room further, examining the intricate designs lining the walls. Some were delicate and ethereal, while others boasted bold lines and fierce imagery. Each piece was a testament to the skill and dedication of the artists Frank Dawson referenced for his work.

"Miss Montgomery, I presume?" a gruff voice called out, snapping Celine back to the present. She turned to face Frank Dawson herself, a tall and slender woman whose arms were adorned with an impressive array of tattoos.

"Frank?" Celine replied, extending her hand.

Frank grasped it firmly. "Francine if you are offended by my preferred name." She released her grip.

I'm Celine Montgomery, owner of the mobile tattoo business you've heard about. I came as soon as I could to introduce myself. Hello, Frank."

Frank's eyes narrowed as she studied her, her skepticism evident. But Celine remained calm and confident, determined to make a good impression. This was her chance to show her that she wasn't just another tattoo artist passing through town – she was something unique, someone worth remembering.

"Nice to meet you, Celine," Frank said grudgingly. "Your reputation precedes you."

"Thank you. I appreciate that," she replied, her heart pounding in her chest. "I hope we can inspire each other and maybe even learn a thing or two from our different approaches to this art form."

"Only time will tell," Frank replied cryptically, leaving Celine to wonder what lay ahead on this thrilling new chapter of her journey.

Frank's voice dripped with skepticism. "The traveling tattoo artist."

"Exactly," Celine confirmed, sensing the doubt in his

tone. "I believe there's room for both traditional parlors and more innovative approaches like mine in this industry."

"Is that so?" Frank raised an eyebrow, scrutinizing her from head to toe. "You really think you can compete with established artists like those working here? With your...mobile setup?"

Celine fought the urge to fidget under her intense gaze. She knew her work was good, but defending it against someone like Frank was intimidating. Still, she couldn't back down now.

"Of course," she replied, meeting her eyes with determination. "My clients appreciate the convenience and personalized experience my mobile services offer. And my skillset speaks for itself."

"Convenience, huh?" Frank snorted, her skepticism undiminished. "This isn't fast food, Miss Montgomery. Tattooing is an art form that requires time, dedication, and a stable environment. How can you possibly guarantee the same level of quality and professionalism when you're constantly on the move?"

Celine clenched her fists, frustrated by Frank's assumptions but determined to prove her wrong. "I understand your concerns, Ms. Dawson, but I assure you that I maintain strict standards for cleanliness and technique in my mobile studio. My work is every bit as good as any parlor-based artist."

"Bold claim," Frank muttered, leaning against the counter, her arms still crossed. "But I'll have to see it to believe it."

"Fair enough," Celine agreed, her heart racing from the challenge in her voice. She knew she had what it took to prove herself to Frank and anyone else who doubted her abilities.

"I brought samples of my work," she said, holding his gaze. "You might just be surprised."

A hint of curiosity flickering in Frank's eyes. Then she brushed aside the portfolio Celine drew out from her carry tote. "It's how a tattoo looks on the client—not on paper," Frank replied, "You won't last against my business." She turned her back to Celine, dismissing her.

Celine took a deep breath, her fingers brushing over the collection of tattoo designs she had brought with her. "Look, Frank," she began, her voice steady and confident. "How about this – we have a friendly competition to see who can attract more customers and deliver the best tattoos? That should give me the chance to show you that my mobile business truly holds up against your parlor, and rather than feel we are competitors, you might want to buy and use some of my designs."

"Alright, Celine," Frank said, turning back to face her,

uncrossing her arms and leaning forward slightly. "I'll admit that you've piqued my curiosity.

Celine's heart raced at his proposal. It was a bold challenge, one that would put her skills and professionalism to the test. But she also recognized the opportunity it presented – a chance to prove herself not only to Frank but to the entire community.

"Deal," she agreed, her determination giving her strength. "Let's show the town what we've got."

"May the best artist win," Frank said, extending her hand.

"May the best artist win?" Celine echoed. "Alright, Frank," Celine said, her voice steady despite the butterflies fluttering in her stomach. "I accept your challenge. Let's prove once and for all which business can truly provide the best experience for our clients."

"Great," Frank replied, her skeptical eyes now alight with excitement. "What do you say we set the date for two weeks from today? That should give us both enough time to prepare and promote our businesses."

"Two weeks it is," Celine agreed, her mind already racing with ideas to make her mobile tattoo business stand out.

"Let's shake on it," Frank suggested, extending her hand across the counter. As their palms met, Celine felt a surge of determination course through her.

"May the best artist win," she echoed, her grip firm and resolute.

"May the best artist win," Frank repeated, a glint of respect beginning to show in her eyes.

With the date set, Celine knew that every moment counted. As she left the parlor, she mulled over various marketing strategies and promotional offers to entice clients to choose her mobile business over Frank's establishment.

"First things first," she thought to herself, "I need to create some eye-catching flyers and spread the word on social media. I'll emphasize the unique, personalized experience my mobile tattoo business provides, as well as any special deals I decide to offer."

As she continued down the street, her phone buzzed with an incoming text message. It was from one of her loyal customers, who had heard about the challenge through the grapevine.

"Hey Celine! Just wanted to wish you luck in your competition with Frank! You've got this!" the message read.

Celine smiled as she typed out her grateful response. The support of her customers meant everything to her, and she knew that they would be instrumental in helping her win the competition.

"Thanks, Emily!" she wrote back. "I really appreciate

your encouragement. I'll make sure to keep you updated on all the exciting promotions and events leading up to the big day!"

With each step Celine took, her excitement and determination grew. She knew that this challenge would be no easy feat, but she also knew that she had the passion, skills, and resilience to come out on top.

"Frank Dawson," she mused, "you have no idea what you're in for."

～

The morning light filtered through the blinds, casting a warm golden glow on Celine's worktable. Surrounded by her art supplies, she dove headfirst into designing eye-catching flyers and social media posts to promote her mobile tattoo business. Every stroke of her brush conveyed the passion that fueled her artistry, and as she layered colors and images, her excitement grew stronger.

"Perfect," she murmured, admiring her latest creation – a vibrant watercolor backdrop with a sleek, minimalist design showcasing her signature tattoo style. "This should definitely grab their attention."

Throughout the day, Celine snapped photos of her work and edited them meticulously before posting on various social media platforms. Each post highlighted not only her artistic talent but also the convenience and unique experience offered by her mobile services. As the likes and shares rolled in, so did the inquiries and appointment bookings.

"Alright, Frank," Celine whispered with a smirk, "let's see what you've got."

The day of the competition dawned bright and clear. Celine could feel the anticipation buzzing in the air as she parked her mobile tattoo station in a bustling area of town. She had chosen this spot carefully – right across from a trendy coffee shop, where she knew foot traffic would be high.

"Okay, Celine," she said to herself as she unloaded her equipment and set up her station, "today is the day. You've worked hard for this moment. Show them what you can do."

People began to gather around her station, intrigued by the colorful display of her artwork and the novelty of a mobile tattoo service. Celine greeted each potential client with a warm smile and confident demeanor, answering questions and showcasing her portfolio.

"Excuse me," a young woman approached, flipping through one of Celine's albums, "is this your work? It's stunning!"

"Thank you so much!" Celine replied, feeling a surge of pride. "Yes, I'm the artist behind these designs."

"Wow, I've never seen a mobile tattoo service before," the woman said, her eyes wide with amazement. "I think it's such an incredible idea."

Celine smiled, her heart swelling with gratitude for the support and validation of her vision. "Thank you! I wanted to create a unique and personal experience for my clients, so I decided to take my art on the road."

As the crowd continued to grow, Celine knew she had made the right decision. She could see the spark of curiosity in each person's eyes, and her confidence swelled with every new client booking and compliment on her work.

"Alright, Frank Dawson," she thought triumphantly, stealing a glance at Frank's tattoo parlor down the street, "let's see if you can keep up with this."

In that moment, standing amidst the throng of eager customers, Celine felt more alive than ever. The fire in her veins burned brighter, fueled by her passion for art and the thrill of proving herself in the face of doubt. And as she prepared to ink her first client of the day, she knew she was ready for whatever challenges lay ahead.

*a*ll day Celine's fingers danced over the sanitized tools, aranging them with precision and care on her gleaming workstation between the frequent clients. Her mobile tattoo studio hummed with energy, the warm sunlight streaming through the windows casting a golden halo around her. Outside, she could hear the buzz of conversation as passers-by stopped to admire her vibrant designs displayed on the easel.

"Hi, are you Celine?" a voice asked tentatively, breaking her focus.

Celine looked up and smiled at the young woman standing in the doorway, her eyes alight with curiosity. "Yes, that's me! What can I do for you?"

"I saw your flyer and just had to come check it out," the woman replied, stepping inside and admiring the cozy, inviting interior. "Your work is incredible, and I've never seen a mobile tattoo studio before."

"Thank you so much!" Celine beamed, feeling a surge of pride. "I wanted to offer something unique to my clients, and this seemed like the perfect way to do it. Do you have a design in mind?"

"Actually, I do," the woman said, pulling out her phone and showing Celine an intricate floral pattern. "Is this something you could do?"

"Absolutely," Celine nodded, her fingers itching to bring the design to life. "Why don't you have a seat and we'll get started?"

As the woman settled into the comfortable chair, Celine thought about how far she'd come since stepping foot in Frank's tattoo parlor. She knew she had to prove herself, not just to him but to all those who doubted the potential of her mobile business. And as she began the delicate dance of needle and ink on her client's skin, she felt more determined than ever.

"Wow, this is amazing!" the woman exclaimed, examining her new tattoo in the mirror. "You're so talented, and getting a tattoo in a mobile studio like this is such a unique experience."

"Thank you," Celine said, her heart swelling with satisfaction. "I'm so glad you enjoyed it."

Word of Celine's skill and the novelty of her mobile tattoo business spread like wildfire throughout the town. A steady stream of clients flowed in and out of her studio, each one leaving more impressed than the last. As the day wore on, she couldn't help but notice how quiet Frank's parlor had become.

The sun dipped low in the sky, casting an orange glow over Celine's mobile tattoo studio. She glanced out the window and watched as Frank approached, a look of surprise etched across his face. As she entered her space,

Celine immediately noticed how different she seemed from their first encounter.

"Hey, Celine," Frank said, her voice softer than she remembered. "I gotta admit, you've really surprised me today."

"Surprised you?" Celine asked, wiping her hands on a cloth after finishing up another tattoo.

Frank scratched the back of her neck, looking almost sheepish. "Yeah, I mean, I didn't expect your mobile studio to be such a hit. But you've got quite a crowd out there, and they're all talking about how great your work is. Y"our know, we could make a great partnership if you would consider it."

Celine smiled, feeling a swell of pride within her. "Thank you, Frank. I'm just doing what I love and trying to offer something unique. I" like working as an independent at this stage."

Frank nodded, meeting her gaze. "Well, perhaps you will come share supper with me when you knock off tonight. Me could chat about the potential if we were to combine. And I have to say, you've earned my respect. I can see now that you're just as dedicated to this craft as I am."

As Frank spoke those words, Celine felt a surge of validation. She had proved herself not only to him but also to the town and, most importantly, herself.

"Thanks, Frank. I'll skip supper tonight. I've been ignoring my hosts, the friend who's putting me up at their home while I'm staying here. I've promised to spend this evening with them," Celine replied. "But it means a lot coming from you, that you are accepting me now." Celine's voice was filled with genuine gratitude.

"Alright, I'd better get back to my shop," Frank said, turning to leave. "But you keep up the good work, Celine. You've got something special here. And I really would like to see more of you—socially as well as professionally.

"Thank you," Celine called after her, watching as she disappeared into the dusky evening.

Once she was gone, Celine allowed herself a moment to reflect on the day's events and her journey so far. She thought back to her initial encounter with Frank and how intimidating it had been to challenge someone so established in the tattoo industry. But she had held her ground, trusted her instincts, and now, she had emerged victorious.

As the last rays of sunlight vanished beyond the horizon, Celine felt a deep sense of accomplishment and validation for her mobile tattoo business. She knew that she still had much to learn and many more challenges to face, but for now, she could relish in the knowledge that she had proven herself as a talented and dedicated artist.

With renewed determination, she mentally prepared herself for the road ahead, knowing that each new customer would be another opportunity to showcase her passion and skill - and to continue building a legacy as unique and lasting as the art she created.

CHAPTER 6

*C*eline Montgomery expertly set up her mobile tattoo booth in the bustling town square. She carefully arranged her inks and needles, feeling a familiar thrill course through her as she anticipated a new day filled with artistic expressions and satisfied customers.

As Celine smoothed the worn leather of her chair, she noticed a young woman with vibrant hair in various shades of purple, pink, and blue, approaching her booth with wide eyes full of curiosity. Celine recognized her instantly as Lily Anderson, a sweet, bubbly woman who had become a regular customer at her mobile tattoo business, always eager to add more color to her already impressive collection of body art.

"Hey there, Celine!" Lily greeted enthusiastically, her infectious smile making Celine's own lips curve into a grin. "I can't believe you're here in Fountain Springs! You never let on before that you were a lesbian."

"Hi Lily!" Celine replied, curiosity in the tone of her voice. "Whatever makes you think I'm a lesbian?" She wiped her hands on a clean towel before extending a hand to shake Lily's. "I'm just following my passion for tattooing and trying to bring my art to as many people as possible. I thought I'd try my luck here in Fountain Springs."

Fountain Springs is predominately a lesbian community." Lily's eyes sparkled with genuine interest as she scanned the numerous tattoo designs displayed on the walls of Celine's booth. "I love your work, Celine. You have such a unique style, and I'm always excited to see what new pieces you've come up with."

"Thank you, Lily," Celine said sincerely, touched by the young woman's compliment. As she watched Lily examine her designs, Celine couldn't help but feel a sense of camaraderie with this fellow artist. They both understood the struggles and triumphs that came with pursuing their passions, and Celine found comfort in that shared understanding.

"Ooh, this one's new!" Lily exclaimed, pointing to a delicate, intricately detailed design of a butterfly perched on a flower. "It's absolutely stunning. I think I might need to add it to my collection."

Celine smiled warmly at her enthusiastic customer, feeling a renewed sense of purpose in her artistic journey. As she prepared to bring another masterpiece to life on Lily's skin, Celine couldn't help but feel grateful for the connection they had forged through their shared love for art and the support they offered each other as they navigated the challenges of their respective careers.

"Let's do it, then," Celine said with determination, picking up her tattoo machine. "I'm more than happy to create something beautiful for you today, my friend." She gestured for Lily to take a seat. "So, tell me more about Fountain Springs. You obviously know more about it than I do." She laughed. "Gosh, I don't think I've ever met a lesbian."

Lily laughed. "Then you are a blind fool. You are working on one who's been following you around, giving you signals they are interested in you for years."

"Oh!" Celine's cheeks burned hot. She felt like a fool. Now, it was so clear to her. Lily had made overtures to her. Who else? Had Francine made a sexual overture to her? She found it hard to focus. "I have been so blind."

"You are waking up and seeing me at last?" Lily exclaimed with joy.

"I'm seeing my friend, the one whose house I've been

staying at as a guest. Oh, my gosh. I feel terrible that I never realised it's more than friendship that Jemima wants from me." Celine turned off the tattoo machine and downed tools. "Give me a moment, please."

She disappeared and returned with two ice cold coffee drinks from the fridge.

Lily sipped her iced coffee, looking thoughtfully at the colorful tattoos that adorned her own arms.

"You know, you don't have to fret it. Your friend is no more a monster than I am," she said, a nostalgic smile gracing her lips. "You are either interested of you're not. We can handle it. I discovered my sexual preference was for women when I was young. My parents didn't appreciate It, but I couldn't help myself."

Celine chuckled, remembering her own early days of sketching in life drawing classes. "That sounds familiar," she admitted. "I far preferred drawing women's bodies. I found them far more beautiful and erotic than men's. "I've just never acted on any of those fantasies I've experienced after seeing naked women." She smiled with understanding. "I guess opportunity and experience is the only thing than separates any of us.

"Well," Lily began, her eyes distant as she recalled the past, "when I was sixteen, my mom took me to an art gallery for the first time. It was like stepping into another world. The colors, the textures... but mainly the paintings of erotically beautiful women. I was completely captivated. That's when I knew I wanted to dedicate my life to featuring women in my art. Loving a woman, and wanting to be loved by a woman, was a natural progression from there."

"Wow," Celine murmured, impressed by Lily's passion. "And I see that reflected in the art you create now?"

Lily's face lit up. "Mostly paintings of women, in acrylics and watercolors these days. But I've also dabbled in sculpture and mixed media. There are so many possibilities, and I love exploring new techniques." She paused, glancing at Celine's tattoo booth. "Actually, your work has been a big inspiration for me lately. The way you blend colors and create such intricate designs is amazing."

Celine felt a warmth spread through her chest at Lily's praise. "Thank you," she said, touched by the compliment. "It means a lot to hear that from a fellow artist."

"Of course!" Lily exclaimed, her enthusiasm infectious. "We all need encouragement and support in this industry, right?"

"Absolutely," Celine agreed, feeling a strong sense of

camaraderie with Lily. "It's reassuring to know that someone else understands the struggles we face as artists."

Lily nodded, "And perhaps now you have a glimpse into the struggles lesbian women face." Her eyes reflecting a depth of understanding that only a fellow female artist could possess. "It's not always easy, but the rewards are worth it. We get to create and live a life that's beautiful and meaningful, something that has the power to touch our hearts more deeply than you would know unless you experience sapphic love for yourself."

Celine smiled, feeling a renewed sense of purpose in her own artistic journey. As she listened to Lily share her experiences and growth as an artist, and as a lesbian, she couldn't help but feel inspired by their connection. The town square seemed to glow with a new vibrancy, as if mirroring the bond between two kindred spirits who had found solace and inspiration in each other's company.

～

Celine felt a surge of gratitude towards the young woman standing before her. It was as if Lily had reached into her chest and pulled out the very fears that weighed on her spirit, only to offer reassurance and support in return. She looked around the bustling town square, the laughter and chatter of the diverse crowd mingling with the scent of fresh flowers and food from nearby stalls. This was the life she had chosen, and despite the challenges, she could see herself fitting into Fountain Springs way of life, given time to adjust.

"Thank you, Lily," Celine said sincerely, her voice thick with emotion. "Your words mean more to me than you could ever know. You have opened my eyes."

"Hey, we artists need to stick together, right?" Lily said with a grin, gently nudging Celine's arm. "Every path has its obstacles, but I've learned that sometimes it's those very challenges that lead us to the most beautiful and unexpected destinations."

Celine smiled, her heart swelling with newfound determination. She knew there would still be difficult moments ahead, but as she stood there in the vibrant atmosphere of Fountain Springs, with the support and understanding of a fellow artist, she felt more prepared than ever to face whatever came her way.

*T*he sun hung low in the sky, casting a warm golden glow over the town square. Celine and Lily sat on a weathered bench beneath a magnificent oak tree, their legs stretched out before them as the soft hum of conversation and laughter from nearby stalls filled the air around them.

"Look at that one," said Lily, pointing to a young girl passing by with her family, her face painted with an elaborate butterfly design. "I remember when I first discovered my love for painting. It was like this whole new world opened up to me."

Celine leaned back against the bench, her head tilted towards Lily as she listened intently. "It's amazing how art can have such a profound effect on us, isn't it?"

"Absolutely," agreed Lily, her eyes lighting up with enthusiasm. "I think that's why I find your tattoo work so fascinating. It's not just about creating something beautiful or meaningful; it's also about helping people express themselves and tell their own stories."

For the first time in what felt like an eternity, Celine felt truly seen and understood. The simple act of sitting on this bench with Lily, sharing stories and experiences from their artistic journeys, their shared attraction to the feminine body, provided a sense of solace that she hadn't even realized she was craving.

"Your unwavering support means the world to me, Lily," Celine confessed, her voice filled with heartfelt gratitude. "At times, it feels like I'm navigating this journey alone, but having someone like you who truly understands what I'm going through... it makes all the difference."

Lily tenderly clasped Celine's hand, her touch radiating comfort. "Celine, I know the weight of self-doubt and the overwhelming challenges that can arise. But I want you to know that your talent as an artist is undeniable, and I have complete faith that you will conquer any obstacles that come your way. Remember, you're never alone."

Celine's smile blossomed, her heart brimming with warmth and an immense appreciation for the genuine friendship that was flourishing between them. In Lily, she had discovered not only a kindred spirit but also an unwavering source of inspiration and support.

"Thank you for guiding me on this journey of self-discovery, Lily," Celine whispered, her eyes shimmering with unshed tears. "I will always be grateful to you for that."

As the sun sank below the horizon, painting the sky with vibrant hues, Celine and Lily remained seated side by side on the weathered bench. Their laughter and conversation intertwined like the delicate threads of a beautiful tapestry, creating an unbreakable connection forged through shared dreams and passions.

"Celine," she nodded, her voice filled with understanding. "Friends?" Emotion tightened her throat. "I'm sorry I can't offer you more."

"Friends," Lily agreed, sealing their pact with a firm handshake and a knowing smile.

CHAPTER 7

Jemima sat on the edge of her bed, her hands running through her dark hair in frustration. Her heart raced at the thought of Celine - her laughter, her warm touch, and the way her eyes lit up when she spoke about her art. It was a feeling that both thrilled and terrified her. Overwhelmed by the intensity of her emotions, Jemima found herself unable to concentrate on anything else.

She had always admired Celine from afar, but ever since they met in person, their friendship had evolved into something so much more powerful than she could have ever imagined. The realization hit her like a ton of bricks: she could not bear the thought of never seeing her again. She loved Celine. And, as frightening as it was, she knew she had to tell her.

"Get it together, Sullivan," she muttered to herself, pacing back and forth across the room. "You're a grown woman, not some lovesick teenager."

Jemima glanced at the clock, realizing that she'd be meeting Celine soon. The anticipation sent butterflies fluttering in her stomach, and she let out a deep breath, trying to calm her nerves. She decided it was now or never; she had to confess her love to Celine. But how would she even begin?

"Hey, Celine," she practiced in front of the mirror, "I just wanted to tell you that... No, no, that's terrible." She shook her head, frustrated with herself. "Come on, you can do this."

As she continued rehearsing, Jemima couldn't help but smile, thinking about the gentle curve of Celine's lips and the way her blonde hair framed her face. Celine had captured her heart entirely, and Jemima hoped beyond hope that Celine might feel the same way.

"Alright," she said to her reflection, taking one last deep breath. "You've got this. Just speak from the heart."

Determined, Jemima grabbed her keys and headed out the door, ready to face her fears and lay her heart on the line.

*T*he sun was beginning to set, casting a warm, golden glow over the small wooden cabin situated on the outskirts of a picturesque small town. The soft chirping of birds and rustling leaves created a serene ambiance around them, as if nature itself was rooting for their blossoming connection.

Inside the cozy living room, a fire crackled in the stone fireplace, its flickering light casting dancing shadows on the walls. Two comfortable armchairs had been pulled closer together near the hearth, a small table between them holding two steaming mugs of hot cocoa. The scent of burning wood mingled with the subtle aroma of chocolate, creating an atmosphere that was both intimate and comforting.

"I can talk now," Celine said softly, her eyes meeting Jemima's as she took a seat in one of the armchairs. "It's been so hectic these past couple of weeks. I gat so obsessed about winning this challenge, I lost sight of what's important. I really do need you as my friend."

"Of course," Jemima replied, her heart pounding as she sat down opposite Celine. She couldn't help but notice how the firelight illuminated the other woman's delicate features, making her look even more beautiful than she had remembered.

"Everything alright?" Celine asked, concern etched

on her face as she noticed Jemima's slightly furrowed brow. Little did she know that it was her presence that caused Jemima's nerves to jumble.

"Actually, there's something I've been wanting to talk to you about," Jemima began, trying to steady her voice as she looked into Celine's eyes. She took a deep breath, reminding herself to speak from the heart. "Celine, ever since we met in person, I've realized that my feelings for you have grown beyond friendship."

She paused for a moment, gauging her reaction before continuing. "I can't stop thinking about you, and the thought of not seeing you again... well, it terrifies me."

Celine's eyes widened, but not in surprise; her conversation with Lily had opened her to this possibility. She didn't interrupt. Instead, she offered a small, encouraging smile, urging Jemima to continue.

"Every time we talk or spend time together, I feel this connection between us," Jemima confessed, her vulnerability shining through with every word. "I know this might be unexpected, but I had to tell you. Celine, I've fallen in love with you."

For a moment, the only sound in the room was the crackling of the fire, as if it were holding its breath along with Jemima. Her heart raced, her palms sweating as she anxiously awaited her response. But despite her nervousness, Jemima knew that she had taken the most important step: opening herself up to the possibility of a future with Celine by her side.

～

*C*eline blinked, her ocean-blue eyes reflecting the firelight as she processed Jemima's words. Confusion danced across her delicate features, and she chewed her lower lip as if searching for the right response to Jemima's heartfelt confession. She glanced away for a moment, taking in the cozy surroundings of the cabin they had chosen for their getaway.

"Jemima," she finally said, her voice soft and uncertain. "I... I don't know what to say." Her gaze met Jemima's once more, revealing an array of emotions swirling beneath the surface.

"Take your time," Jemima replied gently, giving her hand a reassuring squeeze. "I just wanted you to know how I feel."

Celine let out a shaky breath, her chest rising and falling as she collected her thoughts. "I never expected this," she admitted, her fingers tracing absent patterns on the armrest between them. "I mean, I've always felt a connection with you, too. But I guess I never thought about it in that way before today."

They sat in silence for a few moments, the crackling fire and the distant sound of raindrops on the window-pane providing a soothing soundtrack to their conversation. Celine's heart raced at the possibility of exploring her feelings for Jemima. She acknowledged to herself—she felt a strong attraction—but, this was all unexplored and frighteningly new territory.

"Can I ask you something?" Celine ventured hesitantly, her curiosity piqued.

"Of course," Jemima nodded, her blue eyes locked onto hers, full of sincerity and vulnerability.

"Have you ever been in love before?" Celine asked, her voice barely above a whisper.

"Once," Jemima admitted, swallowing hard. "But it wasn't like this. What I feel for you is different, deeper... It feels like coming home."

A warm flush spread across Celine's cheeks at this honest admission. As she stared into Jemima's eyes, she couldn't help but feel a magnetic pull between them, a spark of attraction that had been quietly smoldering, only now being fanned into a flame by this honest conversation and their time spent together.

"Jemima," she began, her voice quivering with emotion. "I'm not sure where this will lead, but I want to explore these feelings with you. I can't deny that there's something special between us."

"Neither can I," Jemima agreed softly, her gaze never leaving Celine. "And while it scares me to think of the unknown, I know that I'd regret it if we didn't give ourselves a chance."

As their conversation continued, Jemima and Celine found themselves growing closer, their hearts intertwining like the branches of a tree reaching for the sky. The sparks of attraction between them grew brighter, the warm glow of possibility illuminating the path before them. And though the future remained uncertain, one thing was clear: together, they would face whatever challenges lay ahead, hand in hand and heart to heart.

⁓

The flickering candlelight cast a warm glow across the cozy living room, illuminating the delicate curve of Celine's cheek as she stared deep into Jemima's eyes. The weight of their conversation hung in the air, mingling with the faint scent of cinnamon from the nearby candles.

"Jemima," Celine murmured, her voice barely above a whisper. "I don't think I've ever met anyone quite like you."

Jemima felt a sudden surge of warmth in her chest, and she knew that this was her chance to express how she truly felt – to show Celine just how much she meant to her. She took a deep breath, her heart pounding in her ears as she mustered the courage to speak her truth.

"Before I met you, Celine, I didn't know what it meant to connect with someone so deeply," Jemima confessed, her voice slightly shaky but sincere. "Your passion and your spirit have captivated me from the moment we first spoke online. And now, having spent time together, I can't imagine my life without you."

Celine's eyes filled with tears, her vulnerability shining through as she listened to Jemima's heartfelt words. Her hands trembled in her lap, and she found herself at a loss for words.

"Jemima, I..." She paused, searching for the right words to convey the whirlwind of emotions swirling within her. "I never expected to feel this way about you, either. It's terrifying and exhilarating all at once."

As she spoke, Celine reached out tentatively, her fingers brushing against Jemima's hand on the armrest between them. The simple touch sent shivers up her spine, igniting a fire within her heart that she hadn't known existed.

"Every time I see your name pop up on my phone or hear your voice, it's like a piece of me comes alive," she admitted, her eyes shimmering with unshed tears. "I'm not sure what the future holds for us, Jemima, but I want to explore this connection – whatever it may be – and see where it takes us."

Jemima felt her heart swell with gratitude and hope as she listened to Celine's honest words. She knew that they were both taking a risk by admitting their feelings, but it was a risk she was more than willing to take – if it meant the possibility of something truly special with her.

"Thank you, Celine," she murmured, her fingers gently intertwining with Celine's. "For being brave enough to explore this with me. I promise you, I won't let you down."

～

The silence that fell between them was heavy with unspoken emotions. The air in the cozy living room seemed to crackle with the electricity of their newfound connection, making every breath feel like an intimate dance.

Jemima's gaze flickered over Celine's face, searching for any hint of doubt or hesitation. But all she saw was a raw vulnerability that mirrored her own. As their eyes locked, it felt as though they were suspended in time – two souls drawn together by fate and now, finally, acknowledging the depths of their feelings.

"Are we really doing this?" Celine whispered, her

voice barely audible over the soft ticking of the grandfather clock in the corner. She shifted closer to Jemima on the couch, seeking the warmth of her body as she tried to wrap her head around the enormity of what they were discussing.

Jemima nodded, swallowing the lump in her throat. "I want to try," she said, her voice steady despite the butterflies dancing in her stomach. "I know it won't be easy, but I believe that what we have is worth fighting for."

Celine bit her lip, her thoughts racing a mile a minute. "What if we mess up our friendship?" she wondered aloud, the fear evident in her eyes. "What if we're not meant to be more than just friends?"

"Those are valid concerns," Jemima admitted, her thumb gently caressing the back of Celine's hand. "But I think we owe it to ourselves to see what could be. We can take it slow, one step at a time. And no matter what happens, I'll always cherish the bond we have."

Celine hesitated, then sighed, her shoulders relaxing slightly. "I guess we'll never know if we don't try, right?" She met Jemima's gaze, the spark of determination in her eyes igniting a fire within her.

"Exactly." Jemima smiled softly, feeling the weight of their shared decision settle around them like a warm blanket. "And I want to be completely honest with you,

Celine. I'm scared, too. But I'm also excited – for all the possibilities that lie ahead and the chance to explore this new side of our relationship."

"Me too," she agreed, her voice barely more than a breath. "I want to be brave with you, Jemima. This is all new for me. But, you can guide me and and we can discover what our future holds."

As they shared their hopes, dreams, and uncertainties with one another. Each confession brought them closer, weaving a tapestry of trust and understanding between them.

As the embers in the fireplace burned down to glowing coals, Jemima and Celine found themselves still entwined on the couch. Their hands clasped tightly, they gazed into each other's eyes, knowing that they had taken the first tentative step towards something extraordinary.

"Here's to us," Jemima murmured, her heart full of hope and anticipation for the journey that lay ahead.

"Here's to us," Celine echoed, her smile lighting up the room as they faced each other.

Jemima took Celine in her arms, her heart racing with a mixture of excitement and tenderness. As she leaned in, their lips met in a gentle, passionate kiss. The world around them faded into the background, and in that moment, there was only the taste of their lips, the warmth of their presence, and the overwhelming rush of emotions that coursed through their hearts. The kiss, a passionate declaration of their love.

~

*T*he sun was setting, casting a warm golden glow over the small town. Jemima and Celine sat side by side on the porch of the quaint cottage, their laughter echoing through the tranquil air. It was a scene right out of a painting, one that Celine wished she could capture with her talented hands.

"Jemima," she began hesitantly, turning to face her as her heart raced in her chest. "I... I've never felt this way about anyone before. It's scary, but it's also exhilarating."

Jemima looked at Celine intently, her blue eyes piercing through any remaining walls she had left. "Celine, neither have I. There's something about you that makes me feel like I'm home – not just in this little town, but within myself."

Jemima's words struck a chord deep within Celine, leaving her breathless. Their shared vulnerability hung in the air between them, binding them together like an invisible thread.

"Promise me," Celine whispered, her voice trembling with raw emotion. "Promise me that we'll take this journey together, hand in hand, no matter where it leads us." She reached out and gently took Jemima's hand, intertwining their fingers as she looked into Jemima's eyes.

"I promise," Jemima murmured, her voice steady and resolute. "We may have our doubts, but I have faith in us, Celine. We can face anything together."

In that moment, time seemed to slow as they gazed deeply into each other's eyes. The warmth from their joined hands spread throughout their bodies, solidifying their decision to give their relationship a chance. Jemima leaned forward, her lips brushing against Celine's forehead in a tender kiss that spoke volumes.

Celine couldn't help but feel a sense of wonder at the path her life had taken. She knew there would be challenges ahead, but with Jemima by her side, she felt an unshakable courage to face them head-on.

"Jemima" she whispered, her voice full of conviction. "I don't know what the future holds for us, but I'm ready to find out."

"Me too," Jemima replied softly, giving her hand a reassuring squeeze as they clung close to each other..

CHAPTER 8

*C*eline stared out the window of the small cottage, her heart pounding with a mix of excitement and trepidation. She knew she had reached a turning point in her life, one that would require her to be brave and vulnerable. The decision to give her relationship with Jemima a chance weighed heavily on her mind, stirring up an internal struggle she hadn't experienced in years.

"Am I really ready for this?" she wondered aloud, her fingers tracing patterns on the fogged-up glass. "Can I truly open my heart again and take this leap?"

Taking a deep breath, Celine closed her eyes and envisioned the woman who had so unexpectedly captured her heart. She remembered their countless late-night conversations, the laughter they shared, and the way she made her feel understood like no one else ever had. With a resolute nod, she decided it was time to trust herself and embrace the unknown.

As if on cue, she heard the crunching sound of tires on gravel outside. Peeking through the window, Celine caught sight of Jemima's SUV making its way down the long driveway. A rush of anticipation surged through her as she quickly grabbed her coat and hat, eager to embark on their adventure together.

"Here goes nothing," she whispered as she stepped outside, greeted by the picturesque countryside that surrounded them.

The beauty of nature seemed to envelope Celine and Jemima as they ventured out together, hand in hand. Rolling hills stretched out as far as the eye could see, adorned with wildflowers that bloomed in vibrant hues of red, yellow, and purple. The sky above was a brilliant canvas of azure, dotted with fluffy clouds that cast gentle shadows on the earth below.

"Isn't it breathtaking?" Celine remarked, her eyes shining with wonder. "I never get tired of seeing this."

"Neither do I," Jemima agreed, her gaze lingering on Celine's face before returning to the landscape. "There's something so peaceful and grounding about being out here, surrounded by nature."

As they continued to stroll through the countryside,

Celine couldn't help but feel a sense of serenity wash over her. The connection she shared with Jemima seemed to be amplified by the beauty that surrounded them, reinforcing her belief that they were embarking on something truly special.

"Jemima," she said softly, squeezing her hand gently. "Thank you for being here with me, for taking this chance together. I know it won't always be easy, but I have faith in us."

"Me too," she responded with a smile, pulling her close and pressing a tender kiss to her forehead. "We'll navigate this journey side by side, come what may."

And with that promise hanging in the air like the sweet scent of wildflowers, Celine and Jemima continued on their path, surrounded by the enchanting beauty of the countryside and the warmth of each other's presence.

As they stood in the quiet embrace of the country-side, their connection deepened. Jemima was over-whelmed by a surge of emotions. She gazed into her eyes, her heart swelling with love and longing.

Their second kiss was a continuation of the unspoken promise they had made to each other. Jemima held Celine close, her hand gently cradling her cheek, her fingers tangling in her soft hair. She leaned in, and their lips met once again, this time with a hunger that spoke of their longing and desire.

Their mouths melded together in a slow, languid dance of passion and tenderness. It was a kiss that lasted, a kiss that explored and expressed their love for one another. Jemima deepened the kiss, savoring the taste of Celine's lips, and she responded in kind, her arms wrapping around Jemima as if to hold her close forever.

In that moment, their world was reduced to the warmth of each other's embrace, the taste of each other's lips, and the unspoken vows of their hearts. Their kiss was a declaration of their love, a promise to stand together through all the challenges and joys life had in store for them.

❧

The sun was beginning to dip below the horizon, casting a warm orange glow that illuminated the rolling hills and lush green fields. Celine couldn't help but marvel at the way the fading light danced on the leaves of the ancient oak tree under which they had decided to set up their picnic.

"Isn't this just perfect?" she sighed, spreading out a checkered blanket on the soft grass beneath them.

"Absolutely," Jemima agreed, smiling as she took in the picturesque scene. "I don't think I've ever seen anything more beautiful."

As they unpacked their wicker basket filled with sandwiches, fresh fruit, and cool lemonade, Celine felt a surge of happiness wash over her. She couldn't remember the last time she had felt so content, her heart swelling with joy as she watched Jemima laugh at her attempts to peel an orange without getting juice all over herself.

"Have you always wanted to be a tattoo artist?" Jemima asked, curiosity lighting up her eyes as she sipped her lemonade.

"Actually, no," Celine admitted, wiping her sticky hands on a napkin. "I originally wanted to be a painter when I was younger. But I fell in love with the intimacy of tattooing – how it allows me to create art that becomes a part of someone's life forever."

"And what about you?" Celine asked. "What's your dream?"

"Me?" Jemima paused for a moment, contemplating her answer. "Well, I've always been passionate about helping others. I'd love to start my own nonprofit some-day, as a part of my existing business. There are a lot of seniors who'd be willing to volunteer their services if they had a fully equipped workshop like mine that they could use. We could restore discarded wooden toys and good quality older furniture and ensure that they find new homes where they will be loved. The profits from these endeavors could go to whichever charities the volunteers want to support. Alternatively, we could directly donate the goods to underprivileged communities."

"That sounds like a wonderful idea," Celine said. "How did you come up with it?"

Jemima smiled, her eyes sparkling with enthusiasm. "Well, it all started when I was a child. I used to spend hours in my grandfather's workshop, tinkering with tools and fixing broken things. He taught me the value of craftsmanship and the joy of giving new life to old objects. As I grew older, I realized that there are so many resources that go to waste, and there are people in need who could benefit from them. That's when the idea of combining my love for helping others with my skills in woodworking and restoration came to me. I wanted to create a space where seniors, who often have valuable knowledge and experience, could contribute and make a difference in our community. It's a way for me to honor my grandfather's legacy and make a positive impact on the world."

Celine listened intently, captivated by Jemima's passion and the thoughtfulness behind her dream. "That's incredible," she said. "You have such a big heart, and I know you'll make a real difference in the world." Celine couldn't help but feel a deep admiration for the woman sitting in front of her, whose heart overflowed with kindness and a genuine desire to make a difference.

As the sun dipped lower in the sky, casting long shadows across the countryside, Celine and Jemima continued to share their dreams and vulnerabilities. They spoke of past heartbreaks, fears about the future, and the courage it took to chase after their aspirations.

"Sometimes I worry that I'm not strong enough," Celine confessed, staring out at the rolling hills. "That I'll let my insecurities hold me back from really going after what I want."

"Hey," Jemima said softly, reaching for her hand. "You are one of the strongest people I know, and I have no doubt that you can achieve anything you set your mind to. Remember, we're in this together – whatever challenges we face, we'll overcome them side by side."

Celine felt a warmth spread through her chest at her words, grateful beyond measure for the unwavering support of the woman beside her. And as they sat beneath the ancient oak tree, wrapped up in each other's company and the beauty of the fading sunlight, she knew without a doubt that together, they were capable of facing anything life had in store for them.

An unspoken connection bound them together as Jemima and Celine stood in a moment of quiet intimacy. Jemima's eyes met hers, and with a soft smile, she traced the curve of Celine's cheek with her fingers, her touch gentle and loving.

Celine's breath caught as Jemima leaned in, her lips brushing against Celine's in a feather-light caress. Their kiss was a slow, unhurried exploration of the depths of their love. Jemima's mouth moved with a tenderness that spoke of devotion, and as they deepened the kiss, their passion flared like a gentle flame.

Their lips met, parted, and met again, each touch igniting a symphony of emotions that washed over them. Jemima's kisses trailed from her lips to her eyelids, placing sweet, lingering kisses on each, before moving to her earlobes, where her warm breath sent shivers down her spine.

Celine's fingers gently grazed Jemima's cheek as she kissed her back, her heart soaring with the depth of her feelings for Jemima. Their mouths found each other once more, exploring the taste and texture of each other's lips, as if they were savoring the sweetness of their love.

Their kiss was a dance of tenderness and desire, a

testament to the deep connection they shared. Jemima held Celine close, and their lips found new places to explore, from the curve of each other's jaws to the delicate skin of their cleavages. They were kisses that expressed the depth of their love and the promise of a future filled with passion and devotion.

And as they finally pulled away, their eyes locked in a silent exchange of love and longing, they knew that their bond was unbreakable, and their love would continue to grow, one sweet, tender kiss at a time. Jemima couldn't help but feel a sense of urgency. She knew that she needed to show Celine just how much she loved her, and that she needed to do it now.

Jemima took Celine's hand, leading her back towards the house, her heart pounding in her chest. They walked in silence, their eyes locked in a deep trance of desire. As they reached the door, Jemima turned to Celine, her eyes burning with passion.

"Celine," she whispered, her voice rough with emotion. "I need you. I need to be with you. Will you come with me?"

Celine's eyes widened, but she didn't hesitate. She nodded, her heart racing with anticipation. Jemima took her hand once more, leading her up the stairs and into her bedroom.

As they stood in the center of the room, Jemima

turned to Celine, her eyes dark with desire. She stepped closer, gently running her hand down the curve of Celene's waist. Celine shuddered, her breath coming in shallow gasps.

Slowly, Jemima leaned in, pressing her lips to Celine's. This time, there was no holding back.

CHAPTER 9

Their kiss was ravenous, their hands roaming each other's bodies with fevered need. Jemima pulled back and hurriedly began to unbutton her shirt, her intent clear to Celine.

As Jemima slipped her shirt from her shoulders, Celine reached out, her hands tracing the outline of Jemima's breasts through her bra. Jemima groaned, arching into her touch.

With one hand, Jemima pulled the front of Celine's dress down, revealing the delicate curve of her breasts. With the other, she reached behind Celine's back, following the line of her spine down to the top of her lacy thong.

Celine gasped as Jemima's hands found the junction of her underwear, and she gasped again as she felt

Jemima pull the material aside, exposing her to the cool night air.

Jemima looked at Celine, desire radiating from her eyes. "You are so beautiful," she whispered, her voice husky with emotion.

Without waiting for Celine's response, she stepped close, pressing her body against Celine's, their bare breasts pressing together. Celine's body shuddered as Jemima ran her hands down her back, finally resting them on the curve of her hips. Then, with a groan, Jemima pulled their hips together, rocking them back and forth suggestively.

Celine moaned, wrapping her arms around Jemima's neck, pressing her breasts against Jemima's.

"Please," she whispered, her voice cracking with passion. "I need you. I need you now."

Jemima's answer was to press her lips to Celine's, her tongue pushing its way into Celine's mouth. Celine moaned, burrowing into her kiss.

Celine felt Jemima's hands slide around her back, unzipping her dress and letting it fall to the floor.

Jemima stepped back for a moment, and Celine's breath caught at the sight of her. Jemima wore her usual uniform of a fitted tank top and comfortable khaki pants, but now the shirt was unbuttoned to the waist, and her pants were unbuttoned and unzipped, revealing a taut stomach and a pair of black panties. And she had undone the few remaining buttons on her shirt, and her bra had slipped down her arms, and the sight of her bare breasts, the sight of them pressed against the black of her bra...

Celine seemed to lose herself in that sight, and Jemima reached out, gently guiding her to the bed. Together they fell on it, Jemima laughing with delight as they land in a heap.

Celine felt Jemima's lips on her neck, her touch light and delicate. Her hand slid up Celine's leg, pushing her dress up as she went. She stopped just below Celine's panties, lightly tracing the outline of her leg.

Celine began to speak, but Jemima's touch sent a bolt of pleasure through her, and she moaned, her words coming out as a gasp.

Jemima laughed, trailing a line of kisses down Celine's chest. Her hand slid up, cupping a breast. Celine could feel Jemima's touch everywhere, all over her body, wrapping around her.

"Mmmm," she murmured, her body pulsing in time with her heartbeat.

Jemima's mouth trailed down, reaching the edge of the lace-trimmed panties. With agonizing slowness, she kissed the top of Celine's mound, then her way down to the edge of the panties.

Celine's breathing quickened. Jemima pulled back, and Celine could see that her eyes were locked on where Jemima's hand was playing with the edge of her panties.

"So beautiful," she whispered, and then her voice shifted, rougher. "So sexy. I want to... I need to..."

Celine felt her panties being slipped down her legs, and then Jemima's hands were running over her body, cupping her naked ass.

Celine felt Jemima shift, and then she felt something warm and soft against her. Her body responded, her lips opening to Jemima's. Jemima's tongue slid into her mouth, and Celine wrapped her arms around her neck.

Jemima's lips began to trail across her cheek, her teeth scraping delicately across Celine's skin.

Celine felt her own breathing quicken, and her whole body was tingling with pleasure, anticipating Jemima's touch. Then Jemima's lips were around one of her nipples, and she could feel her heart pounding, her body tense with the need to move, to grind against Jemima.

"Jemima," she moaned.

Jemima's only response was to bite down softly, the little nip enough to make Celine gasp.

Celine could feel Jemima's fingers, gently pressing her legs apart. She groaned, shifting her hips to make room, and Jemima ran a finger over Celine's clit.

"Oh," Celine gasped. "Oh, please..."

Jemima raised her head, turning to look Celine in the eyes. "Tell me what you want," she said, the lust in her voice almost as strong as the unspoken challenge.

"Please," Celine said. "Oh, please."

Jemima's hands continued their gentle caress, but she was watching Celine, making sure that she kept watching, that she was in no doubt as to what she wanted. She lowered her head, gently kissing around Celine's clit, then pulling back just as Celine felt her muscles begin to tense for release.

Jemima bit down, and Celine came, her body shuddering with release as Jemima looked on.

Jemima climbed up onto the bed, her body sliding against Celine's as she moved. She twisted, reaching to her bedside drawer. From the drawer, she pulled out a long black feather.

"Oh," Celine gasped, watching as Jemima began to trace patterns on her skin. Jemima leaned down to kiss her, her lips soft, her tongue gliding into Celine's mouth "I might never want to leave this bed," Jemima whispered, then kissed her again.

"Then why are we wasting time sleeping?" Celine asked.

Jemima pulled the covers over both of them, drawing Celine close. Then Celine felt Jemima's hand between her legs. She was moist, ready, and Jemima's fingers slid easily inside her, then Jemima's palm was pressing against her clit, and she groaned, shifting, trying to get closer. Jemima slid another finger in, stretching her gently, and Celine moaned again.

"Feather, feather, feather," Jemima murmured, her lips just brushing against Celine's ear, her fingers alone enough to set Celine on fire. Celine thrust her hips up against Jemima's hand, trying to get her deeper. Jemima obliged, twisting her hand slightly as she thrust, the added sensation making Celine gasp.

"I want you," she whispered, and Jemima's fingers slid out of her.

"Yes," Jemima said, her voice rich with desire. "Yes, I know."

Jemima climbed off the bed, and Celine could only watch, her body aching for Jemima's touch. Jemima was wearing a long, low-cut dress, with a slit up the side that would allow her access. It was black, and very, very sheer lace, but Jemima pulled it up over her head without hesitation, tossing it aside.

Jemima was wearing black lace panties, with a delicate white trim. Her breasts were full, her nipples taut. She tossed the panties aside, then slid back onto the bed, leaning over Celine as her hands traced patterns on her skin.

Celine ran her hands over Jemima's arms, then over her breasts. She thumbed Jemima's nipples, then took one breast in her mouth, sucking it in softly as she gave it a gentle love bite. Jemima moaned, her fingers dipping between Celine's legs again.

"I want you," Celine whispered.

"I know," Jemima replied, her voice throaty. "But I want to make you come again, first."

Jemima's fingers found Celine's clit, and she began to stroke her, sliding two fingers into her as Celine's body began to shake. Jemima kissed her, then, her lips soft, her own body aching.

Celine shifted, her knees moving up towards her chest, and Jemima could feel Celine's body on hers, soft curves against hard muscle, and she kissed her again, wrapping her fingers in Celine's hair, tugging gently.

Jemima pulled back, then slid down the bed, kissing Celine's neck, her collar bones, kissing down her body until Celine was almost quivering.

"Oh, Jemima," Celine whispered.

Jemima slid one hand under Celine's body, her fingers probing between Celine's legs as she kissed her. Then she slid a third finger inside Celine, crooking her fingers just right as she began licking Celine's clit.

"Oh, Jemima, don't stop. Oh, please," Celine begged.

Jemima slid her tongue down Celine's slit, then

suckled Celine's clit softly as she curled her fingers inside Celine. Celine came with a sharp cry, her body shaking and shuddering as her pussy clenched around Jemima's fingers.

"Oh, Jemima..." Celine whispered.

Jemima slid up Celine's body, kissing her, tasting herself on Celine's lips.

"That was good," Celine whispered.

"You're a fast learner," Jemima said, kissing Celine again. "But I think you may be a natural."

"I love you," Celine whispered.

"I love you, too," Jemima replied. "And I want to make you come again, like that. Are you ready?"

"Yes," Celine said, softly.

Jemima slid her fingers into Celine, then used her thumb to press against Celine's clit, rubbing it slow at first, then picking up the pace as Celine's breathing picked up. Soon, Celine was begging Jemima, her voice hoarse with need.

Celine came hard, and Jemima slid her fingers out of Celine's body, then brought them to her mouth, sucking Celine's juices off of them.

"Oh, Jemima," Celine whispered.

"I want you, Celine," Jemima whispered.

"I want you," Celine said, softly.

Jemima reached for the drawer of the nightstand,

taking out a vibrator. She then moved it to Celine's entrance, which was still slick with Celine's juices. Jemima pushed the toy inside Celine slowly, and Celine gasped, then took a deep breath, as Jemima turned it on and slid it all the way inside.

"Oh, Jemima," Celine said.

"I love you," Jemima said, then began to move against Celene's hand.

Celine gasped, her back arching as Jemima faced her with the vibrator, moving it in and out of her. Jemima slid one hand under Celine, holding her close as she kissed her.

Jemima slid her free hand under Celine's ass, then began to spank Celine. Celine gasped, then moaned, holding Jemima tightly as pleasure washed over her. Jemima spanked Celine again, then again, then kissed her.

"Oh, Jemima," Celine whispered, as she came, her orgasm making her body shudder.

Jemima kept moving, Celine squeezing her, then slide all the way inside Celine again, thrusting hard and deep. Celine cried out, then held Jemima tightly.

"Jemima," Celine said. "I love you. I want to be with you for the rest of my life."

"I love you, too, Celine," Jemima said, kissing Celine, then began thrusting again.

Celine moaned, then came again, crying out as she did. Jemima thrust into her again, then again, her thrusts harder, faster. Her breath caught, her body tensed, and then she collapsed against Celine, groaning as wave after wave of pleasure poured through her.

Jemima slid the vibrator out of Celine, then kissed Celine.

"I love you," Jemima said.

"I love you, too," Celine said.

Jemima held Celine close, lips pressed together in a long kiss that spoke of love and passion.

⁓

The following morning, the golden light of dawn filtered through the curtains as Celine stretched in the cozy bed, her thoughts still lingering on the heartfelt conversation she had shared with Jemima the evening before. She smiled at the memory of their laughter and the way her blue eyes seemed to dance in the sunlight.

"Morning," Jemima murmured sleepily from beside her, drawing her attention back to the present moment.

"Good morning," she whispered, rolling onto her side to face Jemima. Their eyes met, and she felt a flutter in her stomach, realizing how close they were lying together.

As if reading her thoughts, Jemima hesitated for a moment before leaning in to steal a soft, tender kiss. Celine's heart skipped a beat, her pulse quickening at the delicate contact between their lips.

"Last night was special," Jemima said quietly, her warm breath caressing Celine's cheek.

"It really was," Celine agreed, feeling an undeniable connection between them that went beyond mere friendship. They lay there for a while longer, simply enjoying each other's presence, their fingers entwined beneath the covers.

Later, they decided to spend the day exploring the local village, taking in the charming sights and sounds of the small town life that Celine had always cherished. As they strolled hand-in-hand down the cobblestone streets, she couldn't help but notice the way their fingers fit perfectly together, like two pieces of a puzzle finally finding their rightful place.

"Look at that!" Celine exclaimed, pointing out a whimsical sculpture in the town square. "It's so quirky and fun!" She laughed, and Jemima joined in, her own laughter like music to her ears.

"Only you would find something like that so fascinating," she teased, nudging her playfully with her elbow. The inside joke brought a smile to her face, reminding her of the unique bond they shared.

Throughout the day, the couple continued to share moments of physical affection and laughter, their connection growing stronger with each stolen kiss and shared smile. They explored hidden alleyways, browsed through quaint shops, and stopped for a leisurely lunch at a cozy café.

"Have I told you how much I love your laugh?" Jemima asked as they sipped their drinks, her eyes never leaving Celine's.

Celine blushed, feeling a warm glow spread through her chest at her words. "Well, I could say the same about yours," she replied softly, reaching across the table to squeeze her hand.

The day seemed to fly by in a blur of happiness and contentment, with each small gesture or shared joke only serving to deepen the bond between Celine and Jemima. As they sat on a bench overlooking the picturesque countryside, Celine couldn't help but feel incredibly grateful for the woman beside her and the beautiful journey they had embarked upon together.

CHAPTER 10

$\mathcal{U}$nderneath the vast expanse of the night sky, Jemima worked diligently to create an atmosphere that she knew Celine would adore. The secluded spot she had chosen was a picturesque meadow, nestled in the heart of their small town, away from the hustle and bustle that often consumed them both. As she gently unfolded the soft checkered blanket onto the grass, she couldn't help but feel a sense of pride at the intimate scene she had crafted.

With precision, she placed candles around the perimeter of the blanket, their flickering flames casting a warm glow against the darkness. A gentle breeze whispered through the trees, rustling the leaves as if nature itself was approving of her efforts. The stars above seemed to twinkle in unison, forming a celestial canopy that further heightened the enchanting ambience.

"Jemima, this is absolutely breathtaking," Celine's voice broke through the stillness as she approached the picnic site. Her eyes sparkled with anticipation and excitement, mirroring the stars above. She couldn't help but admire the care and thoughtfulness Jemima had gone to.

"Thank you, Celine," Jemima replied, her cheeks flushing with color. "I wanted it to be perfect for you." Her deep blue eyes met Celine's reflecting her sincerity and warmth.

It was clear to Celine that Jemima wasn't just referring to the picnic, but rather, the connection they shared and the potential for something more.

Celine took in the beautiful scene before her, feeling her heart swell with gratitude and affection for Jemima. As an artist, she had always been captivated by the beauty of the world around her, but it was moments like these - where the magic of life seemed to come alive - that truly took her breath away.

"Shall we sit?" Jemima gestured towards the blanket, offering her hand to her. Celine graciously accepted, allowing herself to be led into the heart of their enchanting escape.

As they settled onto the soft blanket, Celine's excitement bubbled up inside her like champagne. She couldn't help but think about how this night might shift the dynamic between them, moving their relationship into uncharted territory.

"Jemima," she said softly, "I don't know what the future holds for us, but I'm grateful for this moment."

"Me too, Celine," she replied with a smile, her hand gently brushing hers. "No matter where life takes us, moments like these are ones we'll always remember."

And as they sat beneath the canopy of twinkling stars, basking in the warmth of their shared connection, they knew that they were on the precipice of something extraordinary.

~

"Voilà!" Jemima exclaimed, lifting the covered wicker basket's lid to reveal a spread of Celine's favorite foods. The arrangement was meticulous, showcasing her thoughtfulness and attention to detail. Fresh strawberries glistened like rubies alongside an array of artisan cheeses, while golden, flaky pastries emitted a heavenly aroma that made her mouth water.

"Jemima, this is incredible," Celine breathed, her eyes

widening in awe as she took in the delicious spread before her. "You really went above and beyond."

"Only the best for you," she replied with a playful wink, handing her a plate. "I hope everything is to your liking."

Celine couldn't help but smile at Jemima's charming demeanor, feeling a wave of gratitude wash over her. As she took her first bite of a warm, buttery croissant, memories of her childhood flooded back. The familiar taste instantly transported her to Sunday mornings spent in her grandmother's country kitchen, where laughter and love were as abundant as the food that graced their table.

"Jemima, I don't know how you did it, but this tastes exactly like my grandma's croissants," she said, her voice filled with emotion. "It feels like home."

"Really?" Jemima asked, her eyes lighting up with genuine happiness at her reaction. "I'm so glad I could bring a little piece of home to you tonight."

As they continued to enjoy the meal, Celine savored each bite, allowing herself to be fully present in the experience. The flavors danced on her tongue, weaving a tapestry of memories and emotions that only served to deepen her connection with Jemima.

"Thank you, Jemima," she whispered, reaching out to

touch her hand. "This means more to me than you know."

"Anything for you, Celine," she replied, giving her hand a gentle squeeze, their fingers intertwining in a silent promise of support and understanding.

And as they shared their feast beneath the canopy of twinkling stars, the world around them seemed to fade away, leaving only the magic of the moment and the unspoken feelings that filled the air between them.

~

*A*s Celine took another bite of the heavenly croissant, she playfully raised an eyebrow and said in a mock accusatory tone, "You know, you're setting the bar pretty high for any future picnics we might have."

"Future picnics, huh?" Jemima replied with a grin, her blue eyes twinkling mischievously. "Well, I'll just have to keep upping my game then, won't I?"

Celine laughed as she popped a juicy strawberry into her mouth, the sweetness mingling with the lingering butteriness of the croissant. "I'm looking forward to seeing what you come up with next time."

"Is that a challenge, Ms. Montgomery?" Jemima

pretended to look shocked, feigning offense as she placed a hand over her heart.

"Maybe it is," Celine shot back, the corners of her lips curling into a teasing smile.

They continued to enjoy their meal and banter, the comfortable atmosphere settling around them like a warm embrace. The crickets serenaded them from the shadows, their chorus providing a soothing soundtrack to the intimate moment.

As they leisurely sipped on their wine, Jemima hesitated for a moment before asking, "So, Celine, can I ask you something a bit more serious?"

"Of course," she replied, curiosity piqued by the sudden change in tone.

"Where do you see yourself in the future? What are your dreams and aspirations?" Jemima's gaze held Celine's, encouraging her to open up.

Celine took a deep breath, her mind racing through the various possibilities. She had always been hesitant to share her deepest desires with others, but there was something about Jemima that made her feel safe and understood. As Celine pondered her question, she absently traced the rim of her wine glass with a delicate finger, lost in thought.

"Growing up, I've always wanted to live a life filled with art and creativity," she began, her eyes glistening with a faraway look. "I've been fortunate enough to make a living doing what I love, but there's still so much more I want to explore."

"Like what?" Jemima asked gently, her curiosity genuine as she leaned in closer.

"Traveling, for one," she said, the excitement evident in her voice. "I'd love to see the world, soak up the different cultures, and let it all inspire my artwork. And I guess, deep down, I've always wanted a place to call home, where I can feel grounded and connected to something greater than myself."

"Sounds like a beautiful dream," Jemima whispered, her sincerity shining through in the warmth of her gaze.

CHAPTER 11

*C*eline Montgomery sat on the porch, a steaming cup of tea cradled in her hands as she watched the sun dip below the horizon. The warm hues of sunset cast a golden glow across the landscape, and Celine couldn't help but think about the woman who had become such an integral part of her life - Jemima Sullivan. Their friendship had blossomed ever since they met in person, and every shared moment seemed to strengthen their bond. As the evening breeze caressed her face, Celine knew that what she felt for Jemima was a lasting love.

"Jemima deserves something special," she whispered to herself, her heart swelling with affection. "Something that can capture the depth of my feelings." Her eyes scanned the horizon, searching for inspiration, and she suddenly realized the perfect way to express her love – a custom tattoo, designed with all the care and attention to detail that Jemima deserved.

As excitement bubbled within her, Celine hurried inside, eager to begin sketching potential designs. She could already envision the intricate patterns taking shape on Jemima's skin, each stroke a testament to their unique connection. Her fingers moved deftly across the page, drawing upon the countless memories they'd created together, the laughter and tears they'd shared, and the unspoken words that lingered between them.

"Hey there, beautiful," Jemima's voice echoed through the phone as Celine held it between her ear and shoulder, her pencil continuing its dance across the paper. "Whatcha up to?"

"Hi, Jemima," she replied, trying to mask her excitement. "Just working on some new ideas." As much as she wanted to share her plan with him, she knew that keeping it a secret would make the final reveal even more meaningful.

"Can't wait to see what you come up with," Jemima said, the warmth in her voice making Celine's heart flutter. "You always seem to create something extraordinary."

"Thanks, Jemima," she said, blushing at her praise. "I hope this one will be really... special." The word hung in the air between them, a promise of something profound yet to be discovered.

As Celine continued to sketch, she lost herself in thoughts of Jemima, their love fueling every line and curve of the design. She knew that this tattoo would be a true expression of her heart, an indelible mark of their connection – and she couldn't wait to see the look on Jemima's face when she finally laid eyes on it.

~

Celine sat at her drawing desk, sifting through the memories she and Jemima had shared together. Her fingers danced across the paper as she sketched ideas for the tattoo that would symbolize their unique connection. She paused for a moment to sip her coffee, smiling as she remembered their late-night conversations about life and love, the secrets they'd whispered over the phone.

"Maybe something with stars," Celine mused, thinking of the night they'd spent stargazing in a field near Jemima's small-town home. "Or perhaps a compass, to represent our journey together." As each new thought took shape on the paper, she felt herself falling deeper in love with the idea, her heart swelling with anticipation.

Celine knew she needed the perfect materials for the tattoo, so she decided to visit Frank Dawson's tattoo parlor for more tattoo supplies. Dawson's Ink was a cozy little shop, filled with shelves lined with colorful ink bottles and an array of tattoo supplies.

"Hi there, Celine!" Frank said, "I"m thrilled to see you back here again. What can I help you find today?"

"Hey Frank," Celine replied, her eyes scanning the shelves. "I'm working on a really special custom piece, and I need some top-quality inks and needles."

"Absolutely! Let me show you what we've got," Frank said, leading her toward a display of vibrant inks. "These are some of our best sellers – the colors are incredibly vibrant and long-lasting."

Celine nodded, carefully selecting a few shades that would bring her design to life. As she browsed the store, she couldn't help but imagine Jemima's reaction when she saw the completed tattoo – the mixture of surprise and joy that would light up her face, the warmth of their connection deepening even further.

"Frank, I also need some really fine needles for this piece," Celine said, her voice filled with determination. "I want the lines to be as delicate and precise as possible."

"Of course," Frank replied, guiding her toward another display. "These are excellent for intricate work.

They'll give you the control you need for those fine details."

"Thanks, Frank," Celine said, gathering the supplies she needed. As she paid for her purchases, she felt a surge of excitement – she was one step closer to creating the perfect symbol of her love for Jemima.

Returning to her workspace, Celine couldn't help but feel a sense of purpose; every stroke of ink would be an expression of her heart, each line weaving together their shared experiences and dreams. As she prepared to begin the tattooing process, she knew that this intimate moment would bring them closer than ever before, solidifying their bond in a way words alone could never achieve.

~

*C*eline stood in her workspace, meticulously cleaning every surface and arranging her tools with precision. The afternoon sun filtered through the windows, casting a warm glow across the room as she mentally prepared herself for the task ahead. She could feel the weight of anticipation settling in her chest, knowing that each stroke of her needle would be an extension of her love for Jemima.

"Alright," she whispered to herself, taking a deep breath. "Let's do this."

"Hey, Celine," Jemima called out gently from the doorway, her blue eyes shimmering with a mix of excitement and curiosity. "Are you ready for me?"

"Absolutely," she replied, her voice steady despite the butterflies in her stomach. "Come on in and have a seat."

Jemima entered the room, her gaze lingering on the carefully organized workspace. "You've done an amazing job setting up everything," she said, clearly impressed. "I can tell you put a lot of thought into this."

"Thank you," Celine responded, touched by her words. "I wanted it to be perfect for you."

As Jemima settled into the chair, Celine began the process of applying the stencil to her skin, making sure it was perfectly aligned before transferring the design. Her focus was unwavering, her fingers deftly maneuvering the delicate paper with practiced ease. Once the stencil was secured, she turned her attention to preparing her ink and needles, selecting the finest ones for the intricate details of the tattoo.

"Ready?" she asked, her eyes meeting Jemima's.

"More than ever," Jemima replied, offering her a reassuring smile.

With a nod, Celine pressed the buzzing needle to Jemima's skin, the first line of ink flowing smoothly and effortlessly. As she worked, she spoke softly, recounting the memories and experiences that had inspired each element of the design.

"See this part here," she said, gesturing to a series of intertwining lines. "It represents the way our lives have become so beautifully entwined, how we've grown together and supported each other through everything."

"Wow," Jemima murmured, her eyes glistening with emotion. "That's incredible, Celine."

She smiled at Jemima's response, her heart swelling with love as she continued to work. Each line was a testament to their shared journey, an indelible reminder of the connection they had forged. Her hand was steady, guided by the intensity of her feelings for him as she carefully etched each detail into her skin.

As the hours passed, Celine became lost in her work, her entire being focused on capturing the essence of what they meant to each other. Every stroke of the needle felt like a declaration of her love, her devotion to Jemima shining through in each intricate design element.

"Almost done," she whispered, her voice barely audible over the hum of the tattoo machine.

"Take your time," Jemima replied softly, her gaze never leaving Celine's. "This is more than just a tattoo –

it's a part of us, and I want you to be completely satisfied with it."

"Trust me," Celine assured her, pausing to look up from her work. "I am."

With a few final touches, Celine completed the tattoo, setting aside the needle and taking a moment to admire her handiwork. The design was a stunning tribute to their love, a symbol of their shared experiences that would forever bind them together. She couldn't wait to see Jemima's reaction, knowing that this intimate moment would only serve to deepen their connection even further.

~

A smile slowly spread across Jemima's face as she took in the intricate design that now adorned her skin. Her eyes shimmered with emotion, reflecting the intensity of her feelings for Celine and the significance of the tattoo she had just completed. "I can't even begin to tell you how much this means to me," she said, her voice thick with emotion. "Every line and detail... it's like you've captured our entire journey together."

Celine's heart swelled at her words, and she couldn't help but reach out to touch Jemima's arm, her fingers gently tracing the curves and lines of the tattoo. "That's exactly what I was hoping for," she admitted, her own emotions welling up inside her. "This is more than just art – it's a symbol of our love, and I wanted it to be something we could both treasure forever."

"Mission accomplished," Jemima replied, her eyes never leaving Celine's. She reached out, cupping Celine's cheek in her hand, and Celine felt an electric jolt race through her body at the contact. Despite the countless hours they'd spent together over the past weeks, every touch still felt like a new discovery, each one intensifying their connection.

"Thank you," Celine murmured, leaning into the warmth of Jemima's palm. "For trusting me with this, for being so open and vulnerable with me... It's been such an incredible gift."

Jemima's gaze softened, and she let out a breathy chuckle. "I should be the one thanking you," she said, her thumb stroking Celen's cheekbone. "I don't think I've ever met anyone who understands me as deeply as you do, Celine. You've given me so much more than a beautiful piece of art – you've given me hope, and love, and the courage to believe in myself again."

As their eyes locked, time seemed to slow to a crawl, and Celine was struck by the fierce love she saw in Jemima's eyes. It was like staring into the depths of her soul, and she felt herself being drawn inexorably closer, her heart beating in time with Jemima's.

"I love you," she whispered, her breath hitching as their lips brushed against one another. "I love you so much, and I can't imagine my life without you."

"Neither can I," Jemima murmured, closing the distance between them and sealing their words with a tender, passionate kiss. As their mouths moved together, Celine found herself lost in the sensation, her entire world narrowing down to this single, breathtaking moment.

As they pulled apart, their foreheads resting against each other's, Celine knew that what they shared went beyond physical attraction or simple friendship. Their connection was something deeper, more profound – a bond forged in the fires of shared experiences, laughter, and tears. And as they stood there, hands clasped and hearts beating in unison, Celine couldn't help but feel a sense of awe at the incredible journey they were embarking on together.

~

Celine's fingers traced the contours of Jemima's hand as they stood entwined, their breaths mingling in the quiet warmth of the room. The weight of their shared emotions seemed to settle around them, anchoring them to this moment in time.

"I can't believe how lucky I am," Jemima murmured, her voice tinged with wonder. "You've given me so much more than just this tattoo, Celine. You've given me a reason to hope again."

"Jemima, I feel the same way," Celine replied softly, her eyes shining with unshed tears. "You've changed my life in ways I never thought possible. We might have started as friends, but what we have now... it's something truly special."

Their gazes met and held, both sensing the depth of love that coursed between them. It was a connection that defied description, an invisible tether that bound their hearts together. And as they leaned into one another, seeking solace in each other's arms, they knew that there was nothing they couldn't face as long as they were together.

"Promise me something, Celine?" Jemima asked, her voice barely more than a whisper.

"Anything," she breathed, her heart swelling with affection for the woman before her.

"Promise me that we'll face whatever comes our way, side by side. That we won't let anything come between us."

"Of course, Jemima," Celine vowed, her voice steady

and resolute. "Together, we can conquer anything. I promise."

As they sealed their words with a gentle kiss, the world outside seemed to fade away, leaving only the brilliant light of their love shining brightly in the darkness. And as they reluctantly pulled apart, they knew that their journey was only just beginning.

"Come on," Celine urged, giving Jemima's hand a playful tug. "There's a whole world out there waiting for us to explore together."

"Lead the way," Jemima said, her eyes dancing with excitement. "I can't wait to see what our future holds."

As they stepped into the fading light of the day, hand in hand, Celine felt a thrill of anticipation race through her. She couldn't predict what lay ahead, but she knew that whatever challenges and joys awaited them, they would face them together. And that knowledge was enough to make her heart soar.

CHAPTER 12

The sun dipped low in the sky, casting warm hues of orange and pink across the quaint town of Fountain Springs. Nestled at the foot of the mountains, this picturesque community seemed to be frozen in time, its cobblestone streets lined with charming shops and friendly faces. White picket fences bordered manicured lawns, and the scent of freshly baked pies wafted through the air.

It was a place where everyone knew their neighbors and looked out for one another, a close-knit haven that prided itself on traditional values and simple living. But beneath the idyllic surface, there was an undercurrent of rigid conservatism that sometimes stifled those who dared to venture outside the norm.

Celine Montgomery stood in front of her mobile

tattoo studio, a sleek black RV adorned with vibrant murals showcasing her artistic talent. She clutched a piece of paper in her trembling hands, disbelief clouding her blue eyes. The words on the page stung like a slap to the face: "Permission Denied."

"Unbelievable," she muttered, crumpling the paper into a tight ball, her knuckles turning white from the force of her grip. The disapproval of the town council felt like a crushing weight on her chest, threatening to suffocate her dreams. Celine had poured her heart and soul into making her passion a reality, only to be met with unwavering resistance from the very people she hoped to serve.

"Hey, don't let them get you down," a voice called out, and Celine glanced up to find Jemima jogging toward her with concern etched on her features. She reached Celine's side in a heartbeat, her strong arms enveloping her in a comforting hug. "I just heard about it. I came straight away."

"Thanks," Celine mumbled into her shoulder, fighting back tears, but refusing to let them fall. Celine was nothing if not determined, and she refused to let this setback derail her dream. "I just don't understand it."

Jemima sighed, pulling back and gently cupping her Celine's face in her hands. "It's a small town, Celine. People are afraid of change, of anything that challenges their beliefs. But you're strong, and I know you'll find a way to make this work."

Celine looked into Jemima's deep brown eyes, drawing strength from her unwavering support and encouragement. She took a deep breath, steeling herself for the fight ahead. "You're right," she said, straightening her shoulders and wiping away a stray tear. "I can't let them win. I'm going to prove to them that my art is nothing to be afraid of. I'm going to show them that I'm not just some rebel with a cause. I'm an artist, and my love for this craft runs deeper than the ink on my skin."

With a fierce determination burning in her heart, Celine set her jaw and prepared to face the uphill battle that lay ahead. She knew it wouldn't be easy, but she also knew that she couldn't back down now. Not when so much was at stake, not when her dreams were on the line. And with Jemima by her side, she felt ready to take on the world – one tattoo at a time.

~

The tension in the air was palpable as Celine and Jemima stood outside her mobile tattoo studio, parked at the edge of the town's picturesque main street. Their eyes scanned the quaint shops and conservative residents bustling about their daily routines, seemingly unaware of the battle brewing in the hearts of the two outsiders.

"Jemima, I just don't understand," Celine said, her voice cracking with frustration. "I've never faced this kind of resistance before. It's like these people on the town council don't even want to give me a chance."

Jemima sighed, running her fingers through her dark hair as she tried to find the right words to comfort her. "Celine, you have to remember that this is a small, close-knit community. They're not used to something as bold as a mobile tattoo shop rolling into town. Change is scary for them."

Celine crossed her arms defensively, her beautiful features hardening with determination. "Well, they better get used to it. I'm not leaving without a fight."

"Is that really the best approach, though?" Jemima asked gently, concern etched on her face. "Maybe we should try talking to them, getting to know them. Show them that you're not here to disrupt their way of life, but to share your art and passion with them."

"Jemima, are you honestly suggesting that I compromise my values just to appease these closed-minded people?" Celine snapped, her eyes flashing with anger.

"No, I'm not saying that at all," she replied, trying to keep her voice steady despite her growing frustration. "I just think there might be a more diplomatic way to handle this situation."

"Like what? Baking cookies and joining their knitting circles?" she scoffed, rolling her eyes.

"Come on, Celine, you know that's not what I meant," Jemima said, her own temper starting to flare. "It's just... I worry about you. I don't want to see you get hurt or pushed out of this town because they don't understand what you're trying to do."

"Jemima, I appreciate your concern, but I can handle this," Celine insisted, her hands on her hips as she stared Jemima down. "I've faced challenges before, and I'll face them again. I won't back down from this, not when it's something I believe in so strongly."

Jemima took a deep breath, realizing that pushing her further would only drive a wedge between them. "Alright, Celine. I trust you. Just remember that I'm here for you, and I'll support you no matter what."

"Thank you, Jemima," she whispered, her eyes softening as she reached for her hand. Their fingers intertwined, a symbol of their unbreakable bond even in the most trying times.

As they stood there, united against the world, Celine knew that no matter how difficult the road ahead might be, she had someone by her side who believed in her dreams just as much as she did. And with that knowledge, she felt ready to take on anything – even the stubborn resistance of a small, conservative town.

~

*C*eline stood at the living room window, her eyes scanning the quiet streets as her mind raced with potential solutions to her current predicament. Jemima leaned against the wall beside her, her gaze steady and supportive as she watched Celine think.

"Alright," Celine began, taking a deep breath. "Maybe I could talk to some local officials, try to find common ground or work out a compromise that respects the town's values."

Jemima nodded, her dark hair falling over her blue eyes as she considered Celine's idea. "That's a good start, but we'll need to do some research on who would be most open to the conversation. We don't want to waste time and energy on someone who's completely closed off to the idea."

Celine brushed a stray strand of her blonde hair behind her ear and sighed. "You're right. I just feel so helpless, like my future is being determined by people who don't even bother to get to know me or understand my passion for tattoo art."

"Hey," Jemima said softly, stepping closer to wrap her

arms around her. "I know this is tough, but we're going to figure it out together. I'm here for you, every step of the way."

Celine leaned into Jemima's embrace, allowing herself a moment of vulnerability as she absorbed her warmth and unwavering support. Then, with renewed determination, she pulled away and strode to the coffee table, where her laptop sat waiting. Opening it up, she began searching for contact information for local officials while Jemima took a seat beside her, ready to assist in any way she could.

As they delved into research together, Celine couldn't help but marvel at the strength of their connection. Despite the obstacles they faced, Jemima remained steadfast in her loyalty and dedication to their relationship.

"Hey, listen to this," Celine said, excitement lacing her voice. "I found an article about a town official who's been pushing for more progressive policies. Maybe they'd be willing to help us come up with a solution that satisfies everyone."

"Good find, Celine," Jemima replied, her smile proud and encouraging. "Why don't you reach out to them and see if you can set up a meeting? In the meantime, I'll look into other alternative locations or strategies we could explore."

"Deal," she agreed, her fingers already typing up an email to the potential ally. As they continued their research side by side, Celine felt her resolve strengthen. With Jemima by her side, she was ready to face whatever challenges lay ahead and fight for the future they both so deeply desired.

"Jemima," she said, pausing in her typing to glance at her, Celine's eyes filled with gratitude. "Thank you. For everything."

"Always, Celine," she responded, her love for Celine shining through her gaze. "Always."

~

*C*eline stood outside the quaint coffee shop, watching as families strolled by, their laughter filling the air. She took a deep breath, her heart racing with anticipation. Within minutes, she would be meeting with Marjorie Thompson, a local business owner who had faced similar challenges when opening her own art gallery in town.

"Ready?" Jemima asked, her eyes searching Celine's for any signs of hesitation.

"Ready," she replied with a determined nod.

Grasping hands together, they entered the bustling coffee shop, the scent of freshly brewed coffee and warm pastries enveloping them. They spotted Marjorie sitting at a corner table, her silver hair neatly coiffed and her posture radiating confidence.

"Marjorie? I'm Celine, and this is Jemima." Celine extended her hand, and Marjorie shook it firmly.

"Please, have a seat," Marjorie said, gesturing to the empty chairs across from her. As they settled down, Celine couldn't help but wonder if this woman held the key to unlocking a solution for her mobile tattoo business.

"Thank you so much for meeting with us," Jemima began, her tone gracious and sincere. "We've been struggling to find a way to reconcile our business with the conservative values of the town, and we're hoping you might have some advice or guidance."

"Of course," Marjorie replied, her eyes sympathetic. "I understand what you're going through. When I first opened my gallery, I faced resistance from those who believed that certain forms of art were too risqué or provocative. But over time, I found ways to work within the community's guidelines while still staying true to my vision."

"Can you tell us more about how you did that?" Celine asked, her fingers gripping her cup of tea. The warmth seeping into her hands mirrored the hope blossoming in her chest.

"I focused on building relationships and trust with the community," Marjorie explained. "I held local art exhibitions, hosted workshops for children, and even collaborated with the town's schools on various projects. By demonstrating that my gallery was an asset to the community, I slowly gained their support."

"Maybe we can apply a similar approach to Celine's mobile tattoo business," Jemima mused, her eyes filled with optimism. "Perhaps by offering temporary tattoos or hosting art events related to tattoo design, we can show the town that tattoos are a form of art, too."

"Exactly," Marjorie agreed. "It might take some time, but if you're committed to making this work, I believe you can find a way."

"Thank you, Marjorie," Celine said, her voice brimming with gratitude. "Your advice has been incredibly helpful, and we'll definitely explore these avenues."

"Of course," Marjorie replied, her smile warm and encouraging. "I wish you both the best of luck in overcoming this obstacle and pursuing your dreams."

As they left the coffee shop hand in hand, Celine couldn't help but feel a renewed sense of hope. With Jemima's unwavering support and Marjorie's invaluable advice, she felt ready to tackle the challenges that lay ahead. After all, love and determination had a way of making the impossible seem possible.

~

*C*eline sat on the edge of their bed, her eyes tracing the intricate patterns of the quilt as she mulled over the obstacles they faced. Jemima entered the room quietly, concern etched on her face when she saw her lost in thought. The weight of their situation pressed down upon them, and Celine wondered if their love could withstand the strain if she had to leave the town to conduct her business.

"Hey," Jemima said softly, sitting down beside her. "You know we'll figure this out, right?"

"Will we?" Celine replied, her voice cracking with vulnerability. "I can't help but feel like I've dragged you into this mess."

Jemima reached for her hand, her blue eyes full of sincerity. "Celine, we're in this together. Don't ever think you're alone in this. You're my world."

A tear escaped Celine's eye, and Jemima gently wiped it away. She leaned into Jemima, her head resting against her chest, drawing comfort from her steady heartbeat.

"Maybe we should consider moving to a more open-minded town," she whispered, feeling a rush of fear at the prospect of leaving behind the home they had built together. "I don't want our love to suffer because of this."

"Let's give it a little more time," Jemima suggested,

her voice full of hope. "They say love conquers all, right? We just need to find a way to show the town that your art is worth fighting for."

The next day, as they strolled through the local farmer's market, Celine noticed something that caught her attention. A young woman approached them, her arms adorned with stunning henna designs.

"Excuse me," Celine asked, her curiosity piqued. "I couldn't help but notice your beautiful henna tattoos. Where did you get them done?"

"Oh, there's a lovely lady who has a booth here every week," the woman replied, directing them to a nearby stall. "She's amazing, and her henna designs are very popular among the townsfolk."

As they approached the booth, Celine couldn't help but feel a flicker of hope ignite within her. If the town was embracing this temporary form of body art, perhaps there was potential for her own tattoo business after all.

"Jemima," she whispered, excitement bubbling inside her. "This could be our breakthrough! What if I offered henna tattoos alongside my regular ones? It could be a way to bridge the gap between the conservative community and my art."

Jemima grinned, her eyes lighting up with joy.

"Celine, that's brilliant! A perfect compromise that still allows you to share your talent with the world."

With renewed determination, they approached the henna artist together, ready to explore this potential breakthrough and face the challenges ahead side by side. Their love had led them this far, and now, it would guide them through the storm.

~

*C*eline gazed at the intricate henna designs on the artist's hands, her fingers tracing the swirling patterns as she considered the potential solution. Jemima stood beside her, offering her strong presence a comforting reminder that they were in this together.

"Jemima, do you really think this could work?" Celine asked, her voice tinged with both hope and hesitation. "What if the town still refuses to accept my business, even with the henna addition?"

Jemima took her hand, squeezing it gently. "We won't know until we try, Celine. But I believe in you, and I believe in your art. This might just be the bridge we need to win them over."

As they walked away from the booth, their conversation continued, exploring the possible risks and benefits of incorporating henna into Celine's mobile tattoo business.

"Think about it," Jemima said, her blue eyes earnest as she spoke. "Henna is temporary, and it's been embraced by the community here. By offering it alongside your permanent tattoos, you're showing respect for their values while still sharing your incredible talent."

Celine bit her lip, mulling over her words. "But what if it backfires? What if they see it as an attempt to infiltrate their traditional beliefs with something more permanent and rebellious?"

"Then we'll find another way," Jemima replied, her voice steady and unwavering. "But I have a feeling that this town, or at least some of its residents, are more open-minded than we initially thought. We just have to give them the chance to come around."

Celine looked into her eyes, finding solace in their depths. "I'm scared, Jemima. The thought of losing my dream, of losing everything I've worked so hard for...it terrifies me."

"I know," she whispered, pulling Celine close. "But I'm here with you, every step of the way. We'll face whatever comes our way, together."

As they embraced, the sun dipped below the horizon, casting a warm glow across the small town. The market was winding down for the day, but the prospect of a new beginning for Celine and Jemima seemed to illuminate their path forward.

"Alright," Celine said, taking a deep breath. "Let's give it a shot. We won't know unless we try, right?"

"Right," Jemima agreed, her smile contagious as she pressed a tender kiss to Celine's forehead.

With renewed hope, they set off towards home, hand in hand, eager to put their plan into action. But as they turned the corner, they found themselves face-to-face with Mayor Thompson, his stern expression making it clear that he had something important to discuss.

"Ms. Montgomery, Ms. Sullivan," he said, folding his arms across his chest. "I think it's time we had a talk about your...business proposal."

Celine glanced at Jemima, her heart racing. This conversation could either make or break their future – not just as business partners, but as lovers.

CHAPTER 13

*A*s Jemima sat at the kitchen table, sunlight streaming through the window and illuminating the scattered papers before him, she couldn't help but feel a sense of determination. With Celine's mobile tattoo business on her mind, she knew she had to do everything in her power to make it a reality for Celine. The warm scent of freshly brewed coffee filled the air as she focused her gaze on the laptop screen, searching for the local officials' contact information.

"Okay, let's see...Mayor Stevens, Councilwoman Rodriguez, and Councilman Thompson," Jemima mumbled under her breath, jotting down their names and numbers on a notepad. She glanced up at the clock and noticed that time was ticking away. "Alright, time to make some calls."

Her heart raced with anticipation as she picked up her phone and dialed Mayor Stevens' office. As the line rang, she took a deep breath, reminding herself that she was doing this for Celine – for their future together.

"Hello, Mayor Stevens' office, how may I help you?" a polite voice answered on the other end.

"Hi, my name is Jemima Sullivan. I'd like to arrange a meeting with Mayor Stevens and the council members to discuss a new business proposal for our town," she explained, trying to keep her tone confident and steady.

"Of course, Mr. Sullivan. We have an opening next Thursday at 2:30 PM. Will that work for you?"

"Perfect, thank you. I'll be there," Jemima replied, feeling a slight sense of relief wash over her.

"Great, we'll put you on the agenda. Have a good day, Mr. Sullivan," the secretary said before hanging up.

With the meeting set, Jemima allowed herself a small smile. At least they were willing to hear her out. But she knew the real challenge lay ahead. She needed to present a strong case for Celine's mobile tattoo business, emphasizing not only her talent but also the benefits it could bring to the community.

As she began organizing her notes and drafting a persuasive argument, Jemima couldn't help but feel a flutter of excitement in her chest. The stakes were high, but the possibility of making Celine's dream come true made it all worthwhile. She just hoped that the local officials would be open to seeing the potential in her unique venture.

Lost in thought, she didn't notice Celine entering the kitchen until she wrapped her arms around Jemima from behind, resting her chin on Jemima's shoulder.

"Hey there, what are you working on?" she asked softly, her eyes scanning the papers scattered across the table.

"Setting up a meeting with the local officials to discuss your mobile tattoo business," she replied, feeling a surge of warmth at her touch. "I want to make sure we have the best chance possible."

Celine's eyes sparkled with gratitude as she pressed a gentle kiss to Jemima's cheek. "Thank you. I appreciate everything you're doing for me – for us."

Jemima smiled, knowing that no matter what obstacles they faced, they'd overcome them together, side by side. And as they delved into their preparations for the upcoming meeting, Jemima felt more determined than ever to prove that Celine's mobile tattoo business was worth fighting for.

～

*S*unlight streamed through the trees as Jemima pulled her SUV into the small parking lot near the town hall. Celine's heart pounded with anticipation, her fingers tapping nervously on her knees. She took a deep breath, trying to calm herself. She knew Jemima had done everything in her power to prepare for this meeting, and she couldn't help but feel grateful for her unwavering support.

"Ready?" Jemima asked, her voice gentle and reassuring as she turned off the engine.

"Yeah," Celine replied, forcing a smile. "Let's do this."

As they walked toward the entrance of the town hall, Celine couldn't help but admire the quaint beauty of the building. It was built from warm, honey-colored stone, with ivy climbing its walls and large windows that allowed sunlight to pour inside. The picturesque scene was a stark contrast to the uncertainty churning within her.

"Remember," Jemima said, squeezing her hand as they approached the door, "we've got this. We just need to show them what you have to offer, and how it can benefit the community."

Celine nodded, drawing strength from her words. Together, they entered the dimly lit room where the local officials were already seated at a long wooden table. The scent of aged wood and leather filled the air, and Celine could hear the faint ticking of an antique clock on the wall.

"Good afternoon," Jemima began, her voice steady and confident. "Thank you for meeting with us today. My name is Jemima Sullivan, and I'm here to discuss the mobile tattoo business of my friend, Celine Montgomery."

She gestured to Celine, who offered a small wave and forced another smile, feeling the weight of their scrutiny.

"Over the past few years, Celine has gained a reputation as one of the most talented and sought-after tattoo artists in the city. With her skill and unique artistic vision, she has decided to bring her talents to our town by starting a mobile tattoo business that will operate from a custom-designed van."

Jemima paused, allowing the officials to absorb her words. She then continued, presenting a series of detailed proposals and statistics that highlighted the potential economic benefits of Celine's business.

"By offering high-quality tattoos in a comfortable and sanitary environment, Celine's mobile tattoo business can attract visitors from neighboring towns, boosting tourism and local revenue. Moreover, it presents an opportunity to showcase the rich cultural heritage of our town through unique, custom designs inspired by our history and traditions."

Celine watched as Jemima expertly navigated their concerns, speaking with conviction and passion. She couldn't help but feel a swell of pride for him, as well as a deepened appreciation for her unwavering support.

"Furthermore," Jemima added, "Celine has already volunteered her time and expertise to several community events and art workshops, fostering connections with both young and old residents alike. Her presence here would only serve to enrich our town's cultural landscape."

As they awaited the officials' response, Celine felt her chest tighten with anxiety. She knew Jemima had done everything she could to present their case, but the final decision was now out of their hands. All they could do was hope that their arguments had been persuasive enough to sway the minds of those with the power to grant or deny their future together.

～

A stern-looking official cleared his throat, drawing Celine's attention back to the present. "While we appreciate your thorough presentation, Ms. Sullivan, we must express our concerns about the nature of tattooing and the potential impact it may have on our town's image," he said, his furrowed brow casting a shadow over his eyes.

"Many people still associate tattoos with criminality or rebellious behavior, and we wouldn't want our town to be seen as promoting such values," another official chimed in, her tone cautious yet firm.

Celine's heart sank as she listened to their words, fearing that their prejudices might spell the end for her mobile tattoo business before it even had the chance to begin. She glanced at Jemima, watching as she took a deep breath and nodded in understanding.

"Thank you for voicing your concerns," Jemima began, her voice calm and steady. "I understand that the perception of tattoos can be a sensitive topic for some. However, I'd like to emphasize that Celine is a professional artist who has dedicated her life to perfecting her craft. She approaches each tattoo with the utmost care and respect for her clients, creating personalized works of art that celebrate individuality and self-expression."

As she spoke, Celine noticed how her blue eyes seemed to burn with determination, fueling her own resolve to fight for her dream.

"Moreover," Jemima continued, "times are changing, and so too are attitudes towards tattoos. They have become increasingly popular and accepted, transcending stereotypes and misconceptions. By embracing Celine's mobile tattoo business, our town has the opportunity to demonstrate its progressive spirit and openness to change."

Celine could see the officials exchanging glances, their expressions a mixture of curiosity and skepticism. She held her breath, her fingers entwined in her lap, silently praying that Jemima's impassioned plea would resonate with them.

"By supporting Celine's business," Jemima concluded, "we are not only endorsing an accomplished artist, but also fostering a sense of community and inclusivity that benefits us all. I believe our town can only grow stronger by embracing diverse talents and perspectives."

A tense silence filled the room as the officials considered her words. Celine dared to hope that their minds might be swayed, sparing a grateful glance at Jemima for her unwavering support.

~

Despite Jemima's heartfelt speech, the local officials seemed unmoved. One of them, a woman with tightly coiled gray hair and a pinched expression, cleared her throat and addressed the couple.

"Ms. Sullivan, while we appreciate your eloquence and passion, we still have concerns that a mobile tattoo business may not be the best fit for our small town. We pride ourselves on our quaint, wholesome image, and we fear that this venture might tarnish that."

Celine's heart sank at the woman's words, but she could see Jemima's frustration bubbling beneath the surface as her hands clenched into fists at her sides.

"Respectfully," Jemima began, her voice strained but steady, "I believe there is more to consider than just the town's image. Celine's business has the potential to draw in tourists and generate revenue for local establishments. Furthermore, it would add a unique element to our cultural landscape."

"Ms. Sullivan," another official interjected, a portly man with a bushy mustache, "we simply don't see the need to introduce such an unconventional idea into our community. Our citizens are content with the way things are."

Jemima glanced at Celine, who tried her best to offer her a reassuring smile. Taking a deep breath, she continued. "Change can be intimidating, I understand. But progress requires evolution. By welcoming Celine's business, our town embraces diversity and stands out as a forward-thinking community."

The officials exchanged skeptical glances, their pens

tapping impatiently on the table. Celine's stomach churned with anxiety, and she silently pleaded with them to see reason.

"Ms. Sullivan," the gray-haired woman said finally, "while your arguments are well-intentioned, I'm afraid we remain unconvinced that this endeavor aligns with our town's core values. We will take your request under advisement, but cannot promise a favorable outcome."

Jemima's jaw clenched, and Celine could see the frustration etched on her face. Despite the setback, she was immensely grateful for Jemima's unwavering support and solid presence by her side. Beneath the table, their fingers brushed together, an unspoken promise of solidarity as they faced the uncertainty ahead.

～

The room seemed to shrink around them as the officials' decision hung heavy in the air. Celine's heart ached, and she couldn't help but notice the way Jemima's shoulders stiffened with each passing second.

"Thank you for your time," Jemima managed to say through gritted teeth, forcing a tight-lipped smile onto her face. She stood up, pulling out Celine's chair for her as she rose to her feet, a knot forming in her throat.

"Of course, Ms. Sullivan," the gray-haired woman replied, her tone final, leaving no room for further discussion.

As they walked back toward the door, Celine felt the weight of their disappointment settling on her like a crushing fog. The sound of their footsteps echoed down the hallway, mirroring the emptiness that now filled her chest.

"Jemima..." she whispered, her voice barely audible even to herself. "I'm so sorry."

"Hey," Jemima responded softly, pausing just outside the door to meet her gaze. Her blue eyes shimmered with concern, and Celine could see the hurt lurking beneath the surface. "We tried our best, alright? We'll figure this out."

Jemima's words were meant to soothe, but they only served to deepen the chasm between them. As Jemima held the door open for Celine, the sunlight outside seemed too bright, too harsh for the emotions that swirled within her.

"Maybe they'll change their minds," she offered half-heartedly as they stepped into the daylight, her hand instinctively reaching for his. She knew it was unlikely, yet she couldn't help but cling to the smallest sliver of hope.

Jemima exhaled, rubbing the back of her neck as she glanced at their intertwined fingers. "Maybe," she agreed, the word sounding more like an admission of defeat than any semblance of optimism. "But we need to be prepared for whatever comes next. We'll find a way, Celine. I promise."

Celine's heart swelled with gratitude as she looked at Jemima, her unwavering support shining through even in the face of adversity. But the question remained: could their love survive the storm that threatened to engulf them?

"Thank you," she murmured, her voice catching on the words. "For everything."

Jemima looked at her, her eyes softening as she squeezed her hand gently. "Always," she whispered, the single word carrying a world of meaning.

As they walked back to the car, the uncertainty of their future together loomed large and menacing in the distance. And yet, despite it all, Celine knew one thing for certain: they would face whatever challenges came their way, hand-in-hand, their love defying the odds.

· · ·

*T*he sun dipped low in the sky, casting an almost melancholy glow on the small-town as Jemima and Celine sat together on a bench in the town square. The once bustling marketplace now seemed eerily deserted, mirroring the desolation that filled their hearts.

"Can you believe we're here?" Celine asked softly, her voice barely audible above the gentle rustle of autumn leaves. "I mean, everything was going so well...until it wasn't."

Jemima sighed, leaning back against the bench as her gaze followed a stray leaf tumbling across the cobblestone path. "Yeah," she agreed, turning to look at her with a sad smile. "But life has a funny way of throwing curveballs, doesn't it?"

Celine stared at their hands, fingers intertwined in a silent confession of love and support. She took a deep breath and ventured into the heart of the matter. "Do you think we can make it through this, Jemima? I know we love each other, but is that enough?"

Jemima hesitated, searching for the right words. "I wish I had all the answers, Celine. But what I do know is that we've faced challenges before, and we've come out stronger. We just need to stay true to ourselves and keep fighting."

"Are we fighting for our love or are we fighting against the town?" she questioned, her eyes glistening with unshed tears. "I don't want to feel like I'm constantly battling to prove my worth, to prove our worth."

"Neither do I," Jemima admitted, her grip on Celine's hand tightening. "But if there's one thing I've learned from all of this, it's that we have something truly special. And I refuse to let anyone take that away from us."

"Even if it means leaving town?" Celine inquired, her heart pounding in her chest as she awaited Jemima's response.

"Even if it means leaving town," she confirmed, Jemima's eyes filled with determination. "If we have to find a new place to call home, then that's what we'll do. Together."

Celine's chest tightened at the conviction in Jemima's words, her fear and doubt momentarily giving way to hope. "I love you, Jemima. I just hope we can weather this storm."

"Hey," Jemima whispered, gently lifting Celine's chin so she was looking into her eyes. "We've got each other, and that's one hell of a strong foundation. So let's take it one day at a time, alright?"

"Alright," Celine agreed, leaning into Jemima's comforting embrace as they sat beneath the fading light.

Surrounded by uncertainty, their love served as a beacon of hope amidst the darkness, guiding them through the turbulence of life's unpredictable journey.

~

*C*eline stood on the porch, the cool evening breeze carrying the scent of wildflowers as it rustled through her blonde hair. The golden hues of the setting sun cast a warm glow on her face, and she felt a peculiar mix of serenity and unease, knowing that she and Jemima were at a crossroads in their lives.

"Hey," Jemima said softly, stepping outside to join her, her blue eyes reflecting the deepening colors of the sky. She moved closer, gently placing her hands on Celine's shoulders. "I know things are tough right now, but I promise we'll find a way to make this work."

Jemima's touch was like a balm to her troubled heart, and she couldn't help but lean into her warmth. "How can you be so sure?" she asked, her voice barely above a whisper.

"Because I believe in us," Jemima replied with conviction, her gaze never leaving Celine's. "And I believe in you. You're one of the most talented and passionate people I've ever met. If anyone can turn this situation around, it's you."

Tears welled up in Celine's eyes, but she blinked them back, refusing to let her emotions get the better of her. "It's just so frustrating, Jemima. It feels like everyone is against us, and all we want is to live our lives and share our love for art."

Jemima nodded, understanding the weight of Celine's words. "But that's exactly why we have to keep fighting, babe. We can't let other people dictate our future. We'll search for a solution, even if it means exploring options beyond this town."

Celine took a deep breath, drawing courage from Jemima's unwavering support. "You're right. We can't let fear stand in our way. Thank you for always being there for me, Jemima. You're my rock."

Jemima smiled, her eyes crinkling at the corners as she pulled Celine into a tender embrace. "And you're mine, Celine. Together, we can conquer anything."

As the sun dipped below the horizon, the world around them seemed to pause for just a moment, allowing Jemima and Celine to bask in the strength of their love. They knew that challenges lay ahead, but with their hearts bound together, they were ready to face whatever life had in store.

*T*he evening sky stretched out above them, an endless canvas of vibrant oranges and purples that seemed to mirror the emotions swirling within their hearts. As Jemima pulled Celine closer, her head resting against Jemima's chest, they stood together in the fading light, two souls seeking solace in each other's embrace.

"Jemima," Celine whispered, her voice barely audible above the gentle rustling of leaves in the breeze. "I don't know what the future holds for us, but I want you to know that I'm not giving up. We'll find a way – together."

Jemima ran her fingers through Celine's golden hair, marveling at the softness of each strand as it slipped through her touch. "I know, Celine. I believe in us, and I believe in our love. No matter the obstacles, we'll overcome them, side by side."

Her arms tightened around Jemima, and they could feel the warmth of their bodies seeping into each other as they held each other close. In that moment, the doubts and fears that had plagued them seemed to melt away, replaced by a newfound determination to protect the love they had fought so hard to nurture.

"Promise me," Celine murmured, lifting her gaze to

meet Jemima's, "promise me that we'll never let go of this feeling – the strength we find in each other."

Jemima looked down into Celine's eyes that reflected the unwavering resolve in her own. "I promise, Celine. With every beat of my heart, I promise."

As they stood there, wrapped in each other's arms, they found the comfort and reassurance they both craved. The challenges they faced were daunting, but they had discovered something far more powerful: the unbreakable bond between them, forged in the fires of adversity and tempered by the depths of their love.

CHAPTER 14

*C*eline stood on the porch of her quaint country cottage, a steaming cup of coffee in hand. She watched as Jemima's SUV rolled down the long gravel driveway, sending tiny rocks flying like pebbles skipping across water. Her heart skipped a beat at the sight of her; the city lights had never made her feel such warmth, such comfort.

"Jemima!" she called out, setting her mug down and hurrying to meet her as she parked her car. "Perfect timing - I need your help with these boxes."

"Of course," she replied, stepping out of the vehicle with a smile that reached her sincere blue eyes. "Anything for you, Celine."

Together, they loaded Celine's belongings into the back of her SUV, their laughter mingling with the rustle of leaves as a gentle breeze swept through the trees.

"Okay, let's get down to business," Celine said, brushing strands of her blonde hair from her face as they settled onto the porch swing. "We need to find new locations for my mobile tattoo studio."

"Right," Jemima agreed, pulling out a map and unfolding it on her lap. "Let's see what we've got."

They leaned in close, their heads almost touching as they studied the paper. Celine felt an unexpected spark of electricity as she caught a whiff of Jemima's scent – subtle yet intoxicating.

"Here's Helen Springs," she pointed out. "It's a small town, but it's within driving distance from several others. What do you think?"

"Seems like a good starting point," Jemima mused, tracing the route with her finger. "Plus, it's close enough that you can still make trips back home when you want to."

"Exactly." Celine nodded, feeling a surge of excitement at the thought of taking her art on the road. "Now, let's look into space availability and local regulations."

"Right." Jemima pulled out her phone and began to search online. "I'll start with zoning laws and permits, and you can look up any vacant lots or community events where you could set up shop temporarily."

"Deal." Celine's fingers flew across her own phone screen as she researched potential locations.

"Hey, I found something," Jemima announced after a few minutes. "There's an upcoming street fair in Helen Springs next month. It's a popular event with food, live music, and local vendors. Could be a great opportunity for you to showcase your work and attract new clients."

"Amazing! Let me jot that down," Celine replied, excitement bubbling within her. "Now we just need to find a few more places like that – somewhere with good foot traffic and a welcoming atmosphere. We should also research the nearby towns, see if they're open to having my mobile studio there."

"Agreed." Jemima nodded, her focus unwavering as she continued to search online. "We'll consider accessibility, too. You don't want to set up in a spot that's difficult for people to reach."

"Exactly." Celine smiled at her, feeling a warmth spread through her chest. She couldn't help but think how lucky she was to have a friend like Jemima by her side – someone who understood her passion for her art and supported her unconditionally.

Together, they delved deeper into their research, confident that they would find the perfect alternative locations for her mobile tattoo business. And as the sun dipped below the horizon, casting golden hues across the countryside, Celine knew that this journey was one they would embark on together - hand in hand, heart to heart, united in their shared determination to overcome any obstacles that stood in their way.

~

*C*eline's fingers danced across her phone as she reached out to her network of fellow tattoo artists and friends in the industry, seeking recommendations and insights on suitable locations for her mobile business. The faint scent of jasmine wafted through the open window, a gentle reminder of the warm summer evening outside.

"Hey, I've been thinking about setting up my mobile tattoo studio in some new places," she typed, her thumbs moving swiftly over the keyboard. "Do you have any suggestions or advice on where I should go?"

As she waited for responses, Celine glanced over at Jemima, who was busy making phone calls to local business owners and community leaders. Her deep voice resonated confidently in the cozy living room, her blue eyes filled with determination as she inquired about the possibility of setting up Celine's mobile tattoo business in their town or at local events.

"Thank you for considering our proposal, Mr.

Thompson," Jemima said into the phone, her tone both respectful and persuasive. "We believe that Celine's mobile tattoo studio would be a unique addition to your upcoming street fair."

Celine couldn't help but admire her unwavering dedication to helping her find new locations for her business. As her phone buzzed with incoming messages, she read through the replies from her fellow artists, mentally noting their suggestions and words of encouragement.

"Hey Jemima," Celine called out softly, not wanting to interrupt her conversation. "Tasha just mentioned that there's a monthly art walk in Willow Creek that could be a great spot for me to set up shop."

"Perfect! I'll make a note of that," Jemima replied, jotting down the information while still maintaining her phone call with Mr. Thompson.

Celine's heart swelled with gratitude as she watched Jemima multitask effortlessly, balancing her support for Celine with her own work responsibilities. In those quiet moments between conversations, she felt the sweet, undeniable pull of their connection, growing stronger with each passing day.

"Alright," Jemima said as she ended the call, a triumphant smile lighting up her face. "Mr. Thompson has agreed to give us a spot at the street fair next month!

It's going to be a great opportunity for you to showcase your work and connect with potential clients."

"Jemima, that's fantastic!" Celine exclaimed, her own smile mirroring his. "Thank you for all your help. I couldn't do this without you."

"You're more than welcome, Celine," she replied, her eyes warm and sincere. "I just want to see you succeed – in your business and in life."

As they continued to research and network their way through the evening, Celine felt an overwhelming sense of gratitude for the woman sitting beside her. Together, they were a formidable team, ready to tackle any challenge that came their way. And as the soft golden light of twilight painted the room, she knew in her heart that they were destined for greatness – not only in their quest to find alternative locations for her mobile tattoo business but also in the uncharted territory of their blossoming love.

$\sim$

The sun dipped low on the horizon, casting a warm glow over the quaint streets of Helen Springs as Celine and Jemima strolled hand-in-hand down the cobblestone sidewalks. Their laughter mingled with the hum of conversation from the busy cafe patios that lined the street. With each location visited, the excitement between them grew, fueled by their shared passion for helping Celine's mobile tattoo business thrive.

"Alright, this spot here is next on our list," Jemima announced, stopping in front of a bustling farmers market set along a picturesque stretch of parkland. The scent of fresh produce filled the air, while children darted between vendors' stalls with glee.

"Wow, this place is lovely," Celine breathed, her eyes sparkling with delight. "I can definitely see myself setting up shop here."

As they walked through the lively market, Celine imagined her mobile studio nestled among the colorful stalls. She could almost hear the buzz of her tattoo machine as it created intricate designs on the skin of eager clients who had been drawn in by the vibrant atmosphere.

"Let's take a moment to consider the pros and cons of this location," Jemima suggested, guiding Celine to a nearby bench. They sat down, hands still entwined, and began to discuss the various factors that would impact her business here.

"First off, foot traffic is excellent. There's a constant flow of people passing through, which means more potential clients," Celine mused, nodding to the steady stream of market-goers around them. "And the overall atmosphere is so inviting – I think people would be really open to getting a tattoo in such a warm, friendly environment."

"True," Jemima agreed, her blue eyes thoughtful. "But we have to consider the competition – there are already several vendors offering henna and temporary tattoos. You might have to work harder to stand out."

Celine chewed her lip, considering her point. "That's true. But I think my unique artistic style and the fact that I offer permanent tattoos will set me apart from the others."

"Good point," Jemima conceded, giving her hand a gentle squeeze. "What about space availability? Your mobile studio is quite large – do you think there's enough room for it here?"

Celine looked around, her eyes scanning the crowded market. "It might be tight, but I think with a little creativity, we could make it work."

As they continued to discuss the merits and drawbacks of each location, Celine felt a growing sense of confidence. With Jemima by her side, she knew they could overcome any obstacle and chart a course to success for her mobile tattoo business. And as the sun dipped below the horizon, bathing the park in a warm, golden twilight, she couldn't help but feel that their own love story was just beginning to unfold.

~

eline stared out the window of Anna Thompson's cozy gallery, observing the quaint cobblestone streets of Helen Springs. The lively chatter of the town's residents filled the air as they went about their daily activities. She couldn't help but wonder if this charming place could be the perfect location for her mobile tattoo business.

"Anna," Celine began, turning to face the elegant woman who had become a mentor to her. "I was wondering what your thoughts are on the possibility of setting up my mobile tattoo studio here in town?"

Anna thoughtfully sipped her tea before responding, her intelligent gaze fixed on Celine. "Well, I do think there would be a market for your unique talents here. However, considering the conservative nature of some residents, you may face challenges with local regulations."

"Good point," Anna Thompson chimed in, her supportive presence never far from Celine. "What about partnering with local businesses or participating in community events? That might help us overcome any potential issues."

"An interesting idea," Mabel Jenkins added, her greying hair and kind eyes exuding warmth. "As someone who has lived in Helen Springs for years, I can say that there's always room for creative solutions. Perhaps you could collaborate with other artists or even host workshops at the gallery?"

"Or maybe set up a pop-up studio at our town fair?" Lily Anderson suggested excitedly, her bubbly personality shining through. "It's a huge event, and people from neighboring towns flock to it – it could be a great way to gain exposure!"

Celine took in all the suggestions, her heart swelling with gratitude for these wonderful women. Their willingness to help and support her dream was both humbling and inspiring. "Thank you, everyone," she said earnestly, her eyes glistening with unshed tears. "Your input means the world to me."

"Let's make a list of potential locations and events," Jemima proposed, always the practical one. "We can weigh the pros and cons of each and see which ones hold the most promise."

"Sounds like a plan," Celine agreed, her spirits lifted by the possibilities that lay before them.

As the group brainstormed ideas, Celine's thoughts wandered to the love affair that had blossomed between her and Jemima. It was hard for her not to feel over-whelmed with happiness as they navigated this new chapter together – both in business and in life. And as they continued their discussions, deep into the evening, she knew that finding a home for her mobile tattoo studio was just another adventure they would conquer side by side.

~

*T*he sun cast a warm glow over the small-town streets of Helen Springs as Celine and Jemima sat on the porch of the quaint country house Jemima had rented, surrounded by notes, maps, and their steaming cups of coffee. A soft breeze rustled through the trees, carrying the scent of fresh blossoms and the promise of a new beginning.

"Alright," Celine began, combing her fingers through her blonde hair as she focused on the task at hand. "Let's start with the first location: the old farmer's market lot. What do you think about the logistics?"

Jemima leaned back in her chair, her blue eyes thoughtful as she chewed on the end of her pen. "It has plenty of space for your mobile studio and parking for clients," she said slowly. "But it might need some cleanup and landscaping to make it more inviting."

Celine nodded thoughtfully. "True, but that could be an opportunity to collaborate with local businesses – maybe a flower shop or a landscaper. It would not only help us, but also promote them."

"Great idea!" Jemima agreed, her eyes twinkling with excitement. She jotted down a few notes before continuing. "Now, let's talk about costs – rent, utilities, insurance, and so on."

As they delved into the financial aspects of each location, they maintained a steady rhythm of conversation, fueled by their combined determination to make Celine's dream a reality. The discussion was peppered with laughter and playful teasing, highlighting the deep connection that had formed between them.

"Okay, last one: marketing strategies," Celine said with a sigh, rubbing her tired eyes. "How do we get the word out about my mobile tattoo business in these areas?"

"Social media, for sure," Jemima replied without hesitation. "We can create targeted ads for each location and promote any partnerships we make with local businesses. And don't forget the power of word-of-mouth – you've already got a strong reputation in the industry."

"True," Celine smiled, feeling a surge of pride at Jemima's words. "And perhaps I could offer limited-time promotions or discounts to encourage people to give my tattoos a try."

"Brilliant!" Jemima exclaimed, scribbling furiously on their notes. "Now, let's prioritize these locations."

They spent the next hour carefully weighing the pros and cons of each potential location, considering factors such as foot traffic, clientele demographics, and how well they could integrate into the local community. Eventually, they narrowed it down to three top choices: the old farmer's market lot, a spot near the popular Helen Springs Park, and a booth at the upcoming town fair.

Celine looked over their detailed plans, her heart swelling with anticipation and gratitude for all the support she had received. "I can't believe we're actually doing this, Jemima," she whispered, unable to keep the emotion from her voice. "Thank you for being by my side through all of this."

Jemima reached across the table, taking her hand and squeezing it gently. "It's been an honor, Celine," she replied softly. "I believe in you and your talent, and I can't wait to see where this journey takes us."

As they sat there, hands clasped and eyes locked, Celine knew that whatever challenges they faced in bringing her mobile tattoo business to life, they would tackle them together – as friends, as lovers, and as partners in every sense of the word.

❧

The warm sun cast a golden hue over the quaint town of Fountain Springs as Celine and Jemima prepared to present their meticulously crafted plan to the local community. Standing on the charming wooden stage in the park, they exchanged an encouraging glance before addressing the gathering crowd.

"Good afternoon, everyone," Celine began, her voice steady and confident. "Thank you for coming out here today to hear our proposal. My name is Celine Montgomery, and this is my partner, Jemima Sullivan. Together, we have developed a plan to bring a unique mobile tattoo business to your beautiful town."

As she spoke, Jemima set up a small easel displaying a detailed map of the three potential locations they had chosen. The crowd's eyes were drawn to the vibrant colors and intricate designs that decorated the map, showcasing Celine's undeniable artistic talent.

"By setting up shop at the old farmer's market lot, near the popular Helen Springs Park, or at the upcoming town fair, we believe we can offer a fresh, creative outlet for locals and visitors alike," Jemima continued, her blue eyes sincere as she addressed the gathering. "We understand there may be concerns about the impact of such a business on the community, so we'd like to address them head-on."

"Firstly," Celine chimed in, "we want to assure you that we will adhere to the highest standards of hygiene and professionalism. We are dedicated to maintaining a clean, safe environment and providing top-quality service to our clients."

"Furthermore," Jemima added, "we believe our mobile tattoo business can contribute positively to the local economy by drawing in new visitors and encouraging spending at nearby establishments. We also plan to collaborate with other businesses and participate in community events whenever possible."

Nods of approval rippled through the crowd, but Celine could sense lingering doubts among some of the onlookers. She locked eyes with an older woman who seemed particularly skeptical and addressed her directly.

"Ma'am, I understand that tattoos may not be to everyone's taste, and that's okay. Our goal is not to impose our values on anyone but to offer an opportunity for self-expression to those who seek it. We believe Helen Springs is a town that values creativity and diversity, and we hope our mobile tattoo business can contribute to that."

The woman hesitated for a moment before giving Celine a small nod of acknowledgement. Encouraged by this exchange, Celine and Jemima opened the floor to questions, addressing each concern with respect and understanding.

Over the next few days, Celine and Jemima worked tirelessly to secure the necessary permits, licenses, and approvals for their mobile tattoo business. They visited local offices, filled out paperwork, and made countless phone calls, all the while supporting each other through the process.

"Almost there, Cel," Jemima murmured one evening as they sat side by side on the porch, poring over the last of the documents. "Just a few more signatures, and we'll be ready to roll."

Celine looked up from the papers, her eyes shining with gratitude. "I couldn't have done this without you, Jemima." She leaned in, pressing a tender kiss to her cheek. "Thank you for being my rock."

~

s night fell on Helen Springs, the future seemed brighter than ever for Celine, Jemima, and their soon-to-be-realized dream. Hand in hand, they faced the challenges ahead with unwavering determination and love, knowing that together, anything was possible.

The sun dipped low on the horizon, casting a warm glow over the small park in Helen Springs where Celine and Jemima had chosen to celebrate their victories. The scent of freshly cut grass filled the air, mixing with the sound of laughter from children playing nearby.

"Cheers," Celine said, raising her glass of sparkling cider towards Jemima. She grinned and clinked her glass against Celine's, their eyes meeting for a brief moment before they both took a sip.

"Who would've thought we'd make it this far?" she mused, setting down her glass and leaning back on the picnic blanket they had spread out on the soft grass. "I mean, finding all these alternative locations for your mobile tattoo business... it's been quite the adventure."

Celine nodded, her blonde hair catching a stray beam of sunlight. "It has, hasn't it? But I wouldn't have wanted to do this with anyone else." She gave Jemima a warm smile, her green eyes brimming with sincerity.

Jemima returned the smile and reached for her hand, giving it a gentle squeeze. "And I would follow you to the ends of the earth if it meant helping you realize your dreams, Cel."

As they sat there, hands intertwined, Celine couldn't help but think about the roller coaster of emotions and challenges they had faced together. From brainstorming potential locations to navigating local regulations and securing permits, they had tackled each obstacle head-on, always supporting one another.

"Remember that time we almost gave up when we found out about the zoning restrictions in Fountain Springs?" Celine asked, her voice tinged with amusement.

Jemima chuckled. "Oh yeah, I was ready to throw in the towel that day. But you were so determined, Cel. You just refused to let anything stand in your way."

Celine blushed slightly at her praise, but she knew Jemima was right. Throughout this entire journey, she had been driven by her passion for tattooing and her belief in the potential of her mobile business. And every step of the way, Jemima had been by her side.

"Jemima, I just want you to know how much I appreciate everything you've done for me," she said softly, her gaze locked on hers. "I couldn't have done any of this without you."

Jemima smiled, a genuine warmth radiating from her blue eyes. "And I wouldn't have wanted to be anywhere else, Celine. You've taught me so much about perseverance and chasing your dreams, even when the odds are stacked against you."

As the sun dipped below the horizon, bathing the park in a golden glow, Celine and Jemima lay there on the soft grass, their fingers still entwined. They reveled in the knowledge that they had overcome countless obstacles together, and in doing so, had forged a bond stronger than either of them could have ever imagined.

"Here's to us, Jemima," Celine whispered, raising her glass once more. "And to all the adventures yet to come."

"Cheers to that, Cel," she murmured, clinking her glass against Celine's one last time before they both took a sip, sealing their commitment to each other and to the future of their mobile tattoo business.

CHAPTER 15

he sweltering heat of the summer afternoon
weighed heavily on Celine as she wiped the
sweat from her brow, her eyes scanning over the paperwork and scheduling that seemed to have taken over the
small kitchen table. Jemima sat across from her, her
brows furrowed in concentration as she typed away on
her laptop, trying to keep their fledgling mobile tattoo
business afloat.

"Ugh, this is so frustrating," Celine muttered under
her breath, tapping her pen against the open notebook
in front of her. The numbers just didn't seem to add up,
and the mounting challenges they faced threatened to
crush her spirits.

"I know," Jemima sighed, running a hand through her
dark hair. "I wish there was an easy solution, but we're

doing our best. Maybe we could use some outside perspective."

Her blue eyes met Celine's with a glimmer of hope. Celine took a deep breath, knowing that Jemima was right. They couldn't do this alone, not if they wanted the business to survive and thrive. "You're right. Let's reach out to Anna, Mabel, and Lily. They've been so supportive in the past; maybe they can help us figure this out."

Jemima nodded, a faint smile tugging at the corners of her lips. "Anna has always had a keen eye for talent. I'm sure she could offer some insights on how to promote your work better."

"And Mabel, she's like the mother I never had," Celine added, her voice softening as she thought of the kind-hearted woman who was running Jemima's store while Jemima was assisting Celine find a new base for her mobile tattoo studio. "She's seen it all, and I bet she has some wisdom to share."

"Plus, Lily is one of your biggest fans," Jemima said, her eyes twinkling. "She knows firsthand what it's like to be a customer of your mobile tattoo business. Maybe she can give us some ideas on how to make the experience even better for others."

"Alright," Celine said, determination setting in. "Let's reach out to them and see if they can help us get back on track. We need all the support we can get right now."

As they made their decision, a sense of relief washed over them. While the road ahead was still uncertain, at least they knew they had a network of friends who believed in them and were willing to offer their guidance. Celine and Jemima exchanged a hopeful look, ready to face the challenges head-on, together.

~

*C*eline glanced nervously at the screen of her phone as it rang, her fingers tapping an anxious rhythm on the countertop. The sun streamed through the windows, casting a warm glow on the small kitchen table where Jemima sat, her blue eyes fixed on Celine with unwavering support.

"Hello, Anna?" Celine began hesitantly when the line connected. "It's Celine Montgomery. I hope I'm not catching you at a bad time."

"Of course not, dear," Anna replied, her voice soothing and sophisticated. "What can I do for you?"

Celine took a deep breath, mustering the courage to express her concerns. "Jemima and I are facing some challenges with my mobile tattoo business, and we were hoping you might have some advice for us."

"Absolutely, I'd be happy to help," Anna assured her. "Why don't you come by the gallery later this afternoon? We can all sit down together and discuss your concerns."

"Thank you so much, Anna," Celine said, relief evident in her tone. "We'll see you then." She hung up the phone and turned to Jemima. "Anna agreed to meet with us. Let's call Mabel and Lily now."

Jemima dialed Mabel's number, her strong fingers gripping the phone as she prepared to ask for guidance. "Hello, Mabel? It's Jemima Sullivan. Celine and I could really use your wisdom right now."

"Jemima, my dear boy, what's going on?" Mabel asked, concern immediately flooding her motherly voice.

"We're struggling to keep Celine's mobile tattoo business afloat," Jemima admitted, her voice cracking slightly with vulnerability. "Could we come by the B&B this afternoon to talk?"

"Of course, Honey," Mabel replied warmly. "I'll put the kettle on."

Finally, Celine called Lily, her bubbly and infectious enthusiasm bringing a smile to Celine's face. "Hey, Lily! We were wondering if you could join us at Anna's gallery later? We need some advice on how to overcome the challenges we're facing."

"Absolutely!" Lily chirped. "I'll be there with bells on!"

Later that afternoon, the sun casting long shadows across the quiet streets of Fountain Springs, Celine and Jemima arrived at Anna's gallery. The smell of oil paint and varnish filled the air as they stepped through the door, greeted by the sight of their friends waiting for them.

"Thank you all for coming," Celine began, her voice trembling with gratitude. "Your support means the world to us."

"Of course, dear," Anna reassured her, her eyes filled with empathy. "We're here to help you in any way we can."

"Remember," Mabel added, placing a gentle hand on Celine's shoulder, "we're stronger together. This community is built on friendship and mutual support."

Lily nodded vigorously, her colorful tattoos seeming to dance with her enthusiasm. "We've got your back, Celine. Whatever obstacles you're facing, we'll find a way to overcome them, together."

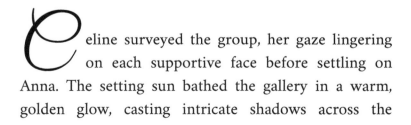

eline surveyed the group, her gaze lingering on each supportive face before settling on Anna. The setting sun bathed the gallery in a warm, golden glow, casting intricate shadows across the colorful paintings and sculptures that adorned the walls. She clutched a small notebook to her chest, feeling the weight of the challenges that lay before her and Jemima.

"Alright," she began, taking a deep breath. "Let's hear your ideas."

Anna leaned forward, her elegant hands folded on the table. "Firstly, I believe we should organize a community event to showcase your work, Celine. It would be an excellent opportunity to raise awareness about your mobile tattoo business and generate support from the townspeople."

Celine scribbled down the suggestion, her eyes brightening at the prospect. "That's a great idea, Anna. We could invite local artists and musicians to participate, too. It could be like a mini arts festival!"

Jemima nodded, her blue eyes filled with determination. "We can reach out to local businesses for sponsorship and collaborate with them to make the event even more successful." Her mind raced with ideas, already envisioning the vibrant atmosphere of the community coming together in celebration of art and creativity.

"Absolutely," Lily chimed in, her enthusiasm contagious. "I know several people who would love to attend an event like this. Plus, it would give you a chance to showcase your incredible talent to a wider audience, Celine."

Celine's heart swelled with gratitude as her friends offered their insights and encouragement. She jotted down notes furiously, filling page after page with potential solutions and ideas. All the while, Jemima stayed by her side, offering unwavering support and contributing her own suggestions.

"Thank you all so much," Celine said, her voice thick with emotion as she looked around the table. "I can't express how much this means to me. With your help, I truly believe we can overcome these challenges and keep my mobile tattoo business alive."

"Of course, dear," Mabel said warmly, reaching across the table to squeeze Celine's hand. "This is what friends are for. We'll do whatever it takes to help you succeed."

As they continued discussing potential solutions, Celine felt a renewed sense of hope and optimism. With the guidance and support of Anna, Mabel, and Lily, she knew that she and Jemima could face whatever obstacles lay ahead and emerge stronger than ever before.

$\sim$

The sun dipped low in the sky, casting a warm golden glow over Mabel's cozy living room. Celine watched as dust particles danced in the light, her mind momentarily distracted from the weight of her worries. Jemima sat next to her, with hand resting reassuringly on her knee.

"Overcoming obstacles is never easy," Mabel began, her voice rich with the wisdom of years. "But I can tell you from experience that it's worth every bit of effort you put into it."

Celine looked up at Mabel, her green eyes reflecting the firelight flickering in the hearth. The older woman leaned forward, her kind eyes meeting Celine's gaze.

"Many years ago, when my dear husband passed away, I thought I'd never be able to keep this bed and breakfast running on my own," Mabel recounted, her fingers tracing the delicate embroidery on the armchair she occupied. "But with determination, resilience, and the help of good friends, I managed to not only keep the business going but to make it thrive."

A soft smile played on Mabel's lips, and Celine felt a surge of admiration for this strong, nurturing woman who had become a steadfast friend.

"Never underestimate the power of perseverance, my dear," Mabel continued, her words sinking deep into Celine's soul. "You and Jemima have what it takes to overcome these challenges, just as I did. But you must stay resilient and determined in pursuing your dreams."

Celine squeezed Jemima's hand, feeling a renewed

sense of determination course through her veins. She nodded silently, vowing to follow Mabel's advice and fight for her mobile tattoo business.

"Thank you, Mabel," Jemima said sincerely, smiling warmly at the older woman. "Your words mean more than you know."

Lily chimed in, her bubbly energy filling the room. "I've got an idea for expanding your clientele, Celine! Have you ever thought about partnering with local businesses or hosting pop-up tattoo events in nearby towns?"

Celine's eyes widened at the suggestion. "That's a brilliant idea, Lily! I never considered it before, but it could be the perfect way to reach new clients and showcase my work."

"Exactly!" Lily enthused, her colorful tattoos peeking out from beneath her sleeves. "You could collaborate with businesses that share your artistic vibe, like clothing boutiques or art galleries. And pop-up events would create excitement and buzz around your mobile tattoo business."

Celine felt her heart swell with gratitude as she took in Lily's suggestions, her mind alight with possibilities. She couldn't help but steal a glance at Jemima, whose blue eyes shone with pride and support.

"Thank you, Lily," Celine whispered, her voice thick

with emotion. "I never would have thought of that on my own."

"Hey, what are friends for?" Lily grinned, her dimples deepening.

As the group continued their discussion, Celine marveled at the love and support that surrounded her. With Mabel's wisdom, Anna's ingenuity, and Lily's enthusiasm bolstering her spirit, Celine knew that she and Jemima could face any challenge that came their way. And with each step they took, their dreams would grow ever closer to becoming a reality.

~

*C*eline stood in the soft afternoon light that filtered through the window, her eyes glistening with unshed tears. The warmth of Anna's hand on her arm grounded her as she looked at the faces of the three women who had supported her and Jemima so much.

"Thank you," Celine said, her voice wavering slightly. "Your advice and encouragement mean the world to us. We couldn't do this without you."

"Of course, dear," Mabel replied gently, her kind eyes crinkling at the corners. "We're here for you both, every step of the way."

"Absolutely," Anna agreed, nodding her head firmly. "It's important to lean on your friends and community when you need it most."

"Let's take all of this amazing advice and use it to make a plan," Jemima suggested, her blue eyes filled with determination and hope.

"Great idea," Celine breathed, feeling a renewed sense of purpose wash over her.

Gathering around the cozy living room table, they began to brainstorm. Celine wrote down their ideas, while Jemima kept the conversation focused and flowing. Each suggestion was given its due consideration, from organizing community events to showcase Celine's work to partnering with local businesses.

~

"*A*nna mentioned collaborating with clothing boutiques or art galleries," Celine mused aloud, scribbling the idea down. "I could create custom tattoo designs inspired by their products, maybe even offer exclusive discounts for their customers."

"Sounds perfect," Jemima chimed in, her excitement palpable. "And we can't forget Lily's idea about hosting pop-up tattoo events. That would definitely generate buzz and help expand your clientele."

"Definitely," Celine agreed, her mind racing with possibilities. She could already envision herself mingling with potential clients, surrounded by her artwork and the hum of her tattoo machine.

"Let's not forget Mabel's advice about staying resilient and determined," Jemima added softly, glancing over at the older woman with gratitude. "We need to be patient and persistent, even when things get tough."

"Absolutely," Celine nodded, feeling a resolve settle within her. She knew that with Jemima by her side and the support of their friends, they could overcome any obstacle.

As they continued to brainstorm, Celine felt a warmth spread through her chest – a mixture of gratitude, hope, and excitement for the future. As she gazed around the room at the faces of Anna, Mabel, and Lily, she knew that they had forged a bond that would see them through all of life's challenges.

"Thank you all again," she murmured, her eyes meeting each of theirs in turn. "We'll make you proud, I promise."

"Darling," Mabel said, her voice full of love, "you already do."

*T*he sun cast a warm glow through the window, illuminating the cozy nook where Celine and Jemima sat with their laptops open, ready to tackle the challenges ahead. It was as if the universe was smiling upon them, infusing them with a renewed sense of purpose. The rich aroma of freshly brewed coffee filled the air, mingling with the scent of lavender from the nearby fields.

"Alright," Celine began, her fingers tapping rhythmically on the table, "let's divide and conquer. Based on everything we've discussed, I think it's best if I focus on the creative side of things – you know, designing new tattoo concepts, refining my technique, and connecting with potential clients."

Jemima nodded in agreement, her blue eyes serious yet warm. "That sounds perfect. And I can handle the logistics – reaching out to local businesses for partnerships, organizing the community event Anna suggested, and managing our social media presence."

"Great," Celine said with a smile, feeling a spark of excitement at the prospect of working together. "What about Lily's suggestion? Do you think you could take the lead on planning those pop-up events?"

"Absolutely," Jemima confirmed enthusiastically, already envisioning himself scouting locations and coordinating schedules. "I love the idea of bringing your art to people who might not have considered getting a tattoo before."

"Me too," Celine agreed, a vision of her mobile studio filled with eager, excited faces playing out in her mind.

"Okay, so let's set some goals and deadlines," she continued, pulling out a calendar to map out their plan of action. "We should aim to have the community event within the next two months. That way, we'll have enough time to generate interest and prepare without feeling rushed."

"Sounds good," Jemima concurred, making a note on her laptop. "And what about the pop-up events? How often do you think we should aim to host those?"

"Let's start with one every three months," Celine suggested, her brow furrowed in concentration. "That way, we can see how they go and adjust accordingly."

"Perfect," Jemima said, adding the information to her growing list of tasks. "And don't forget to set aside some time for yourself, too. I know how passionate you are about your art, but it's important to maintain a balance."

Celine smiled at Jemima's thoughtfulness, touched by her concern for her well-being. "You're right," she admitted, making a mental note to schedule some downtime. "I'll make sure to pencil in some self-care."

"Good," Jemima replied, her eyes softening with

affection. "Now, let's get to work and breathe new life into this mobile tattoo business of ours."

With their plan in place and hearts full of determination, Celine and Jemima dove into their respective tasks, each fueled by a desire to succeed and the knowledge that they had the unwavering support of their friends behind them. As they worked side by side, the line between friendship and something deeper began to blur, adding an undercurrent of electricity to the air that neither could deny.

And as the sun continued to shine on their small town, it brought with it a promise of hope, growth, and the chance for two kindred spirits to find their way through life – together.

$\sim$

The sun cast golden rays across the quaint streets of Helen Springs as Celine and Jemima set about implementing the advice they had received. The vibrant colors of the town seemed to mirror the renewed sense of excitement that now thrummed between them.

"Okay, first up, we need to start promoting the community event," Celine said, tapping her pen against her notebook. "I'll design the flyers, and you can help me distribute them around town."

"Sounds like a plan," Jemima agreed, her blue eyes reflecting the determination that matched Celine's. "And I'll reach out to some local businesses to see if they'd be interested in partnering with us or hosting a pop-up tattoo event."

"Perfect," Celine replied, her heart swelling with gratitude for Jemima's unwavering support. "I'll also work on updating my portfolio, showcasing a range of designs that cater to different tastes."

As they spoke, their words were laced with enthusiasm, each suggestion and task carrying them closer to their goal. With every passing day, they ticked off items on their to-do list, feeling the momentum build.

"Hey, Celine," Jemima called out one afternoon as she returned from speaking with a local café owner. "Guess what? They've agreed to display your flyers and even offered to host a pop-up event next month!"

"Really?" Celine exclaimed, her eyes lighting up at the news. "That's amazing, Jemima! Thank you so much for all your hard work."

"Of course," Jemima replied, her cheeks warming under Celine's appreciative gaze. "We're in this together, remember?"

Celine nodded, touched by Jemima's dedication.

"We are. And I've got some good news, too. Lily stopped by earlier to see my new designs, and she loved them so much that she booked an appointment on the spot!"

"Fantastic!" Jemima grinned, sharing in her excitement. "It's all starting to come together."

As the days turned into weeks, Celine and Jemima continued to experience small victories along the way. Their community event drew an impressive crowd, with people eagerly lining up to admire Celine's artwork and book their own tattoo appointments.

"Look at this," Celine whispered to Jemima as they stood side by side at the event, watching the bustling scene before them. "We did this – together."

Jemima smiled, her heart swelling with pride. "We certainly did. And it's just the beginning, Celine. With our friends' support and our own determination, there's no limit to what we can achieve."

Jemima's words resonated within Celine, forging a bond between them that went far beyond friendship. As they continued working together, that connection only grew stronger, fueled by the triumphs they shared and the challenges they overcame.

And in those quiet moments, when their gazes lingered just a little longer than necessary, they both knew that something extraordinary was blooming between them – something that had the power to change their lives forever.

~

 eline stood in the doorway of her mobile tattoo studio, the morning sun casting a warm glow over her face as she surveyed the bustling town square. The scent of fresh flowers from a nearby stand filled the air, and the cheerful chatter of townspeople floated on the breeze.

"Can you believe how far we've come?" Jemima asked, stepping up beside her with a tray of steaming coffee cups in hand. Her blue eyes sparkled with pride and hope, mirroring the optimism that now filled Celine's heart.

"Thanks to our friends, we've turned this dream into a reality," she replied, gratefully accepting a cup from Jemima. "Anna's idea for the event was genius. And Mabel's advice on resilience...I don't know if we would have made it without them."

"Or Lily's suggestions on expanding our clientele," Jemima added, her gaze softening as she looked at Celine. "And all the while, we've been by each other's side, supporting one another."

"Exactly," Celine agreed, her heart swelling with gratitude. She looked around, taking in the sight of people admiring her work displayed on the walls and the steady stream of clients booking appointments. A newfound sense of confidence surged through her, fueled by the knowledge that they had the unwavering support of their friends.

"Remember that time when we first reached out to Anna, Mabel, and Lily for help? We were so nervous," Jemima recalled, her voice tinged with nostalgia.

Celine chuckled, recalling the butterflies in her stomach as they awaited the responses of their wise confidantes. "But their guidance gave us the strength to keep going, even when things seemed impossible. And look where we are now!"

"Here's to many more successes and the incredible journey that lies ahead," Jemima toasted, raising her coffee cup towards Celine.

"Cheers to that!" Celine replied, clinking her cup against his. As they sipped their coffee, she caught Jemima's gaze and held it for a moment longer than necessary. A familiar warmth spread through her chest, reminding her of the deep connection they shared – one that had blossomed over time, nurtured by their shared experiences.

CHAPTER 16

*J*emima made her way back to Fountain Springs, finding solace in the familiarity of her cabin. Her primary objective was to fulfill a commissioned order and replenish the store's inventory.

While she could entrust the sales duties to her capable team, she knew that the craftsmanship of the carpentry goods and the completion of commissioned projects were her personal responsibilities.

Until the day came when she would sell the Fountain Springs business and relocate to be nearer to Celine, she recognized the necessity of spending a minimum of four days per week managing the affairs of the business on-site.

~

*C*eline Montgomery sat alone in her temporary studio, a small converted garage filled with the intoxicating scent of ink and the clutter of art supplies. The late afternoon sun filtered through the dusty window, casting a warm glow over her latest creation – a delicate sketch of intertwining rose vines that seemed to dance across her drafting table.

As she dipped her fine-tipped brush into a pool of black ink, Celine couldn't ignore the creeping sensation of unease that knotted itself tighter in her stomach. Her hand trembled slightly, the bristles leaving an unintentional splatter of ink on the paper. She sighed and set the brush down, leaning back in her chair to survey the room.

"Is this really what I want?" she murmured, her voice barely audible above the hum of the overhead fan.

Her thoughts turned to the challenges she had encountered in the past months since starting her mobile tattoo business. While some towns welcomed her with open arms, others had been less receptive, their conservative values clashing with her vibrant body art and free-spirited nature. Those rejections stung deeply, but she persevered, driven by her love for her craft and the connections she forged with her clients.

"Maybe I should have expected it," she admitted to herself, recalling the cold stares and whispered comments as she'd packed up her equipment after being turned away from yet another town square. "But it still hurts."

The uncertainty of her nomadic lifestyle weighed heavily on her mind. Where once it had seemed like an exhilarating adventure, now it began to feel like she was running from something, rather than towards it. Celine longed for more stability, a place where she could put down roots and truly belong. But would that mean giving up the freedom and independence she cherished?

"Can I really have both?" she wondered aloud, her fingers tracing the intricate patterns of ink that adorned her own forearm. "Or am I just chasing a fantasy?"

Lost in thought, Celine barely noticed the shadows growing longer in her studio, the sun gradually sinking behind the distant hills. She knew something had to change, but what? And how could she make that decision without losing herself – or those she cared about – in the process?

"Sometimes, I wish life was as simple as ink on paper," she whispered wistfully, picking up her brush once more. "But it isn't...and maybe that's what makes it beautiful."

As she carefully retraced the lines of her sketch,

Celine allowed herself a small smile, taking solace in the familiar dance of ink and skin. It might not solve all her problems, but for now, it was enough.

~

*C*eline stared at her latest creation, a colorful phoenix in flight that seemed to defy gravity as it soared across the canvas. She couldn't help but feel envious of the mythical creature – so free and unrestrained, yet also bound to be reborn from its own ashes. Was that what she wanted? To fly away, only to return and start anew?

"Jemima," she murmured, her thoughts drifting towards the kind-hearted woman who had unexpectedly captured her heart. Her sincerity and unwavering loyalty were like a balm to her restless soul, but the thought of settling down with him in one place filled her with both excitement and trepidation.

"Is this really what I want?" Celine asked herself, her hands absentmindedly wiping away stray flecks of paint from her fingertips. "Can I give up my freedom for love?"

She paced around the small studio, her thoughts whirling like a storm within her. The more she considered the consequences of her decision, the heavier her heart felt. It was as if the weight of the very skies pressed down on her shoulders, threatening to crush her beneath their immensity.

"Freedom or love?" she whispered, her voice barely audible even to herself. "I never thought I'd have to choose."

Her fingers found solace in the soft bristles of her paintbrush, gently caressing them as if seeking comfort from their familiar touch. The brush seemed to understand her turmoil, empathizing with her struggle between independence and commitment.

"Maybe...maybe I can find a balance," she mused, her chest tightening at the possibility. "But is it fair to ask Jemima to wait while I figure this out?"

Celine paused in her pacing, her gaze drawn back to the phoenix on the canvas. Like her, it faced an uncertain future, its fiery wings spread wide as it prepared to embrace change. And like her, it clung to the hope that it could rise above its fears and find a new life amidst the ashes of its old one.

"Jemima," she whispered again, her heart aching with the weight of her decision. "Would you still love me if I can't promise forever? Can I ask you to share your life with someone who may never truly belong?"

As the last rays of sunlight disappeared beneath the horizon, Celine found herself at a crossroads – torn between the freedom that had shaped her identity and the love that offered her a chance at true happiness. It was a choice she knew she must make, but one she feared would ultimately define her as an artist, a lover, and a woman.

*C*eline's fingers trembled as she clutched the paintbrush, the vibrant colors on the canvas before her a stark contrast to the storm brewing inside her. She could feel the pressure building, like an impending thunderclap that threatened to shatter the fragile balance she had maintained for so long. She closed her eyes for a moment, taking a deep breath and exhaling slowly, trying to steady her racing thoughts.

"Jemima" she whispered, her heart heavy with a growing sense of unease. "What am I going to do?"

Her phone vibrated on the nearby table, startling her from her reverie. The screen displayed Jemima's name, and a wave of warmth washed over her at the sight of it. She hesitated for a brief moment, then answered the call.

"Hey, Celine," Jemima said gently, her voice laced with concern. "I just wanted to check in and see how you're doing. You seemed a little off earlier."

Celine looked around her temporary studio, the

scattered art supplies reflecting her own chaos within. She nibbled at her bottom lip, wondering how much she should reveal to Jemima – how much she dared to let Jemima see of her internal struggle.

"Jemima, I..." she began, her voice faltering. She took a steadying breath, determined to be honest with her. "I'm having a bit of a hard time right now."

"Talk to me, Celine," Jemima urged softly, the sincerity in her words wrapping around Celine like a warm embrace, offering her the strength to continue.

"I've been thinking about us, and...and my life," she confessed, her words tumbling out in a rush. "I've been trying to find a balance between my passion for my art and my desire for a simple life with you, but I'm scared. Scared of what I might have to give up, and what it means for our relationship."

Celine could almost feel Jemima's steadying presence through the phone, her unwavering loyalty anchoring her amidst the storm. She could hear her take a deep breath before she spoke.

"First of all," Jemima began gently, "I want you to know that I'm here for you, no matter what. But I also understand that this is something you need to figure out for yourself."

Celine's heart swelled with gratitude for Jemima's

understanding, but she couldn't help feeling the weight of her decision bearing down on her.

"Thank you, Jemima," she whispered, tears pricking at the corners of her eyes. "I just...I don't know how to find that balance without losing myself – or losing you."

"Take your time, Celine," Jemima reassured Celine, her voice steady and calm. "Remember why you fell in love with your art in the first place. And remember that whatever path you choose, I'll be by your side."

As they continued their conversation, Celine found solace in Jemima's unwavering support, her words offering a lifeline amidst Celine's tempestuous thoughts. But even as the storm within her began to subside, she knew that the choice before her was one only she could make – and one that would shape the course of her life forever.

~

*C*eline stared at the worn wooden floorboards of her temporary studio, her fingers tracing patterns on her sketchbook as she gathered the courage to voice her deepest fears. Her heart raced in her chest, and she took a deep breath before speaking.

"Jemima, I've been struggling with something," she began, her voice trembling slightly. "I love the idea of a simple country life here in Helen Springs, but I also can't imagine giving up my art and the freedom of my nomadic lifestyle."

She could hear the rustle of leaves outside, carried by a gentle breeze that seemed to echo her own restlessness. The scent of wildflowers and freshly cut grass filled her senses, grounding her in the moment.

"I'm worried that if I choose one path, I might lose the other—or worse, lose myself in the process," Celine confessed, her eyes glistening with unshed tears. "And I'm scared that if I can't find a way to make it work, I might end up losing you too."

Jemima remained silent for a moment, allowing Celine's words to settle between them. She could almost see Jemima in her mind's eye, her blue eyes reflecting the sincerity and compassion that had drawn her to him in the first place.

"Celine," Jemima finally said, her voice warm and steady, "I understand your fears, and I want you to know that I support you no matter what decision you make. But I also believe that there's a way to balance both your passions and your desire for a simpler life."

As Jemima spoke, Celine felt a strange mix of relief and uncertainty wash over her. Jemima's faith in her abilities was comforting, yet the weight of the decision still weighed heavily on her shoulders.

"Try to remember why you fell in love with your art and the open road, and consider how those things might also bring happiness to your life there in Helen Springs," Jemima suggested gently. "There's more than one way to find adventure, and I'm confident that together, we can find a path that leads to the life you're dreaming of."

Celine closed her eyes for a moment, allowing Jemima's words to sink in. In her heart, she knew Jemima was right–that there was a way to blend her love for art, freedom, and the simple beauty of small-town life. But finding that path would require courage, determination, and a willingness to embrace the unknown.

"Thank you, Jemima," she whispered, her voice filled with gratitude and love. "Your support means more to me than you'll ever know. I just hope I can find a way to make this work without losing what makes me... me."

"Take all the time you need, Celine," Jemima reassured her. "And remember that no matter what path you choose, I'll be here for you, every step of the way."

With those words, Celine felt a glimmer of hope begin to shine through the fog of doubt and uncertainty, guiding her towards a future where her dreams and desires could coexist harmoniously. And as she hung up the phone, she knew that whatever challenges lay ahead, she wouldn't face them alone.

~

*C*eline's heart raced as she clutched her paintbrush tightly, the bristles hovering just above the canvas. Her thoughts were a whirlwind, torn between her love for Jemima and her passion for adventure. The support she had offered was a balm to her soul, but it wasn't enough to quell the doubts that gnawed at her.

"Come on, Celine," she muttered to herself, attempting to shake off the uncertainty and focus on her art. She dipped the brush into a dollop of rich cerulean paint and pressed it against the canvas, her hand trembling ever so slightly.

She tried to lose herself in the brushstrokes, but her thoughts kept drifting back to Jemima. It was maddening, this internal tug-of-war between the life she had always imagined and the one that was now within her grasp.

"Damn it," she whispered, setting down her brush and wiping her paint-stained fingers on a nearby rag. She could feel the weight of her decision pressing down on her like a heavy fog, clouding her vision and suffocating her creativity.

"Hey, Celine," Jemima's voice crackled through the phone as she dialed Jemima number, seeking solace in her comforting presence. "Is everything alright?"

"Hi, Jemima," she sighed, trying to steady her voice. "I'm sorry to bother you, but I... I still can't seem to shake these doubts, no matter how hard I try."

There was a pause, and Celine could almost hear the wheels turning in Jemima's mind as she searched for the right words to say. "Listen," she began, her voice gentle yet firm. "I think maybe we should consider taking some time apart. Not because I don't care about you—I do, more than anything—but because I want you to have the space you need to figure things out."

The suggestion hung in the air between them, and for a moment, Celine's heart tightened with fear. But as she let the idea sink in, she knew that Jemima was right. This decision was too important to make on a whim, and if she wanted to give their relationship a real chance, she needed to confront her doubts head-on.

"Thank you, Jemima," she said quietly, a mix of gratitude and sadness washing over her. "I think you're right. I need some time to think."

"Take all the time you need," Jemima reassured her, her voice warm despite the distance. "And remember, Celine... no matter what you decide, I'll be here for you."

As they hung up, Celine's gaze drifted back to the canvas, its unfinished image a reflection of the uncertainty that still lingered in her heart. But beneath the doubt, there was a flicker of determination—a resolve to face her fears and find the path that would lead her to happiness, wherever it may lie.

~

*T*he following morning, Celine awoke to the sound of birdsong filtering in through the open window. She lay there for a moment, allowing the golden sunlight to warm her face and listening to the gentle rustling of leaves outside. As she slowly rose from the bed, she inhaled deeply, catching a whiff of freshly cut grass and dewy earth.

"Alright," she murmured to herself as she stood up, determination settling in her chest. "Time to find some answers."

She pulled on her favorite pair of worn jeans and a soft flannel shirt, then laced up her boots and headed out the door. She couldn't help but smile at the sight of Helen Springs' picturesque countryside stretching out before her, its rolling hills and lush meadows beckoning with the promise of solace and clarity.

For the next few days, Celine immersed herself in nature's beauty. Each morning, she would set off down a different path, wandering through fields of wildflowers, traversing dense forests, and climbing rocky outcrops that offered stunning panoramic views.

"Hey, Jemima," she whispered one afternoon as she sat on a moss-covered log, gazing out at a tranquil pond where dragonflies danced above the water's surface. "I wish you were here with me. Everything is so... peaceful."

As she spoke, a delicate butterfly fluttered past her, its vibrant wings like stained glass against the dappled sunlight. Celine watched it dance from flower to flower, lost in thought.

"Is this what I want?" she wondered aloud, tracing her fingers along the rough bark of the log. "A life of quiet beauty, far from the chaos and excitement of the city?"

Her heart ached as she considered the question, torn between the allure of the simple country life she had always dreamed of and the passion for her art and nomadic lifestyle that pulsed through her veins.

"Jemima," she sighed, leaning back against the log and closing her eyes. "What am I supposed to do?"

Over the next few days, Celine continued her solitary exploration of Helen Springs' countryside, each new landscape offering a fresh perspective on the decision that loomed over her. She found herself drawn to the vibrant colours and intricate patterns of the natural world, her fingers itching to capture them in ink and paint.

"Maybe... maybe there's a way to bring my love for art and this place together," she mused as she stood atop a hill, gazing out at the picturesque valley below. "Maybe there's more adventure waiting for me here than I ever realized."

"Hey," she called out softly into the breeze, as if Jemima could hear her thoughts. "I think I'm getting closer to figuring it all out. Thank you... for giving me the space to do so."

With renewed determination and a growing sense of clarity, Celine knew that soon, she would be ready to return to Fountain Springs and have an honest conversation with Jemima about their future – whatever it may hold.

~

*T*he sun cast warm, golden hues on the serene meadow as Celine wandered through it, her eyes tracing the delicate lines of wildflowers that danced in the gentle breeze. The soft rustle of leaves overhead played a calming melody, and for a moment, she felt the weight of her impending decision lift from her shoulders.

"Nature has a way of putting everything into perspective, doesn't it?" Celine whispered to herself, a small smile tugging at the corners of her lips. She continued her peaceful stroll, her fingers brushing against the velvety petals of the flowers that lined her path.

As she walked, an idea began to take shape in her mind – an idea that brought with it a sense of excitement and possibility. "What if," she pondered aloud, "what if I could find a way to combine my love for art with this incredible place?" Her heart raced at the thought, her creative spirit ignited by the potential for a new kind of adventure.

"Imagine capturing the beauty of these landscapes in ink, or even incorporating local folklore into my tattoo designs," Celine mused, her eyes sparkling with inspiration. "I could create something truly unique, something that celebrates the charm and warmth of small-town life."

Lost in her thoughts, Celine barely noticed the rustling of wings as a vibrant butterfly alighted on a nearby bloom. Its intricate markings reminded her of the tattoos she'd spent years perfecting, and she couldn't help but smile at the unexpected connection between her passion and the natural world around her.

"Jemima would understand," she murmured, her

resolve strengthening. "He'd support me in finding a balance between my desire for stability and my need for artistic freedom."

With newfound determination, Celine decided to use the remaining days of her retreat to explore this idea further, sketching plans for a new direction in her work that would honor both her love for art and Helen Springs' enchanting allure. The thought of sharing her vision with Jemima filled her with anticipation, as well as a sense of peace – for it seemed that, at last, she had found the answer to her heart's conflict.

"Thank you," she whispered to the breeze, as if expressing gratitude to nature itself for helping her find clarity amidst the chaos of her emotions. "Thank you for showing me that there's more than one way to live an extraordinary life."

～

*T*he sun dipped low in the sky, casting a warm golden glow over the quaint streets of Fountain Springs as Celine approached the town. She felt an odd mix of excitement and trepidation, her heart racing at the thought of seeing Jemima again after their time apart. The scent of freshly mown grass and honeysuckle filled her nostrils as she parked her car outside Jemima's cozy little cottage.

"Hey there," Jemima called out, stepping onto the porch with a smile that reached her deep blue eyes. "I missed you."

"Missed you too," Celine replied, feeling a flutter in her chest at the sight of Jemima. She took a deep breath, steeling herself for the conversation that lay ahead. "Jemima, I need to talk to you about something important."

"Of course," she said, concern etching itself across her handsome features. "Let's sit down inside. Do you want some tea?"

"Tea would be lovely," she agreed, following her into the warmly lit living room. As they settled on the comfortable sofa, Celine couldn't help but notice the tenderness with which Jemima prepared their cups, stirring in just the right amount of honey before handing her one.

"Alright," she said gently, taking a seat beside her. "What's been on your mind, Celine?"

She hesitated for a moment, gazing into the swirling steam rising from her cup. "I've spent the past few days reflecting on my life, my art, and our relationship," she began, her voice barely more than a whisper. "And I realized that I can find a way to combine my love for adventure and creativity with the warmth and charm of small-town life."

"Go on," Jemima prompted, his eyes filled with genuine interest.

"Instead of constantly traveling, I could create a unique, intimate tattoo studio right in Helen Springs," Celine continued, her excitement growing. "One that would blend my passion for art with the authentic, welcoming atmosphere that drew me to the town in the first place."

"Wow," Jemima breathed, clearly moved by her words. "That sounds amazing, Celine. I'm so proud of you for finding a path that feels right."

"Thank you," she murmured, her cheeks flushing with happiness. "But it's not just about my career, Jemima. It's about us, too. If we're going to be together, I want to make sure we build a life that honors both our dreams and desires."

"I couldn't agree more," Jemima replied, reaching out to take her hand. "And if this is what you truly want, Celine, then I'm here to support you every step of the way."

"Really?" she asked, her eyes shimmering with unshed tears.

"Absolutely," Jemima confirmed, her gaze steady and sincere. "As long as we're honest with each other and communicate openly, there's no reason we can't navigate this adventure together."

"Thank you, Jemima," Celine whispered, leaning in to rest her head on Jemima's shoulder. "I don't know what the future holds, but I'm grateful to have you by my side as we face it together."

"Always," she promised, wrapping an arm around Celine as they sat in companionable silence, savoring the warmth of their love and the endless possibilities that lay ahead.

CHAPTER 17

*J*emima Sullivan sat on the edge of her bed, her hands gripping her tousled dark hair in despair. The weight of doubt pressing down upon her felt unbearable, threatening to smother the warm embers of love she held for Celine. Her blue eyes stared blankly at the wall, reflecting the turbulent emotions churning within her.

"Enough," she muttered under her breath, rising to her feet. She couldn't bear the uncertainty any longer; she needed guidance from someone who would understand. And there was only one person in hor life who could provide the wisdom and comfort she desperately sought - Mabel Jenkins.

As she pulled up to Mabel's cozy bed & breakfast

nestled amidst the greenery of Fountain Springs, Jemima took a deep breath, attempting to steady her racing heart. Mabel's presence had always been a balm to her soul, Mabel's nurturing spirit soothing even the deepest of Jemima's wounds.

"Jemima, my dear girl!" Mabel exclaimed as she opened the door, her greying hair framing her kind eyes that sparkled with warmth. "What brings you here today?"

"Hello, Mabel," Jemima managed a small smile, her voice cracking slightly. "I... I need your help. May I come in?"

"Of course, dear," she replied, stepping aside to let Jemima enter. "You know you're always welcome here."

Mabel led Jemima into the quaint sitting room, where an inviting fire crackled in the hearth, casting flickering shadows across the well-loved furniture. As Jemima sank into the plush armchair, Mabel busied herself in the adjoining kitchen, returning moments later with a steaming cup of tea.

"Here you go, my boy," Mabel handed her the teacup, its delicate porcelain warming Jemima's chilled hands. "Now, tell me what's troubling you."

Jemima hesitated, staring into the swirling depths of her tea. How could she put into words the doubts that plagued her, the fears that clouded her heart? But as she glanced up at Mabel's gentle, expectant gaze, she knew she owed it to herself - and to Celine - to be honest.

"Thank you, Mabel. I... I'm not sure where to begin," she spoke softly, her fingers tightening around the teacup. "I've been feeling so lost lately, so uncertain about my relationship with Celine. And I don't know what to do."

"Ah," Mabel sighed, her eyes filled with understanding. "Love can be a fickle thing, Jemima. But sometimes, all we need is someone to help us see the light amidst the darkness."

~

The dim, flickering light of the fire danced across Mabel's face as she leaned forward in her chair, her eyes never leaving Jemima's.

Jemima felt a sense of calm wash over her, knowing that she could trust Mabel with her deepest fears.

"Ever since Celine and I started dating, everything has been so...intense," Jemima confessed, her voice shaky. "It's like we were swept up in this whirlwind of passion and adventure, but now I find myself wondering if it's all too good to be true."

Mabel clasped her hands together in her lap, nodding empathetically. "I understand how you feel, Jemima. Love can be overwhelming at times, and when it comes on strong, it's natural to wonder if it's built to last."

Jemima sighed, fidgeting with the teacup in her hands. "But that's just it – I'm terrified that if I give in to these doubts, I'll ruin what Celine and I have. And I don't think I could bear to lose her."

"Jemima, dear," Mabel said gently, reaching across the small space between them to place a reassuring hand on her arm. "Doubt is an inevitable part of any relationship. It doesn't mean your love for Celine is weak or flawed – it simply means that you're human."

Jemima's gaze flicked up to meet hers, searching for the reassurance she so desperately needed. "But how do I know if our love is strong enough to withstand these doubts, Mabel? How do I know if we're truly meant to be?"

"Life doesn't come with guarantees, my boy," Mabel replied softly, squeezing Jemima's arm. "But what I've learned is that love isn't about certainty – it's about trust and resilience. It's about having faith in one another, even when the road gets bumpy."

Jemima's thoughts turned inward, contemplating

Mabel's words. Trust and resilience – she knew those were qualities she and Celine possessed, but were they enough to conquer the doubts that threatened to tear them apart?

"Remember," Mabel continued, her voice a soothing balm, "love is not without its challenges. But it's how you face those challenges together that truly defines the strength of your bond."

As Jemima absorbed Mabel's wisdom, she felt a flicker of hope ignite within her. Mabel was right – doubt was a part of the human experience, and she couldn't let it define her relationship with Celine. They had shared so many beautiful moments together, and she couldn't let fear overshadow them.

"Thank you, Mabel," she whispered, her grip on the teacup finally relaxing. "You've given me a lot to think about."

"Anytime, my dear," Mabel replied, her eyes warm with affection. "Just remember that you're never alone in this journey, and if you need someone to talk to, I'm always here."

With renewed determination, Jemima took a deep breath and set down her empty teacup. It was time to face her fears head-on and trust in the love she shared with Celine.

~

A warm breeze drifted through the open window, carrying with it the scent of freshly baked apple pie. Jemima gazed at Mabel, her soft eyes filled with understanding and compassion. Surrounded by the cozy ambiance of her bed & breakfast, Jemima felt a sense of safety that allowed her to lower her guard.

"Jemima, dear," Mabel began gently, "I've had my own share of doubts throughout my life, even in my marriage. But I learned that the key to overcoming them is trust and communication."

She paused, a distant memory flickering in her eyes. "When my husband was alive, we had our rough patches, but we always made a point to talk things through. We shared our thoughts and fears without holding back, knowing that we could rely on each other's support."

Jemima listened intently, her heart aching for the comfort of such a connection. Jemima knew that trust and communication were vital in any relationship, but their importance seemed magnified when confronted with the challenges she and Celine faced.

"Recently, Celine and I have encountered some obstacles," Jemima admitted hesitantly, her fingers tracing the rim of her teacup. "And sometimes, I can't help but wonder if these challenges are a sign that maybe... our love isn't meant to be."

Mabel's expression softened as she reached across the table, placing a comforting hand on Jemima' forearm. "My dear boy, don't let your fears cloud your judgment. Challenges will always arise in life, but they're not there to break you apart; they're there to make you stronger."

Her words resonated within Jemima, stirring a longing for the strength and resilience needed to face the trials ahead. Yet, doubt still lurked in the corner of Jemima's mind, sowing seeds of uncertainty.

"You know," Mabel continued, her voice laced with sincerity, "I truly believe that the universe has a plan for each of us. And even if you can't see it right now, I'm confident that your love for Celine is meant to be."

"Thank you, Mabel," Jemima murmured, her eyes glistening with unshed tears. "I appreciate your wisdom and guidance more than words can express."

"Of course," she replied, giving Jemima's forearm a reassuring squeeze before releasing her grip. "Just remember, whatever happens, always trust in yourself and the love you share with Celine."

In that moment, as the late afternoon sun cast golden hues throughout the room, Jemima felt a renewed sense of determination take root within her. With Mabel's wise words echoing in her mind, she resolved to face her fears and embrace the challenges that lay ahead, trusting in the bond she shared with Celine.

~

*G*olden sunlight filtered through the lace curtains, casting intricate patterns on the hardwood floor as Jemima fidgeted in her seat.

Mabel sat across from her with fingers gently tapping against the porcelain teacup. She regarded Jemima with a thoughtful gaze, and Jemima couldn't help but feel exposed under her scrutiny.

"Jemima," she began, her voice soft yet firm, "every relationship has its obstacles. It's how you both navigate through them that truly tests the strength of your love."

Her words seemed to hang in the air, leaving Jemima to ponder their weight. Jemima shifted in her seat, her thoughts drifting back to Celine – the warmth of her smile, the way her laughter filled the room, the countless moments of joy they had shared together.

"Love isn't easy," Mabel continued, her eyes reflecting the wisdom of someone who had weathered countless storms. "But when it's real, it's worth fighting for. Have faith in your connection with Celine, and remember those moments of happiness you've shared. They're the foundation of what you two have built together."

Jemima closed her eyes, allowing Mabel's words to seep into her core. She pictured Celine's face, the way her eyes sparkled when she was excited, and the curve of her lips when she was deep in thought. A small, genuine smile spread across Jemima's face as she thought of the simple, yet profound happiness they brought each other.

"Thank you, Mabel," she whispered, her voice raw with emotion. "You're right. I know deep down that our love is strong enough to overcome anything. I just need to trust in that."

"Trust in yourself too, dear," she replied, her voice warm and comforting. "And trust in Celine. Together, you can face whatever challenges come your way."

With a sigh, Jemima picked up her teacup and took a slow, deliberate sip. The warm liquid seemed to infuse her with a newfound sense of purpose and resolve. She knew that Mabel was right – she needed to have faith in their love and trust that they could navigate through any obstacle together.

"Thank you, Mabel," she said sincerely, setting the

teacup down gently before standing up. "Your words mean more to me than I can express."

Mabel smiled warmly at her, her eyes crinkling with affection. "You're welcome, Jemima. Remember, love is a journey, not a destination. Just keep moving forward, hand in hand with Celine, and you'll find your way."

~

*T*he sun dipped below the horizon, casting a warm, golden glow over Mabel's cozy bed & breakfast. Its rays illuminated the delicate lace curtains that framed her windows and danced across the polished wooden floors, creating an aura of serenity in the quiet, small-town haven.

"Thank you again, Mabel," Jemima said sincerely, her heart swelling with gratitude as she stood to leave. "I can't express how much your guidance means to me."

Mabel smiled warmly at her, eyes twinkling with understanding and compassion. "You're always welcome here, Jemima. Remember, love is worth fighting for, and I have faith that you and Celine will find your way through this together."

As Jemima walked towards the front door, she paused for a moment, absorbing the comforting atmosphere of Mabel's home. The soft scent of lavender and the faint crackle of the fireplace in the next room cocooned him in a sense of security, bolstering her resolve as she prepared to face the challenges ahead.

With a final nod of appreciation to Mabel, Jemima stepped out into the crisp evening air, inhaling deeply as she closed the door behind him. The cool breeze carried the scent of fresh pine and the distant murmurings of the nearby creek, grounding her in the present moment.

"Alright, Jemima," she whispered to himself, steeling her nerves. "Time to talk to Celine."

As she strode toward her car, Jemima's mind raced with thoughts of how she would approach the conversation. She knew it wouldn't be easy, but the memory of Celine's tender touch and the warmth of her laughter reminded her of what was at stake. Celine's vibrant spirit had captured Jemima's heart, and now it was up to her to ensure that their love could flourish.

Jemima slid into the driver's seat, gripping the steering wheel tightly as she visualized the upcoming discussion. Jemima knew she needed to be honest about her fears, but she also wanted Celine to understand the depth of her love for her.

"Trust and communication," she repeated Mabel's sage advice, her voice a low murmur in the otherwise silent car. "Be open, be vulnerable, and trust that our love will see us through."

With a deep breath, Jemima started the engine and pulled away from the bed & breakfast, leaving behind the cocoon of safety that Mabel had provided. The road stretched out before her, winding its way through the picturesque town of Fountain Springs, each turn bringing her closer to her destiny with Celine.

As she drove, Jemima felt her determination solidify, fueled by the hope and love that Mabel had helped her rediscover. She would face her doubts head-on, trusting in the strength of their connection and their shared desire to build a future together. And no matter what challenges lay ahead, Jemima knew one thing for certain: she would fight for Celine, and for the love they had found in one another.

～

Jemima' heart raced as the familiar silhouette of her home appeared on the horizon, its cozy exterior beckoning her in to face the conversation that lay ahead. She could almost see Celine's beautiful blonde hair catching the light, her soft features framed by the warmth of their shared sanctuary. As she approached the house, she took a deep breath, steeling himself for the pivotal moment that would define the future of their relationship.

"Trust and communication," Jemima reminded herself, stepping out of her SUV and into the cool evening air. The gravel crunched beneath her feet, grounding her in the present as she made her way to the front door. Inhaling deeply, she allowed the familiar scent of their home to wash over her, filling her with a sense of calm and determination.

Inside, she found Celine waiting, her perceptive eyes scanning Jemima's face for any hint of what was troubling her. Sensing Jemima's unease, she set aside the boxes she had been packing for their upcoming move and stepped towards Jemima, concern etching her delicate features.

"Jemima, what's on your mind?" Celine asked gently, her voice a soothing balm to Jemima's frayed nerves.

Jemima hesitated, her heart pounding in her chest as she grappled with how to begin. "Celine, I... I've been thinking about us and our relationship lately," she started, her voice barely above a whisper. "And I need to talk to you about my doubts and fears."

Celine's gaze never wavered as she listened, her hand reaching out to gently touch Jemima's arm in a gesture of support. "Of course, Jemima. Let's sit down and talk," she said softly, guiding her towards the living room.

As they settled onto the couch, the warmth of Celine's body pressed against Jemima, who felt a swell of love and gratitude for the woman beside her. Jemima took a deep breath, gathering her thoughts as she prepared to lay bare her heart and soul.

"First, I want you to know how much I love you, Celine," Jemima began, her voice filled with emotion. "But lately, I've been plagued by doubts and fears about our relationship – if we're truly meant to be together, if our love is strong enough to overcome the challenges we've faced."

Celine's eyes shimmered with unshed tears as she listened, her hand tightening around her in a show of solidarity. "Jemima, I understand," she murmured, her voice thick with emotion. "I know that doubt is natural, and I'm here to listen and support you. Let's work through this together."

With those words, Jemima felt the last of her hesitation fall away, replaced by a renewed sense of hope and determination. Trusting in their love and the strength of their connection, Jemima knew that together, they could face whatever doubts and fears lay ahead. And in that moment, as they sat hand in hand, it seemed as if nothing could stand in their way.

*J*emima takes a deep breath and opens up to Celine, sharing her doubts and fears, but also expressing her unwavering love for her.

Jemima felt the weight of her heart in her chest, as if it were tethered by the very words she needed to say. She clung to the warmth of Celine's hand, drawing strength from their connection as she prepared to share her deepest insecurities.

"Thank you, Celine," she murmured, her voice thick with gratitude. "I... I guess my biggest fear is that our love won't be enough to withstand the obstacles we've faced. We come from such different worlds, and I can't help but wonder if that will eventually drive us apart."

Celine's gaze locked onto hers, with eyes filled with empathy and understanding. She squeezed Jemima's hand, her touch grounding her like an anchor amidst a stormy sea. "Jemima, love isn't about being exactly the same or living the exact same life. It's about finding someone who complements you, who makes you better, and who supports your dreams and passions."

As she spoke, Jemima felt the truth in her words resonate within her. With each syllable, her doubt began to dissolve, giving way to the memories of shared laughter, whispered secrets, and stolen kisses beneath moonlit skies. The moments when she had witnessed Celine's fierce independence meld effortlessly with the quiet strength of her own spirit. And in those instances, she knew their love was unlike any other.

"I understand," she admitted softly, her voice barely audible above the sound of her own heartbeat. "But I also worry about how our lives will change as we continue to grow. What if we're not strong enough to adapt to those changes together?"

A gentle smile tugged at the corners of Celine's lips, and she leaned in closer to Jemima, her breath warm against her cheek. "Jemima, life is always changing – that's just a part of being alive. We can't predict or control everything that happens, but we can choose to face it together, side by side. And if our love is true, it will grow along with us."

The conviction in Celine's voice stirred something deep within Jemima, awakening a newfound sense of clarity and purpose. She knew that every relationship had its challenges, that doubt was an inevitable aspect of love. But with Celine by her side, she felt as though they could conquer anything.

"Thank you for believing in us," Jemima whispered, her words laced with unspoken emotion. "I love you, Celine Montgomery. Always and forever."

As their eyes met and held, their fingers still

entwined, it seemed as if time itself had stilled around them. In that moment, the weight of doubt and fear vanished, replaced by a certainty that their love was indeed worth fighting for. Together, they would face whatever lay ahead, secure in the knowledge that their bond was unwavering and unbreakable.

CHAPTER 18

*J*emima stood on the porch of Mabel's cozy bed and breakfast, the warm glow of the setting sun casting long shadows across the lawn. She felt a renewed sense of hope and determination swell in her chest, fueled by Mabel's advice to follow her heart and make a grand romantic gesture for Celine.

"Alright, Jemima," she muttered to himself, running a hand through her dark hair. "Let's plan something unforgettable."

She paced along the porch, blue eyes focused on the distance as she brainstormed ideas for an art exhibit that would showcase Celine's incredible talent. Her artwork deserved to be seen and celebrated, and she was determined to make it happen.

"Maybe we could find a venue with rustic charm, like an old barn or a renovated warehouse," Jemima mused aloud, envisioning the contrast between the weathered wood and Celine's vibrant, intricate designs. "Or perhaps a more intimate setting, like a small gallery or café, where people can truly appreciate her work up close."

As she contemplated different themes, she knew she needed to find something that captured the essence of Celine's spirit: her adventurous nature, her passion for her craft, and her love for the simple life she craved. "What if we create an outdoor exhibit, surrounded by nature? We could illuminate her artwork with soft fairy lights, and let the natural beauty of the landscape enhance her pieces."

"Or how about a theme that combines the country life she adores with the city life she's drawn to?" Jemima continued, growing increasingly excited as her ideas began to take shape. "We could incorporate elements of both worlds - the textures of the countryside, the energy of the city - and celebrate the duality of her artistic identity."

"Jemima, dear," Mabel called from inside the house, her kind voice interrupting her reverie. "Would you like some tea?"

"Ah, yes please, Mabel" she answered, a smile tugging

at the corners of her mouth. She knew that with the help of her dear friend and the unwavering support of the tight-knit community, she could create a memorable experience that would show Celine just how much she meant to her - both as an artist and as the woman who had captured her heart.

~

*J*emima took a deep breath, inhaling the rich aroma of freshly brewed tea Mabel had prepared for her. She felt warmth radiating from the cup in her hands as she sat at the kitchen table, phone in front of her and a list of local artists and gallery owners scribbled on a notepad. The sun streamed through the window, casting golden flecks across her dark hair and reflecting the determination in her blue eyes.

"Alright," she whispered to himself, "time to make this dream a reality."

She started with a call to a well-respected artist in town, whose work she admired. "Hi, Maggie, it's Jemima Sullivan. I'm organizing an art exhibit to showcase Celine's talent and celebrate our community's love for art. I was hoping you'd be interested in contributing a piece or two and perhaps help spread the word to other artists?"

Maggie's enthusiastic response filled Jemima with even more excitement for the event. "Absolutely, Jemima! I'd be honored to be part of such a lovely idea. You can count on me to reach out to my fellow artists."

"Thank you so much, Maggie. Your support means the world to both me and Celine." With each call, Jemima emphasized the collaborative nature of the event, ensuring that everyone understood the importance of coming together to showcase their unique talents.

As the list of participating artists grew, Jemima dove into the logistics of the exhibit. She spent hours researching the best way to arrange the artwork, create a visually striking layout, and find the perfect lighting to highlight each piece's beauty. She made detailed notes and sketches, meticulously planning every aspect of the exhibit.

Her mind buzzed with ideas for promoting the event: designing eye-catching posters, crafting engaging social media posts, and reaching out to local newspapers and radio stations. She wanted the entire town to know about Celine's talent and the incredible celebration of art they were about to witness.

Jemima' thoughts raced as she envisioned the perfect

moment when Celine would see her work displayed alongside other talented artists. Jemima imagined the pride and joy that would light up Celine's face, and she knew that every detail, every phone call, every late-night planning session would be worth it for that priceless expression of gratitude and love.

"Jemima, dear," Mabel's voice brought her back to reality. "You've been working so hard. Why don't you take a break and enjoy this lovely afternoon?"

"Thank you, Mabel," Jemima replied, her eyes filled with gratitude. "But I can't rest just yet. There's still so much to do, and I need to make sure everything is perfect for Celine."

As the sun began to dip below the horizon, casting an orange glow across the sky, Jemima continued her tireless efforts to create a once-in-a-lifetime experience for the woman who had captured her heart. And amidst the flurry of preparations, she couldn't help but daydream about the enchanting evening that awaited them, surrounded by beauty, love, and the magic of art.

∼

The morning light streamed through the windows, casting a golden glow on Jemima' kitchen table as she sipped her coffee and reviewed her list of potential venues for the art exhibit. She knew the importance of choosing the perfect location - somewhere that would capture the essence of Celine's work while providing ample space to showcase the diverse talents of the participating artists.

"Alright," she muttered to himself, "time to hit the road." She grabbed her jacket and keys, stepping out into the cool morning air and climbing into her SUV. As she drove through the picturesque streets of their small town, she considered each venue carefully. Her first stop was an old warehouse with exposed brick walls and high ceilings, creating an industrial yet intimate atmosphere.

"Interesting," Jemima thought as she walked through the vast space, taking in the details of the building and imagining Celine's artwork displayed against the rustic backdrop. "But it might be too dark in here. I need something that can really showcase her talent."

Her next stop was a bright, airy gallery with large windows and plenty of natural light. The owner greeted him with a warm smile and showed her around the pristine space. Jemima admired the sleek, modern aesthetic but couldn't help feeling that it lacked the warmth and charm she wanted for Celine's exhibit.

"Thank you for showing me around," she told the

owner before moving on to the next location. "I'll be in touch."

As Jemima continued her search, she debated the merits of each venue, weighing the pros and cons in her mind. She knew she had to find the perfect balance between a welcoming ambiance and adequate space to accommodate all the artists she had invited. After visiting several more locations, she found himself drawn to the final venue on her list: a charming historic building with wooden floors, exposed beams, and an inviting atmosphere.

"Ah, this feels right," Jemima mused, envisioning Celine's vibrant artwork juxtaposed against the building's rich history. "This is the place."

With the ideal venue secured, Jemima turned her attention to finalizing the list of participating artists. She knew she wanted a diverse range of styles and mediums to create a dynamic exhibit that would complement Celine's work.

"Alright," she sighed as she sat down at her kitchen table once again, spreading out her notes before her. "Let's make some calls."

"Hello, Jane?" she began, calling one of the local artists she had met during her search. "I'd love for you to be a part of the exhibit. Your watercolor landscapes would be a beautiful addition."

As she continued making calls, Jemima felt a sense of excitement building within her. Each artist she spoke to seemed genuinely thrilled to participate in the event, and she could feel the collaborative spirit she had hoped for beginning to take shape.

"Wow," she thought with a grin. "We're really doing this. This is going to be an amazing night for Celine and everyone involved."

And as she dialed the final number on her list, Jemima couldn't help but feel that she was one step closer to making her grand romantic gesture a reality.

~

Jemima glanced at her calendar, the large red circle around the chosen date seeming to mock her as she juggled coordinating with gallery owners and artists. She had worked tirelessly to ensure that the exhibit would be a success, but the weight of responsibility was beginning to settle heavily on her shoulders.

"Alright," Jemima muttered to herself, tapping her pen against the notepad filled with names and phone numbers. "We need to find a date that works for everyone."

She picked up her phone and dialed the first number

on her list, one of the gallery owners who had agreed to participate in the exhibit.

"Hello, Mark? It's Jemima. I'm just calling to discuss the scheduling for the upcoming exhibit featuring Celine's work. What dates do you have available?"

As she spoke to each gallery owner and artist, Jemima methodically crossed off dates on her calendar, narrowing down the options until finally, they settled on the perfect date and time for the event.

"Perfect, thank you," she said with relief, scribbling down the final details. "I'll send out an email to everyone confirming the date and time."

Once she hung up the phone, Jemima allowed herself a moment to breathe. The exhibit was officially scheduled, and everything seemed to be falling into place. But as the days leading up to the event began to disappear, her excitement was slowly being replaced by a gnawing anxiety.

"What if she doesn't like it?" Jemima wondered aloud, pacing back and forth in her living room. "What if no one shows up?"

She shook her head, trying to dispel the negative thoughts. "No, this is going to be amazing," she told himself firmly. "Celine deserves this, and I'm going to make sure it's a night she'll never forget."

As the day of the exhibit drew closer, Jemima found

herself consumed by the preparations. Her nights were spent fine-tuning the details, from creating promotional materials to coordinating with the artists on the delivery of their work. Each task was completed with Celine in mind, her love for Celine driving him to make this event as perfect as she was.

"Alright, it's showtime," Jemima murmured to herself on the morning of the exhibit, her hands shaking slightly as she buttoned up her blouse. "You've got this, Jemima. You can do this."

She took a deep breath, trying to calm her racing heart. The day had finally arrived, and all that remained was for her to bring everything together and make this a night that Celine would cherish forever. And as she stepped out of her front door, ready to face whatever challenges lay ahead, Jemima knew that she wouldn't rest until she had done just that.

~

The vibrant colors of the setting sun bathed the gallery in a warm, inviting glow as Jemima stood at the entrance, meticulously arranging the easels that would soon display the exquisite artwork. She could feel the weight of her responsibility pressing down on her like a heavy blanket, and yet she couldn't help but revel in the excitement of it all. With each brushstroke of light she adjusted, every carefully chosen placement of an art piece, Jemima felt a growing sense of pride and anticipation.

"Alright, let's move this one a bit to the right," she directed, guiding the gallery assistant as they positioned Celine's painting just so. "Perfect. That's exactly how it should be."

As the participating artists began to arrive, Jemima made it her mission to greet each one with warmth and enthusiasm, eager to share their collective passion for art. "Welcome! I'm so glad you could make it," she said, ushering them inside the gallery with a broad smile.

"Thank you for having us," replied one artist, a woman with a vibrant shock of red hair. "This is an incredible opportunity for all of us."

"Absolutely," chimed in another, adjusting his glasses as he surveyed the room. "I've never seen such a diverse and exciting collection of work."

Jemima' heart swelled with pride as she led them through the exhibit, pointing out the different styles and techniques on display. "Celine's watercolor landscapes are over here," she explained, gesturing toward a series of delicate, ethereal pieces that seemed to shimmer in the soft light. "And these bold, abstract acrylics are by

Marcus – an up-and-coming talent from our very own town."

As they moved through the gallery, the artists exchanged stories about their inspirations and personal journeys, creating an atmosphere of camaraderie that filled the space with a palpable energy. It was a celebration of art, of talent, and of the connections that brought them all together.

Jemima couldn't help but steal glances at the door every few minutes, er heart skipping a beat each time she thought Celine might walk in. This was it – her grand gesture, her declaration of love, and her unwavering belief in Celine's incredible abilities. But as much as she wanted to see Celine's reaction, a part of her also feared it, the uncertainty gnawing at the edges of her mind. What if Celine didn't feel the same? What if this was too much?

"Hey," said Marcus, placing a hand on Jemima's shoulder and snapping her out of her thoughts. "You did an amazing job putting this together. Just breathe, woman. She's going to love it."

"Thanks," Jemima replied, trying to swallow the lump in her throat. "I just want it to be perfect for her."

As the artists continued to mingle and admire the artwork, Jemima allowed herself a moment to take it all in. The room was alive with creativity and passion, and it was all because of her love for Celine. Whatever the outcome, she knew that she had given her all to make this night unforgettable.

"Here goes nothing," she whispered to herself, her eyes fixed on the door and her heart pounding in her chest.

~

*T*he door to the gallery creaked open, and a burst of cool evening air swept through the room. Celine stepped inside, her eyes wide with wonder as she gazed upon the stunning display of art before her. The walls were adorned with an eclectic mix of paintings, sculptures, and photographs, each piece thoughtfully arranged and bathed in warm, inviting light.

"Surprise!" Jemima exclaimed, her voice filled with excitement as she approached Celine, who still stood frozen in awe at the entrance. "Welcome to your very own art exhibit."

Celine's gaze swept across the room, lingering on each artwork as if trying to take it all in at once. Her eyes finally landed on one of her own paintings, prominently displayed and surrounded by the creations of other talented artists. She turned to face Jemima, her eyes shimmering with unshed tears.

"Jemima... this is incredible," she breathed, her voice barely audible over the hum of admiration and conversation that filled the room. "You did all this for me?"

Jemima nodded, her heart swelling with pride and affection as she watched Celine's reaction. "I wanted to show you just how much I believe in you and your talent," she said earnestly. "I know you've always been hesitant about sharing your work, but I hope this helps you see what the rest of us have known all along – you're an amazing artist."

Celine took a shaky breath, her emotions threatening to spill over as she tried to find the words to express her gratitude. "Thank you, Jemima," she whispered, reaching out to place a trembling hand on her arm. "This means more to me than you'll ever know."

As the two lovers shared a tender moment amidst the bustling gallery, Celine couldn't help but feel that her life had somehow come full circle. She had once dreamed of a travelling country existence, but her passion for art had led her into the arms of Jemima – a woman who not only admired her talent, but was willing to go to extraordinary lengths to prove it.

"Come on," Jemima said gently, offering Celine her arm. "Let's take a tour of your exhibit."

As they moved through the gallery, Celine couldn't help but marvel at the love and effort that had gone into creating this special night for her. And as she looked into Jemima's eyes – those deep blue pools filled with warmth and sincerity – she knew that she had found something even more precious than success: a true partner who believed in her, supported her, and cherished her just as much as she cherished Jemima.

~

Celine's gaze swept over the gallery, taking in the lively interactions between guests and artists. The atmosphere was charged with excitement and appreciation for the artwork on display. As she and Jemima strolled arm in arm, they were approached by various artists whose work was being showcased alongside hers.

"Ah, Celine!" exclaimed a woman with vibrant red hair and a wide smile. "Your use of color and texture is simply captivating. I'm honored to have my sculptures sharing the same space as your paintings."

"Thank you so much," Celine replied, her cheeks tinted pink with pride. "And your sculptures are amazing – they bring such depth and emotion to the room."

"Excuse me," interrupted a tall man with a goatee and round glasses, extending his hand to Celine. "I'm Mark, another artist featured here tonight. Your work is truly inspiring. The way you blend different art styles is just magnificent."

"Nice to meet you, Mark," Celine said, shaking his hand warmly. "I appreciate the kind words. Your photography is stunning – it captures the essence of the subjects so well."

Throughout the evening, Celine and Jemima mingled with the other artists, discussing techniques, inspirations, and the power of creative expression. The sense of community among them was palpable – a celebration of their shared passion for art.

"Look at that piece," a young couple whispered, pointing at one of Celine's paintings. "The way she plays with light and shadow is just mesmerizing."

"Indeed," agreed an older gentleman, nodding approvingly. "It's bold, yet delicate. She has a unique touch."

As more attendees admired Celine's work, animated conversations about the pieces filled the air. The gallery buzzed with energy, creating a vibrant atmosphere that only served to emphasize the magic of the night.

Amidst the flurry of activity, Celine caught Jemima's eye and offered her a grateful smile. She could see the pride in her gaze, and she realized that this night was not only about her – it was about them and their connection through art. The sense of belonging, the appreciation for each other's talent, and the love that bound them together were all encapsulated in this extraordinary event.

"Thank you," she mouthed silently to Jemima, who simply nodded in response. Her eyes sparkled with emotion, reflecting her unwavering faith in her abilities and the beauty of their shared journey.

As the night wore on, Celine couldn't help but feel humbled by the outpouring of support from the art community and overwhelmed by the love that radiated from Jemima. In that moment, surrounded by the vibrant energy of the gallery, she knew that she had found her true home – both in art and in the arms of the woman who believed in her unconditionally.

～

The vibrant energy of the gallery seemed to hum around them, a symphony of colors and emotions that encapsulated the spirit of the evening. Celine watched as Jemima made her way over to her, weaving through clusters of attendees engaged in animated discussions about the artwork on display. As she approached, she noticed the slight flush on Jemima's cheeks – a testament to the excitement and nerves that had carried them both through the planning and execution of this extraordinary event.

"Hey," Jemima said softly, standing close enough for their fingertips to brush against each other. "I hope you don't mind me stealing you away for a moment."

Celine smiled up at her, heart swelling with gratitude and affection. "Not at all. I think I could use a little break from all the attention."

Together, they slipped into a quiet corner of the gallery, the sounds of laughter and conversation fading into a gentle murmur behind them. For a moment, they simply stood in silence, basking in the glow of shared accomplishment.

"Jemima, I don't even know where to begin," Celine whispered, her voice thick with emotion. "This night… it's more than I ever could have imagined. Thank you so much for everything you've done."

Jemima looked down at Celine, her blue eyes shining with sincerity. "I couldn't be happier to see you getting the recognition you deserve, Celine. Your work is incredible, and I just wanted to help showcase it in the best possible way."

"Still," she insisted, reaching out to clasp Jemima's hand, "you went above and beyond. You brought together such an amazing group of artists, created this beautiful atmosphere… and you did it all because you believe in me."

"Of course I believe in you," she murmured, squeezing Celine's fingers gently. "You're an incredibly talented artist. And more than that, you're an amazing person. I'm so grateful to have you in my life."

"Jemima," she began, her voice wavering slightly as she struggled to find the words to express the depth of her feelings. "I'm so grateful for you, too. You've been my rock through all of this, and I don't know what I would do without you."

Their eyes locked, and for a moment, time seemed to stand still – just the two of them, surrounded by the beauty of art and love. And then, as if drawn together by some magnetic force, they leaned in and shared a tender, lingering kiss.

"Here's to us, and to many more adventures together," Jemima whispered against her lips, her breath warm and sweet.

"To us," Celine agreed, her heart swelling with love and happiness. And as they stood there, wrapped up in each other's arms amidst the symphony of color, laughter, and conversation, they knew that whatever lay ahead, they would face it together.

CHAPTER 19

A kaleidoscope of emotions swirled within Celine as she stood in front of the art exhibit, her heart pounding in her chest. She blinked back tears that threatened to spill over, astonished by the grand gesture Jemima had made. The gallery was a testament to her talent and passion, each piece carefully curated and displayed with reverence.

"Wow," she whispered under her breath, taking in the incredible sight before her. The walls were adorned with her most striking creations, from intricate ink drawings to vibrant watercolors that seemed to leap off the canvas. Each piece was like a window into her soul, capturing moments of joy, pain, and self-discovery. As she moved through the exhibit, she could feel the energy her work radiated, like ripples on the surface of a pond, touching the hearts of all who beheld it.

The viewers, a mix of locals and city dwellers, were visibly enthralled by Celine's artwork. They whispered excitedly amongst themselves, pointing out minute details and marveling at the depth and complexity of her craft. Even those who were new to the world of art couldn't help but be drawn in by the sheer magnetism of her pieces. Their eyes widened in wonder, their faces reflecting a mixture of awe and admiration.

"Your work is truly breathtaking," a woman in a chic black dress commented, her voice filled with genuine admiration. "I've never seen anything quite like it."

"Thank you," Celine replied, her cheeks flushing with pride and gratitude. It was one thing to receive praise online, where words often felt hollow and insincere, but to have people standing before her, moved by her creations – that was something else entirely.

"Did you organize this?" another man asked, his eyes scanning the room as if searching for someone responsible for the stunning display.

"Actually, my friend Jemima did," Celine explained, a warmth spreading through her chest as she thought of Jemima. "She wanted to surprise me."

"Ah, he must be quite a woman," the man chuckled, a

knowing glint in his eyes. "And she's clearly smitten with you."

Celine couldn't help but smile, her heart swelling with love and appreciation for the woman who had done so much for her. Jemima had taken a simple idea – showcasing her art – and turned it into something magical, a night that would live on in her memory forever. And though she knew there would be challenges ahead, she couldn't imagine facing them without Jemima.

~

The warmth of Jemima's affection enveloped Celine like a gentle embrace, leaving her breathless and dizzy with euphoria. The sweet scent of roses mingled with the aroma of freshly brewed coffee, awakening her senses. Laughter and soft murmurs of admiration echoed through the gallery, creating a symphony that stirred her soul.

"Wow," she whispered under her breath, her eyes roaming over the walls adorned with her own creations which included the intricate tattoo designs that told stories of love, pain, and redemption. Each piece was a fragment of her heart, a testament to her passion for her craft and her connection to her clients.

"Jemima did all this for me," she thought, her chest tightening as she realized the depth of Jemima's feelings for her. The way Jemima had transformed this space into a celebration of her art spoke volumes about her dedication and devotion. Jemima believed in her, even when she doubted herself.

"Hey Cece," said Jemima, materializing at her side, her blue eyes shimmering with genuine happiness. "I hope you don't mind that I kept this as a surprise."

"Mind?" she repeated, blinking back tears of gratitude. "This is... incredible. I can't even begin to express how much this means to me."

As they stood side by side, surveying the room, Celine felt the familiar spark of electricity between them. It was a sensation that had grown stronger over the months, evolving from friendship to something more profound and meaningful. She knew that their connection had the potential to change everything, but uncertainty still flickered at the edges of her mind.

"Are we ready for this?" she silently wondered, her heart pounding in her chest. "Could our friendship and romance stand the weight of commitment?"

"Cece," Jemima whispered, breaking into her thoughts. Her hand brushed against Celine's, sending a jolt of warmth up her arm. "I've always believed in you and your talent. I just wanted to share it with the world and show you how amazing you truly are."

Jemima's words were like a balm to Celine's soul, soothing her doubts and fears. She felt a surge of love for this woman who had stood by her through thick and thin, supporting her dreams and aspirations even when they seemed impossible.

"Thank you, Jemima," she murmured, leaning into her as their fingers intertwined. "I couldn't have done any of this without you. You've always been there for me, and I can't imagine my life without you in it."

"Then let's not imagine it," she replied softly, gazing into Celine's eyes. "Let's make it our reality."

In that moment, Celine knew that no matter what challenges lay ahead, she and Jemima would face them together, their bond unbreakable and their love unwavering.

~

Celine could feel the warmth of tears gathering at the corners of her eyes, as she looked at Jemima with a newfound appreciation for the depth of her love. The air around them seemed to shimmer with emotion, charged with the intensity of their unspoken words.

"Jemima," she whispered, her voice trembling slightly. "I didn't know – I mean, I never realized just how much this all meant to you."

Jemima reached out and gently wiped away a tear that had escaped down her cheek. "Cece, you have no idea how much joy your art brings to people. And seeing you happy, doing what you love...that's everything to me. I want to be there for you, every step of the way, cheering you on."

Celine's heart swelled with gratitude and love, unable to contain the torrent of emotions that threatened to overwhelm her. She took a deep breath, steadying herself and meeting Jemima's gaze. "What does that look like? Us, together?"

Jemima smiled, her blue eyes sparkling with sincerity. "It looks like building a life together, hand in hand. Chasing sunsets and laughter. Sharing our hopes, our dreams, and yes – even our fears. It means standing by each other through it all, knowing that we have each other's backs. It means making memories that will last a lifetime and beyond."

"Wow," Celine breathed, her eyes shining with unshed tears. "That sounds...beautiful."

"I think so too," she murmured, pulling Celine close and letting her forehead rest against Celine's. "But we'll make it our own, Cece. Together, we can create something more beautiful than either of us could ever imagine on our own."

And as they stood there, wrapped up in each other's arms, Celine knew that she had found something truly special with Jemima. A love that would only grow stronger with time, a partnership that would endure the challenges ahead. And in that moment, she couldn't have asked for anything more.

~

ears glistened in Celine's eyes as she took a step closer to Jemima, her heart pounding with the weight of the emotions swirling within her. The air between them was charged with anticipation, their connection palpable and undeniable. With every fiber of her being, Celine knew that this was a turning point, a defining moment in their relationship.

"Jemima," she whispered, her voice barely audible as she wrapped her arms around Jemima, clinging to her like a lifeline. Their bodies pressed against one another, and Celine felt the steady rhythm of Jemima's heartbeat, a comforting reminder that they were in this together. She tightened her embrace, her grip on Jemima conveying the depth of her commitment and belief in their love.

"Thank you," she murmured into Jemima's ear, her breath warm against her skin. "For everything. For believing in me, for supporting me, for never giving up on us. I love you, Jemima. More than words can say."

Jemima's arms wrapped around her, holding her close as she gently rocked her back and forth. "I love you too, Cece," she replied softly, her voice filled with emotion. "You've brought so much light and joy into my life. I'm grateful for every moment we spend together, and I can't wait to see what the future holds for us."

Celine leaned back, her gaze locked onto Jemima's, her eyes reflecting the sincerity in her voice. "I'm ready, Jemima," she declared, her cheeks flushed with excitement and determination. "I'm ready to take our relationship to the next level. To face whatever challenges life throws at us, hand in hand. Together, there's nothing we can't overcome."

"Nothing at all," Jemima agreed, her eyes shining with love and admiration. They stood there, enveloped in each other's arms, knowing that their love story had only just begun. With every beat of their hearts, they renewed their commitment to each other and the journey that lay ahead.

As they stood there, basking in the warmth of their embrace, Celine knew with unshakable certainty that she had found her partner, her confidant, her rock. And together, they would build a life more beautiful than either could have ever imagined alone.

~

*S*ilence enveloped them as they continued to hold each other, the world around them fading into the background. Celine could feel the steady rhythm of Jemima's heartbeat against her chest, and she focused on its comforting cadence. The significance of the moment weighed heavily upon them both, but it was a weight they gladly bore, anchored by their love for one another.

"Have you ever seen something so perfect?" Jemima murmured, her breath warm against Celine's ear as she broke the silence. She gestured towards the exhibit that surrounded them, showcasing Celine's extraordinary talent and their unique connection.

Celine smiled, feeling a surge of pride and gratitude course through her. "I couldn't have done any of this without you, Jemima," she admitted, her voice soft yet full of emotion. "You've been my rock, my inspiration."

"Cece, you've always had it in you," Jemima replied, her blue eyes brimming with sincerity. "All I did was help you see what was already there."

As she spoke, Celine noticed the subtle changes in her expression, how her eyes seemed to dance with anticipation for their future together. She found herself getting lost in those eyes, drowning in their depths and allowing herself to truly believe in the possibility of the life they would build together.

"Jemima," Celine whispered, her voice barely audible as she took a deep breath, steadying herself before continuing. "I know we have an incredible journey ahead of us, and I can't wait to see where it takes us. We'll explore new places, chase our dreams, and make memories that will last a lifetime."

"Right by your side, Cece, always," Jemima promised, her hand reaching up to gently cup Celine's face. Her thumb traced Celine's cheekbone, sending shivers down her spine.

"Promise me one thing, though," Celine said, her eyes searching hers for reassurance. "Promise me that no matter what happens, we'll always find our way back to each other. That love will be our compass, guiding us through the darkest of times."

"Cec, I promise," Jemima vowed, her voice filled with conviction. "Our love will be the beacon that lights our path, and together, we'll conquer any storm that comes our way."

As they stood there, locked in each other's gaze, Celine felt a surge of hope and joy course through her veins. She knew that their future was uncertain, but one thing was clear: no matter what life had in store for them, they would face it together, hand in hand, hearts intertwined.

With renewed determination, Celine leaned forward, pressing her lips against Jemima's. As they kissed beneath the gentle glow of the gallery lights, she knew that this was only the beginning of their incredible journey together, a journey that would be written in the stars and etched upon their very souls.

～

*A*s Celine and Jemima stood there, wrapped up in the intensity of their connection, the world around them seemed to fade away. The smell of oil paints and varnished wood filled the air - a testament to the hours Jemima had spent curating this beautiful exhibit of her work.

"Hey, it won't always be easy, you know," Jemima whispered, breaking the silence. Celine looked into her eyes, seeing a hint of vulnerability beneath her unwavering gaze. "There will be times when we'll have to make tough choices, or when life throws us curveballs we can't control."

Celine nodded, understanding that the road ahead wouldn't be without its challenges. There would be moments of doubt, fear, and uncertainty. But she also knew that the love they shared was strong enough to endure anything.

"Whatever comes our way, Jemima, I know that we can overcome it together," she said with conviction. "No matter how difficult things might get, I believe in us and in our love."

Jemima smiled at her words, their fingers intertwining as they stood among the vibrant artwork that had brought them closer than ever before. "I believe in us too, Cece," Jemima said softly, pressing a tender kiss to her forehead.

The gallery hummed with the energy of their newfound commitment, and Celine couldn't help but feel a sense of joy and contentment wash over her. She knew that the future held many unknowns, but the thought of facing it alongside Jemima filled her with excitement and anticipation.

"Come on," Celine urged, her eyes sparkling with determination. "Let's start our journey right here, right now. We've got a lifetime to create our own masterpiece, and I can't wait to see what we paint together."

With their hands clasped tightly and hearts beating in unison, Celine and Jemima stepped forward into their future - a future filled with love, laughter, and the promise of endless possibilities. And as they left the gallery that night, the shadows cast on their intertwined figures seemed to whisper a tale of a love story that was just beginning to unfold.

CHAPTER 20

*C*eline sighed as she stared at the worn tabletop, her fingers tapping out a rhythmic pattern. The flickering light from the small candle danced across the surface, casting shadows on the creased map of Fountain Springs that lay before her. It was an intimate evening in the cozy corner of Jemima's living room, with the sound of raindrops trickling against the windows.

"Jemima," Celine began, her voice carrying a hint of frustration, "I'm grateful for all the support you've given me since I moved here, but I don't think it is right that you should have to upend and move your home and business to Helen Springs to be near me. I need to find a way to be allowed to run my mobile tattoo business in this, your small town."

Celine took a deep breath then said quickly. "I realise how selfish I've been, allowing you to sacrifice a business and home you love, to be near me."

Jemima looked up from her warm cup of herbal tea, her blue eyes reflecting concern and empathy. She ran her hand through her dark hair and leaned forward, ready to offer unwavering assurance. "Celine, I know we can figure this out together. We just need some creative ideas." Her voice was steady and reassuring, exactly what Celine needed in moments like this.

Celine, who had been passionately listening to Jemima's words, suddenly felt a spark of inspiration ignite within her. A determined look crossed her face as she realized that perhaps there was a way for her mobile tattoo business to become a beloved part of Fountain Springs' vibrant community. She had always admired the town's strong sense of togetherness, and now she was determined to contribute to its charm.

～

With newfound determination, Celine set out to make her vision a reality. She retrieved a list of guests who had attended her recent art exhibition, a gathering that had showcased her incredible talent and garnered much attention. These were the very people who appreciated art and creativity, and Celine believed they would understand the value her mobile tattoo business could bring to Fountain Springs.

One by one, Celine reached out to each guest, explaining her aspirations and the positive impact her business could have on the community. She highlighted the unique artistry and personal connections that her mobile tattoo service offered, emphasizing that it could be a beautiful addition to the cultural fabric of Fountain Springs.

To her delight, many of the guests eagerly embraced Celine's idea and expressed their support. They recognized the potential and were captivated by her passion. As word spread, more and more people added their names to the petition, pledging their support for Celine's cause.

On a crisp morning, the day of the council meeting arrived. Celine, accompanied by a group of enthusiastic supporters walked alongside her as she made her way to the council's office. Nervous anticipation filled the air as they approached the grand doors.

Inside the council chamber, Celine found herself facing a panel of councilors, their stern expressions revealing the weight of their responsibility. The mayor, a wise and respected figure, presided over the meeting, exuding an air of authority.

Celine presented the petition with a mix of anxiety and hope, her voice steady as she outlined her business proposal and the overwhelming support she had garnered from the community. The councilors listened intently, their expressions gradually softening as they absorbed the genuine passion behind her words.

After a brief deliberation, the mayor cleared his throat and addressed Celine directly. "Ms Celine, on behalf of the council, I am pleased to inform you that your request has been granted," he announced, a warm smile spreading across his face. "You are most welcome to stay and operate your mobile tattoo business in Fountain Springs."

A surge of joy and relief washed over Celine, her eyes welling up with tears of gratitude. The room erupted in applause, a collective celebration of Celine's victory and the council's recognition of her creative endeavor. It was a triumph for the power of community and the belief in following one's dreams.

As Celine thanked the councilors and the mayor, she couldn't help but race back to where stood at the back of the room, her eyes glistening with pride. In that moment, they both knew that their journeys were intertwined, and their shared dreams were now one step closer to becoming a beautiful reality in the embrace of Fountain Springs.

~

*L*iving together in Jemima's house, they planned their interconnected while still independent lives.

Jemima pondered for a moment, her eyes scanning the quaint room, taking in the familiar faces of family photos and cherished mementos. "Well, they love community events here - the farmers market, holiday festivals, things like that. Why don't we create something similar for your business?"

"Like a... Tattoo Pop-Up event?" Celine's face lit up as the idea took form. "We can host it right here in Fountain Springs, showcase my work, and offer discounted tattoos to attract new clients. It could be a one-day event to start, and if it goes well, maybe we can make it a regular thing!"

"Exactly!" Jemima agreed enthusiastically, her heart swelling with pride at Celine's excitement. "We'll make it an event that people will want to attend, something they can be a part of and enjoy."

"Thank you, Jemima," Celine whispered, her eyes glistening with gratitude. "I couldn't do this without you."

As they continued to discuss the details of their plan, the rain outside slowed to a gentle patter, and the candle's flame flickered with renewed vigor. A sense of hope and determination filled the room, wrapping itself around Celine and Jemima like a warm embrace. Together, they would breathe life into her mobile tattoo business and create a legacy in Fountain Springs.

~

*C*eline glanced at the array of watercolor paints and brushes spread across the dining table, her hands deftly tracing the edges of the blank canvas before her. She dipped a brush into the cerulean hue, gently swirling it around as she envisioned the design for the Tattoo Pop-Up event's promotional flyer.

"Jemima, what do you think about incorporating some floral elements in the design?" Celine asked, turning to face her. "I feel like it'll really capture the essence of Fountain Springs."

"Absolutely," Jemima agreed, her eyes locked on Celine's every graceful movement. "Your art always has this incredible, otherworldly quality that I think people will be drawn to."

Celine smiled at the compliment, her face flushing with pride. Her hand glided across the canvas, creating intricate patterns and swirls that seemed to burst to life with each delicate stroke. As the design took shape,

Jemima couldn't help but feel a sense of awe wash over him, captivated by the raw talent and passion that radiated from Celine like a beacon of light.

"Here's an idea," Jemima suddenly suggested, leaning closer to get a better look at the canvas. "Why don't we add a catchy slogan? Something like, 'Unveil Your Inner Artistry' or 'Ink Outside the Lines'? It'll show that this event is more than just tattoos – it's a celebration of creativity and self-expression."

"Ooh, I love 'Ink Outside the Lines,'" Celine murmured, her eyes sparkling with excitement. "It's playful, yet meaningful. Let's go with that."

As they worked together, laughter and playful banter filled the air, forging a deeper bond between them. After hours of meticulous work, they finally stepped back to admire the finished flyer – a stunning masterpiece that encapsulated the essence of Celine's artistic vision and the spirit of the Tattoo Pop-Up event.

"Alright, now comes the next step," Jemima said, rolling up her sleeves. "We need to get the word out there. Let's make a list of local businesses and community organizations we can approach for partnerships and sponsorships."

Celine nodded, her determination unwavering. "You're right. The more support we have, the better this event will be."

They spent the afternoon reaching out to various establishments – from cozy coffee shops to bustling boutiques – each conversation brimming with enthusiasm and warmth. Celine was touched by the kindness and encouragement that flowed from the small-town community, her heart swelling with gratitude.

"Jemima, I don't think I can thank you enough for everything you've done," Celine whispered, her voice thick with emotion. "This wouldn't be possible without you."

Jemima met her gaze, her blue eyes crinkling with a warm smile. "I'm just happy to be a part of your journey, Celine. Remember, we're in this together."

～

*C*eline perched on the edge of the couch, her laptop balanced on her knees as she clicked through various social media accounts. Jemima sat beside her, her fingers flying over her phone screen as they brainstormed ideas for their campaign.

"Okay, so we've got our flyers and posters ready," Celine murmured, "but we need to make some noise online too. Let's start with Instagram. We can post pictures of your past work, maybe even a few videos of you in action?"

"Great idea!" Jemima agreed, her eyes lighting up. "And how about Facebook? Maybe create an event page and invite everyone we know? Get them to share it with their friends, spread the word that way."

"Perfect." Celine nodded, her fingers tapping away at her keyboard. "We'll use hashtags too, so people searching for tattoos in the area can find us easily. And don't forget to tag our location! That way, potential clients can see where we're setting up shop."

"Speaking of which," Jemima said, glancing out the window, "we should scout for the perfect spot to host the Tattoo Pop-Up. Somewhere visible, accessible, and with lots of foot traffic."

"Right," Celine agreed, saving her progress on the laptop and closing it. "Let's go take a walk around town and see what we can find."

They set off down the sidewalk, the warm sunlight streaming through the trees as they explored Fountain Springs. Celine marveled at the charming storefronts and friendly faces that greeted them along the way, her heart swelling with hope for their upcoming event.

"Look at this place," Jemima pointed to an empty lot nestled between a popular café and a trendy boutique. "It's right in the heart of downtown, plenty of people passing by every day. What do you think?"

"Definitely has potential," Celine replied, surveying

the area. "Plus, it's close to shops and restaurants, so people can grab a bite to eat while they wait or browse nearby stores."

"Exactly," Jemima grinned, snapping a few pictures of the location with her phone. "I'll upload these to our social media accounts, give everyone a sneak peek of where the magic will happen."

As they continued their search, Celine couldn't help but feel grateful for Jemima's unwavering support. Her enthusiasm and genuine belief in Celine's abilities had given her the courage to chase her dreams, and she knew she couldn't have done it without him.

She glanced at Jemima, her blue eyes sparkling with excitement, and felt a warmth spread through her chest. "Thank you, Jemima," she whispered, reaching out to squeeze her hand. "For everything."

"Always," she replied, returning the squeeze and smiling softly at Celine. "Now, let's find the perfect spot for your Tattoo Pop-Up and make this event unfor-gettable."

❧

*C*eline's heart raced as she and Jemima entered the Fountain Springs Town Hall, their foot-steps echoing through the quiet corridors. The scent of old wood mingled with a faint trace of lemon-scented cleaner. The afternoon sun filtered in through the tall windows, casting a golden glow on the polished floors.

"Remember, we're doing this together," Jemima whispered, offering her a reassuring smile. "You've got this."

"Thanks," Celine murmured, taking a deep breath to steady herself. She clutched the folder containing their detailed plans for the Tattoo Pop-Up event, praying that the local officials would see its potential benefits for the community.

The council chamber doors opened, revealing an impressive room adorned with portraits of past mayors and town founders. A group of council members sat at a long table, watching them expectantly. As Celine and Jemima approached, they exchanged quick nods before diving into their well-rehearsed presentation.

"Good afternoon, esteemed council members," Jemima began, her voice confident and clear. "We appreciate the opportunity to present our plans for an upcoming community event - the Tattoo Pop-Up. This unique event will showcase the incredible talent of local artist Celine Montgomery and provide an opportunity for residents to experience the art of tattooing in a safe and welcoming environment."

"Furthermore," Celine added, her nerves fading as passion for her craft took over, "our goal is to highlight the value of artistic expression and create a sense of camaraderie among Fountain Springs residents. We believe that by hosting this event, we can help break down misconceptions about tattoos and foster understanding and appreciation for this beautiful art form."

She watched as several council members nodded thoughtfully, encouraged by their positive reactions. With a final flourish, she unveiled a mock-up of the event space, complete with colorful banners, artistic displays, and cozy seating areas for consultations.

"By partnering with local businesses and community organizations, we hope to create a truly memorable experience for all involved. Your support is crucial to the success of this event, and we humbly request your endorsement."

After a brief moment of tense silence, the council members began murmuring amongst themselves. One by one, they offered their approval, impressed by the passion and dedication Celine and Jemima had shown.

"Congratulations, Ms. Montgomery and Ms. Sullivan," the mayor declared, extending his hand. "We look forward to seeing the Tattoo Pop-Up come to life in our town."

"Thank you so much," Celine breathed, relief washing over her. As they left the chamber, she could hardly believe that their plan was coming together.

"Time to enlist some help," Jemima suggested, pulling out her phone to send a group message to their friends, asking for volunteers to set up the event space.

"Make sure it's both inviting and organized," Celine stressed, her eyes lighting up with excitement. "I want everyone who walks in to not only feel comfortable but also be able to appreciate the artistry of tattooing."

"Trust me, Celine," Jemima reassured Celine, her blue eyes meeting hers. "You have the vision, and we'll bring it to life."

As their friends responded with enthusiasm, Celine felt a renewed sense of purpose. With the support of the local government, and the help of their friends, they were well on their way to making the Tattoo Pop-Up a reality. And as they walked side by side, united in their shared goal, Celine couldn't help but feel grateful for Jemima's unwavering presence in her life.

~

Celine flipped through the pages of her portfolio, the dim glow of the desk lamp casting a warm light on her previous masterpieces. The ink on each piece seemed to dance off the page, telling stories of love, loss, and triumph. She felt a sense of pride well up inside her as she admired her work, knowing that this collection would be the key to attracting potential clients and making the Tattoo Pop-Up a success.

"Your work is amazing, Celine," Jemima said sincerely, looking over her shoulder at the portfolio. "People are going to be blown away."

"Thanks, Jemima," she replied, feeling a blush rise to her cheeks. "But I couldn't have done any of this without you."

"Hey, we're in this together," she reminded her with a reassuring smile. As Celine continued organizing her artwork, Jemima busied herself with making sure everything was in place for the event. She contacted vendors, confirmed the event space layout, and made sure they had all necessary permits. Her attention to detail and unwavering support allowed Celine to focus solely on her art.

On the day of the Tattoo Pop-Up, the sun shone brightly overhead, casting playful shadows on the bustling streets of Fountain Springs. The scent of fresh flowers from the nearby park filled the air, creating an atmosphere of excitement and anticipation.

"Ready to make some magic?" Jemima asked, her eyes sparkling with enthusiasm.

"Absolutely," Celine agreed, her heart racing with anticipation. Together, they stood at the entrance of the event space, welcoming visitors with warm smiles and open arms.

"Hi there!" Celine greeted a young couple who approached, their curiosity piqued by the colorful posters advertising the event. "I'm Celine, the tattoo artist, and this is Jemima, our event coordinator. Welcome to our Tattoo Pop-Up!"

"Wow, your work looks incredible," the woman exclaimed, flipping through Celine's portfolio. "What inspired you to create this piece?"

Celine glanced down at the page, her eyes falling on a stunning design of a phoenix rising from the ashes. "Ah, that one," she said, her voice filled with emotion. "That tattoo was for a client who had survived a terrible accident. The phoenix symbolized their strength and resilience in overcoming such a difficult time."

"I love how personal each piece is," the man added, impressed by Celine's passion for her work.

"Thank you," Celine replied, feeling a surge of pride. "I believe that a tattoo should be as unique as the person wearing it."

As the day continued, more and more visitors streamed into the event space, drawn in by the lively atmosphere and the promise of captivating artwork. Jemima expertly managed the logistics, ensuring everything ran smoothly while Celine engaged with potential clients, sharing the stories behind her art and answering questions about the tattoo process.

"Will it hurt?" a nervous-looking young woman asked, fidgeting with her sleeve.

"Everyone's pain tolerance is different," Celine answered gently, her calm demeanor soothing the woman's nerves. "But I'll do my best to make sure you're comfortable throughout the entire process."

"Thank you," the woman whispered, visibly relieved.

As the sun began to set, casting a golden glow over Fountain Springs, Celine and Jemima shared a victorious smile. They knew that, together, they had created not only an unforgettable event but also a strong foundation for Celine's mobile tattoo business to flourish within the community. And as they stood side by side, their hands brushing against each other's, Celine couldn't help but feel that their friendship had evolved into something even more beautiful than any tattoo she had ever created.

$\sim$

*C*eline's fingers traced the outline of a delicate butterfly, the design taking shape on paper as her client excitedly shared her ideas. The warm scent of freshly brewed coffee filled the air, mingling with the faint buzz of conversation and laughter from the curious visitors exploring the Tattoo Pop-Up.

"Is there any particular symbolism behind the butterfly?" Celine asked, her blue eyes meeting the young woman's eager gaze. "I'd love to incorporate your story into the design."

"Actually," the woman began, hesitating for a moment before continuing, "I've been through some tough times lately, and butterflies represent transformation to me. They signify hope and new beginnings."

Celine understood the power of such symbols; after all, she had built her career on translating them into art. As she nodded in understanding, her thoughts briefly wandered to Jemima, who was currently bustling around the event space, making sure everything was in order. Her unwavering support had given her the confidence to embrace this new chapter of her life wholeheartedly.

"Let's work together to create something truly unique and meaningful for you," Celine said, her voice warm and encouraging.

"Thank you so much," the woman replied, her eyes shining with gratitude.

Throughout the day, Celine offered personalized consultations to interested clients, discussing their tattoo ideas and collaborating with them to create unique designs that reflected their individuality. The room seemed to hum with creative energy as she sketched out concepts, her pencil dancing across the page.

Meanwhile, Jemima took on the role of Celine's assistant, helping her set up her equipment, sterilize tools, and provide a comfortable and safe environment for clients. She moved with practiced ease, anticipating her needs before she even voiced them. Watching Jemima work so diligently, Celine couldn't help but marvel at the depth of their connection, which seemed to grow stronger with each passing moment.

"Jemima, can you pass me that disinfectant spray, please?" Celine asked, her focus momentarily shifting from the intricate design she was creating.

"Of course," Jemima replied, handing her the spray with a reassuring smile. "Anything else you need?"

"Actually, yes," she said, her heart swelling with gratitude for her unwavering support. "Can you make sure we have enough clean towels and that the sterilizer is working properly? I want everything to be perfect for our clients."

"Consider it done," Jemima replied. She set about completing the tasks, her strong hands moving with a quiet efficiency that spoke volumes about her commitment to their shared goal.

As the day wore on, Celine found herself reflecting on how far they had come since they first met, the seeds of friendship blossoming into something infinitely more profound. And as she watched Jemima deftly care for the needs of both her and her clients, she knew without a doubt that they were creating not just beautiful art but a future filled with endless possibilities, side by side.

❧

The sun dipped lower in the sky, casting a warm golden light over the Tattoo Pop-Up event. Amidst the hum of conversation and laughter, Celine's focus remained unwavering as she brought another client's vision to life. The buzz of her tattoo machine harmonized with the cheerful ambiance, creating a symphony of creativity and connection.

"Wow, that looks amazing!" the young woman in Celine's chair exclaimed, catching a glimpse of her fresh tattoo in the mirror. "I can't wait to show this off on Instagram!"

"Thank you," Celine replied, beaming with pride. "And please do! We have a hashtag for the event – #FountainSpringsInk – and don't forget to tag our location too."

"Of course!" the woman agreed enthusiastically,

snapping a selfie with Celine before leaving the chair with a bounce in her step.

Jemima, ever attentive to the needs of the event, approached Celine with a fresh bottle of water and a reassuring smile. "You're doing an incredible job, Celine. Everyone is blown away by your talent."

"Thanks, Jemima," she said, taking a sip of water and pausing for a brief moment to appreciate her support. "But we're doing an amazing job together. I couldn't have done any of this without you."

"Still," she insisted, "your passion and skill are truly inspiring. It's no wonder people can't stop talking about you and sharing their experiences online."

Celine blushed at the praise but knew deep down that their combined efforts were making a difference. While she continued to work on her clients, Jemima mingled with the growing crowd, reminding them to document their time at the event and share it on social media.

"Hey there!" she greeted a group of friends who had just arrived, their excitement palpable. "Welcome to the Tattoo Pop-Up! Feel free to take pictures and share your experience using our hashtag, #FountainSpringsInk."

"Will do!" one of them replied, already snapping away on their phone.

As the day progressed, Celine's steady hand and

undeniable artistry continued to captivate her clients and onlookers alike. Each tattoo she created was a testament to her passion for her craft, leaving people in awe and eager to spread the word about her talents.

"Seriously, Celine, this is beyond incredible," marveled a young man, admiring the detailed design that now adorned his forearm. "I'm definitely telling everyone I know about you."

"Thank you so much," Celine responded sincerely, touched by his enthusiasm. "Your support means the world to me."

Throughout the event, Celine found herself not only immersed in her work but also reflecting on the journey that had brought her to this point. With Jemima by her side, their collaboration had transformed the Tattoo Pop-Up into a celebration of creativity, friendship, and the power of shared dreams. And as the sun began to set, casting its warm glow over the happy faces around them, Celine knew that together, they were creating something truly special – a legacy of love, art, and community that would endure long after the last tattoo needle fell silent.

*a*s the sky deepened to a rich purple, signaling the impending end of the Tattoo Pop-Up event, Celine glanced around at the satisfied faces of her clients. The air buzzed with excited chatter as they admired her handiwork. She couldn't help but feel a surge of pride and accomplishment.

"Hey Celine, I've got a friend who's dying for a tattoo from you," said a woman in her early thirties, showing off her new ink – a delicate butterfly on her ankle. "Can she book an appointment?"

"Absolutely!" Celine replied, her heart swelling with gratitude. "Have her give me a call or send me a message on my website."

"Thanks! She'll be thrilled," the woman gushed before walking away with a bounce in her step.

Jemima approached, grinning widely. "I think we can safely say this event was a huge success, Celine. You've definitely left your mark on Fountain Springs."

"Quite literally," she quipped, flashing him a playful smile. Inside, though, she knew that this moment wouldn't have been possible without Jemima's unwavering support and belief in her vision.

"Seriously, though," she continued, her voice taking on a more earnest tone. "You should be incredibly proud of what you've accomplished today."

Celine felt her eyes misting over and blinked back tears. "Thank you, Jemima. I couldn't have done it without you."

"Hey, we're a team. And I'm just as invested in your success as you are." She squeezed her hand gently. "Now then, let's start packing up. We've got a whole lot of appointments to schedule!"

Together, they began dismantling the makeshift tattoo station, chatting and laughing as they worked. As the last of the equipment was stowed away, Celine took one final look around the space that had been transformed into a hub of creativity and connection for just one day. The echoes of laughter and conversation still seemed to linger in the air, whispering promises of future successes and deepened bonds within the community.

"Ready to go?" Jemima asked, her hand on Celine's shoulder, grounding her in the present moment.

"Definitely," she replied with a nod, feeling more confident than ever that her mobile tattoo business would not only survive but thrive in Fountain Springs. With new clients eager to book appointments and a strong support system in place, Celine felt ready to take on whatever challenges lay ahead – knowing that she and Jemima could face them together.

CHAPTER 21

The room was bathed in the soft, flickering glow of candlelight, casting warm shadows that danced on the walls. The intimate atmosphere embraced Celine and Jemima as they stood amidst the dimly lit space, their eyes locked on each other, revealing a depth of emotion that words could not express. The scent of lavender floated gently through the room, further enhancing the sense of romance and tranquility.

"Jemima," Celine breathed, her voice barely audible, "I've never felt like this before."

"Neither have I, Celine," she replied tenderly, her eyes brimming with sincerity.

As they stood together, their fingers intertwined, Celine marveled at the warmth radiating from their touch. It was as if their very souls were fusing, creating an unbreakable bond that would stand the test of time. With every beat of their hearts, their connection grew stronger, more profound, and more resilient.

"Promise me something, Celine," Jemima whispered as she drew closer, her breath hot against Celine's ear.

"Anything," Celine replied, her pulse quickening at the sound of her voice.

"Promise me that we'll never lose this," Jemima murmured, squeezing Celine's hand gently. "That no matter what happens, we'll always find our way back to each other."

Celine's eyes filled with tears as she nodded, overcome by the intensity of their love. "I promise, Jemima. You're my anchor, my source of strength. I can't imagine my life without you."

Their bodies pressed against each other as they embraced, the warmth of their love shielding them from the world outside. The room seemed to disappear as they stood there, lost in the depths of their connection. As they held each other tightly, the warmth of their touch served as a reminder of the love that had grown between them—a love that would continue to flourish and strengthen, guiding them through every challenge and triumph that lay ahead.

～

*A*s Celine's gaze drifted over the room, she couldn't help but feel a swell of pride and admiration for the journey that lay behind them. The dimly lit space was adorned with her artwork - pieces that had once been mere figments of her imagination, now serving as tangible remnants of their struggles and growth.

"Jemima," she began, her voice barely audible above the soft crackling of the candles. "Do you remember when I first showed you my art?"

"Of course," she replied, her eyes twinkling in the candlelight. "I knew right then that you were something special, Celine."

Celine smiled, recalling her initial fears about sharing her passion with him. It felt like a lifetime ago when they had weathered those early storms together, navigating the choppy waters of doubt and uncertainty.

"Back then, I never imagined we'd be here today," she whispered, her fingers tracing the lines of a painting depicting the open road - an embodiment of their shared spirit of adventure.

"Neither did I," Jemima admitted, her hand brushing against Celine's as they stood side by side, surveying the room. "We've faced so many challenges, but look at us now - stronger, wiser, and more in love than ever."

Celine nodded, feeling the weight of their shared history and the triumphs they had achieved together. She recalled countless moments when she had leaned on Jemima for support, finding solace in her unwavering faith in her abilities.

"Every obstacle we've overcome has made our love deeper, hasn't it?" she mused, reflecting on the transformation that had taken place within them both.

"Absolutely," Jemima agreed, her voice filled with conviction. "Those challenges have only served to make us appreciate what we have even more. And I wouldn't change a thing about our journey, Celine."

"Neither would I," she replied, resting her head on Jemima's shoulder and breathing in the familiar scent of her. In that moment, their shared history enveloped them like a warm embrace, reminding them of the strength and resilience of their love.

~

Celine stood at the window, her heart swelling with pride as she gazed upon their small corner of the world, now a reflection of their love and accomplishment. The sun dipped below the horizon, casting golden hues across the walls adorned with her artwork – each piece a testament to the journey they had shared.

"Look at us," Jemima said softly, joining her at the window, her hand sliding around Celine's waist. "We've built something truly special here, together."

Celine leaned into Jemima's embrace, feeling the warmth of her body pressed against hers. She smiled, recalling how their love had blossomed and grown over the years. From tentative beginnings to unshakeable devotion, they had faced every challenge head-on, growing stronger as individuals and as a couple. And here they were, standing in the home they had created together, surrounded by the tangible evidence of their success.

"Remember when we first met?" Celine asked, her eyes twinkling with amusement. "I was so nervous to let you into my life, afraid of what might happen if we took that leap."

Jemima chuckled, her fingers tracing delicate patterns along her arm. "I was just as terrified, you know. But look at us now - we've conquered our fears, and it's made our love unstoppable."

"Unstoppable," Celine repeated, savoring the word and all it represented. She felt a surge of gratitude for the woman who had walked beside her through thick and thin, who had believed in her dreams and helped make them a reality. Together, they had forged a bond that could withstand any storm.

"Can you imagine where we'll be in another few years?" Jemima whispered, her breath warm against Celine's ear, sending shivers down her spine.

"Wherever it is, I know we'll face it together," Celine replied, her voice full of conviction.

Their eyes met, and they shared a knowing smile, the unspoken language of lovers who had weathered life's challenges and emerged victorious. As they held each other tightly, their bodies pressed together as if trying to merge into one, Celine couldn't help but think that their love was a living, breathing entity - an unstoppable force that would carry them through whatever lay ahead.

"Here's to us," she murmured, her eyes shining with love and determination. "And to all the adventures yet to come."

"Here's to us," Jemima echoed, her grip on Celine tightening, as if to say, 'I'm not letting go.' And in that moment, Celine knew they were ready for whatever the future held, anchored by their love and the strength they found in each other.

~

*T*he dimly lit room bathed in the soft glow of candlelight, casting flickering shadows that danced upon their intertwined fingers. As they stood together, Celine's heart swelled with a mixture of love and anticipation. She could feel the warmth radiating from Jemima's touch, the familiar sensation sending tingles up her spine, reminding her of how far they had come.

"Here's to our beautiful journey," she whispered, her voice barely audible above the crackling fire that burned brightly behind them. Their eyes locked, conveying a depth of emotion that words could never express.

Celine leaned in, her lips brushing against Jemima's as they shared a tender kiss, filled with love, passion, and the promise of a future together. The taste of Jemima on her tongue was as intoxicating as ever, a reminder of the connection they had forged through laughter, tears, and endless nights spent exploring each other's souls.

As their lips parted, Celine breathed in deeply, filling her lungs with the scent of Jemima – a combination of woodsy cologne and the faintest hint of sweat from a day spent working in workshop. It was a scent that had become synonymous with comfort and belonging, and she couldn't help but smile as they held each other tightly, cherishing the bond they had created.

"Jemima…" she murmured, her voice full of affection. "I can't believe how far we've come."

"Neither can I," she admitted, her blue eyes reflecting the sincerity that had always endeared her to Celine. "But I wouldn't trade any of it for the world. We've built something beautiful together, Celine."

She nodded, her heart swelling with pride at the thought of their achievements – both personal and professional. As an artist, she had grown and flourished under her unwavering support, while she had found solace and healing in her unconditional love.

"Promise me," she whispered, her voice wavering with emotion, "that we'll always be there for each other, no matter what life throws our way."

"Of course," Jemima vowed, her grip on Celine tightening as if to physically cement their commitment. "I promise, Celine. We are stronger together than we could ever be apart."

With that, they held each other close, the warmth of their bodies and the steady beat of their hearts a testament to the love that had been forged through trials and triumphs, and the unbreakable bond that would carry them into the future. Together, they faced whatever lay ahead, knowing that they were anchored by a love that could withstand any storm and conquer any challenge.

~

The subtle scent of Celine's perfume wafted through the air as they stood there, their embrace a tangible testament to the deep connection forged between them. She leaned back slightly, her blonde hair cascading gently over her shoulders, to gaze into Jemima's eyes with a radiant smile that illuminated the dimly lit room.

"I love you, Jemima," she whispered softly, her words echoing with the sincerity and warmth that had come to define their relationship.

Jemima's blue eyes sparkled with adoration as she responded, "And I love you, Celine. You are my everything."

A shiver of delight ran down her spine at her declaration, the intensity of her feelings palpable in the air between them. They shared an intimate moment, surrounded by the soft glow of candlelight and Celine's artwork, which showcased their journey together. Hand in hand, they had built a life that was both beautiful and meaningful, overcoming obstacles and fears together.

As they held each other tightly, Celine couldn't help

but marvel at the sense of security and unity they felt in this moment. Their love had grown stronger with each passing day, blossoming into something that had become the cornerstone of their lives. It had given them the strength to face anything together, knowing they could rely on one another for support, encouragement, and understanding.

Jemima brushed a stray lock of hair away from Celine's face before gently cupping her cheek, her touch sending a warm sensation coursing through Celine's veins. She closed her eyes, reveling in the feel of Jemima's skin against hers, and allowed herself to be swept up in the tenderness of the moment.

Celine's mind wandered to the countless memories they had made, the laughter shared, and the tears shed. Through it all, their love had been the anchor that kept them steady amidst the stormy seas of life. And as they stood there, basking in the closeness of their embrace, Celine knew that they had forged something truly special – a love that would continue to grow and thrive as they journeyed through life together, hand in hand.

CHAPTER 22

*C*eline stood on the sunlit porch of Jemima's small cottage in Fountain Springs, the warm breeze playing with her blonde hair. She breathed in deeply, savoring the scent of blooming wildflowers and freshly cut grass. A sense of peace washed over her, something she hadn't felt in the bustling cities where her tattoo career had taken her. As she exhaled, she knew she belonged here.

Hearing the familiar rumble of an engine, she glanced up to see Jemima's SUV coming down the long gravel driveway. Her heart fluttered at the sight of Jemima, their passion having blossomed ever deeper.

"Celine, there's still time to change your mind," Jemima called out as Celine dashed forward to get into her car.

"Never," she replied with a smile, grateful for her unwavering support. "I want to be, permanently. Fountain Springs feels like home," Celine confessed, her cheeks flushing.

"You re sure?" Jemima smiled, her eyes lighting up. "This town has a way of making you feel like you belong, doesn't it?"

"Yes, exactly!" Celine exclaimed. "And I think we could create an amazing life here, together."

"Absolutely," Jemima agreed, reaching for Celine's hand and giving it a gentle squeeze. "I'd love to settle down here with you, Celine."

"Jemima, we can build on our dreams for the future?" Celine said.

Jemima's gaze drifted towards the horizon as she answered, "I want to make a difference in this community, to be a part of something bigger than myself. And I want to keep growing as an artist, just like you."

"Those are beautiful dreams," she murmured, her eyes misting over with emotion. "I want that too. We could support each other in achieving those dreams, right?"

"Of course," Jemima affirmed, her face serious but filled with warmth. "We're stronger together, Celine. We can push each other to do better, to reach higher."

"Then let's do it," she whispered, her voice filled with

conviction. "Let's make Fountain Springs our home and chase our dreams together."

"Nothing would make me happier," Jemima replied, pulling her closer and gently kissing her forehead. They sat there, hand in hand, the beginning of their future together felt full of promise and possibility, and they knew they were ready to embrace it, side by side.

❧

"So, we agree?" Jemima asked as she and Celine sat, sipping their morning coffee. The scent of freshly baked cinnamon rolls wafted through the air as they discussed their plans for the day. Celine's eyes sparkled with excitement as she leaned forward, her hands wrapped around her mug.

"Let's do it!" Celine exclaimed, her eyes shining with anticipation. "I can already picture us working side by side in our shared creative space. What an incredible adventure this will be!"

With renewed energy, they cleared away their breakfast dishes and grabbed their coats, ready to embark on the exciting journey of finding their dream home. As they stepped outside, Celine paused for a moment, taking in the picturesque scene before her: the charming main street lined with small businesses and friendly neighbors waving hello, the lush green park where children played together, and the breathtaking view of the surrounding hillsides.

"Jemima," she whispered, her voice filled with awe. "We're really doing the full comitmen, aren't we?"

"Absolutely," Jemima replied, wrapping an arm around her shoulders and pulling her close. "Together, we'll flourish."

With their hearts full of hope and determination, Celine and Jemima ventured out into the town, eager to begin the next chapter of their lives.

~

With purposeful strides, Celine and Jemima entered the local real estate office, where the clang of the doorbell announced their arrival. The aroma of freshly brewed coffee filled the air, mingling with the scent of polished wood from the vintage furniture.

"Good morning! How can I help you today?" asked a cheerful woman behind the reception desk.

"Hi, we're here to meet with Mr. Thompson," Jemima replied. "We have an appointment to discuss our housing needs."

"Of course! He's expecting you. Please, have a seat

while I let him know you've arrived." The receptionist disappeared into a back room, leaving Celine and Jemima to take in their surroundings.

Celine marveled at the rows of stunning photographs on the walls, showcasing the picturesque beauty of Fountain Springs. She could envision the life they were about to build together, and her heart swelled with excitement.

"Are you ready for this?" Jemima, her eyes searching hers for reassurance.

"More than ever," she answered, offering him a warm smile. "I can't wait to find the perfect place for us to call home."

Soon, Mr. Thompson appeared, shaking their hands firmly before guiding them to his office. As they settled into their seats, he began inquiring about their preferences and requirements for their new home.

"We need enough space for both of us to work comfortably," Celine explained as she brushed a strand of her blonde hair behind her ear. "I'm a tattoo artist, and I'll be using one of the rooms as my studio. And Jemima is a woodworker, so she'll require a workshop as well."

"Proximity to town is also important," Jemima added, leaning forward in her chair. "We want to be part of the community and close to the amenities it offers."

Mr. Thompson nodded, scribbling down notes as he listened intently. "I understand. I'll put together a list of properties that meet your criteria, and we can start exploring the different neighborhoods in Fountain Springs."

"Thank you," Celine said gratefully. "We appreciate your help."

Over the next few days, Mr. Thompson guided them through various neighborhoods, highlighting their unique features and the sense of community each one offered. They wandered along tree-lined streets, taking note of the parks, shops, and schools that would shape their new lives.

"Jemima, look at this charming café!" Celine gushed as they passed by a quaint storefront adorned with colorful flowers. "Can't you just picture us coming here for our morning coffee?"

"Absolutely," she replied, her eyes crinkling at the corners as she smiled. "And that park over there would be perfect for evening strolls together."

As they continued their exploration, they found themselves drawn to a particular neighborhood near the heart of town. The friendly atmosphere and close-knit community resonated with them both, and they knew they had found the ideal location for their future home.

"Mr. Thompson," Jemima said decisively, "we'd like to

focus our search in this area. We feel it's the perfect place for us to build our lives together."

"Excellent choice," Mr. Thompson agreed, beaming at their enthusiasm. "I'll refine our search based on your preferences, and we'll find the perfect property for you both."

With their hearts brimming with hope and anticipation, Celine and Jemima eagerly awaited the day when they could call Fountain Springs their forever home. Together, they were certain they could make their dreams a reality.

~

*C*eline stood in the doorway of the first open house, her eyes widening as she took in the high ceilings and sunlit space. She could already envision her tattoo studio set up near the large window that overlooked the backyard. Jemima walked in beside her, a smile tugging at the corner of her lips as she imagined the potential of the room.

"Can you see it, Celine? Your art displayed on these walls, and clients admiring your work while they wait?" she asked, excitement evident in her voice.

"Definitely," Celine replied, her gaze moving to the

adjacent room. "And that space over there could be perfect for your woodworking workshop."

They continued through the house, discussing how they could customize each room to suit their needs. As they climbed the stairs, Celine's hand brushed against Jemima, sending a thrill down her spine. She couldn't help but think about the life they would build together within these walls.

"Jemima, do you think we could really make this place our own?" She looked into her eyes, searching for reassurance.

"Absolutely," she said with certainty. "We just need to weigh the pros and cons. The location is great, and the layout has potential. But we might need to do some renovations to make it exactly what we want."

As they moved on to the next property, Celine found herself comparing every detail to the first house. This one had a smaller backyard, but a larger kitchen where they could cook together and share intimate meals. They discussed the possibilities of each space, imagining the laughter and conversations that would fill the rooms.

"Although I love the kitchen here, I'm not sure if it's worth sacrificing the outdoor space," Celine admitted, leaning against the countertop. "What do you think, Jemima?"

"True," she agreed, running her hand along the smooth surface. "And the first house has more potential for customization. Plus, I think we both felt a stronger connection to that space."

Celine nodded, her heart swelling with the knowledge that they were on the same page.

As they continued their search, attending open houses and debating the merits of each property, Celine found solace in knowing that Jemima was by her side, supporting her dreams just as passionately as she supported his. Together, they would create a space where their talents could flourish, and their love could continue to grow.

"Jemima," Celine whispered as they left the final open house of the day, "I think we've seen enough to make a decision. I can't wait to start this new chapter with you."

"Me neither," Jemima replied, her blue eyes filled with warmth and determination. "We'll find the perfect place, and together, we'll make it our home."

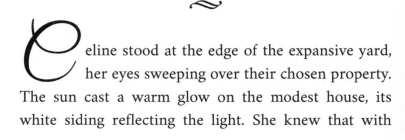

eline stood at the edge of the expansive yard, her eyes sweeping over their chosen property. The sun cast a warm glow on the modest house, its white siding reflecting the light. She knew that with some work, this place could become the home they'd both been dreaming of. Jemima walked up beside Celine, their hands found each others as they admired the view.

"Can you believe it? This could be ours soon," Celine said, her voice filled with excitement and anticipation.

"I can see it now," Jemima replied, giving her hand a gentle squeeze. "The two of us, building our dreams together right here."

"Let's not get ahead of ourselves," Celine cautioned playfully, her eyes dancing with mischief. "We still need to talk to the contractor about renovations."

They met with the local contractor, a sturdy middle-aged man named Frank, at a nearby coffee shop. Over steaming cups of java, they discussed the modifications they hoped to make to their potential new home.

"So, we're thinking about expanding the workshop for my woodworking," Jemima began, her blue eyes earnest. "And Celine needs a dedicated space for her mobile tattoo business."

"Of course," Frank nodded, scribbling notes onto a pad of paper. "What sort of changes are you considering for the interior?"

Celine chimed in, describing her vision for an airy, open-concept living area that would seamlessly flow into a cozy kitchen. As she spoke, she could see the sparks of inspiration igniting in Jemima's eyes, further fueling her own excitement.

"Sounds like you've got a clear idea of what you want," Frank said, closing his notepad. "I'll put together an estimate for you within the next couple of days."

"Thank you, Frank," Celine smiled warmly, grateful for his expertise.

With the contractor's guidance, they felt more confident about making an offer on the property. They approached the seller, eager to negotiate a mutually beneficial agreement. As they sat around the dining room table, Celine couldn't help but imagine the countless memories they'd create in this very space.

"Alright, we've looked over your offer," the seller, an older woman with kind eyes, said as she set down the papers. "We're willing to accept it, on the condition that you allow us a few extra weeks to move out."

"Of course," Jemima answered without hesitation, her hand instinctively reaching for Celine's beneath the table. "We understand that moving is a big process, and we want this transition to be as smooth as possible for all of us."

"Thank you," the woman said, her voice trembling with emotion. "This house has been our family home for years, and it means a lot to know that it's going to people who will cherish it just as much as we have."

Celine felt her heart swell with pride and gratitude as the final details were ironed out. She knew that this was just the beginning of their journey together, but she couldn't wait to see what the future held for them in Fountain Springs.

~

*C*eline stood at the edge of their newly acquired property, her eyes scanning the horizon as the sun dipped below the tree line. She inhaled deeply, relishing the scent of fresh grass and damp earth as a cool breeze rustled her golden hair. Beside her, Jemima let out a low whistle, her blue eyes alight with excitement.

"Can you believe this is ours now?" she asked, her voice tinged with awe.

"Hardly," Celine admitted, grinning as she nudged him playfully. "But I'm beyond excited to make this place our home."

"Then let's get started!" Jemima declared, wrapping an arm around her shoulders as they made their way inside.

The house was spacious but cozy, filled with natural light that streamed through the large windows. They wandered from room to room, discussing potential layouts and color schemes, their voices echoing off the bare walls.

"Okay, hear me out," Celine began as they entered the living room. "What if we painted this wall a deep teal and hung some of my artwork over there?"

"Ooh, I love that idea!" Jemima enthused, nodding vigorously. "And maybe we could have some built-in shelves for my woodworking pieces? We could even find a nice spot for a reading nook."

"Absolutely," Celine agreed, her imagination already racing with possibilities. "We'll have the most unique and beautiful home in Fountain Springs."

As they continued to plan, Celine couldn't help but marvel at how easily their ideas melded together. It felt like a testament to the strength of their bond, proof that their relationship was something truly special.

"Hey, what do you think about turning that small room into a workshop for me?" Jemima asked, interrupting her thoughts. "I've always wanted a dedicated space where I can work on my woodworking projects."

"Perfect!" Celine replied, her eyes sparkling with enthusiasm. "And maybe we could convert the garage into a studio for my tattoo business? It would be amazing to have everything right here at home."

"Absolutely," Jemima said, her warm smile making

Celine's heart skip a beat. "We'll make this place our very own creative haven."

Over the following weeks, they threw themselves into transforming their house into a home. Armed with paintbrushes and power tools, they worked side by side, laughter and music filling the air as they brought their vision to life.

As Celine stepped back to admire their handiwork one evening, she felt a surge of pride and contentment wash over her. This was more than just a house; it was a tangible representation of the life they were building together. And as she looked over at Jemima, covered in paint and grinning like a child, she knew without a doubt that they were exactly where they were meant to be.

~

Celine stood on the porch, a warm breeze rustling her hair as she surveyed the sprawling yard. The vibrant green grass was a stark contrast to the barren landscape they had inherited upon moving in. With the help of their new friends and neighbors, the once neglected property was now brimming with life. She couldn't help but smile at the thought of how far they'd come.

"Hey Celine, where do you want these potted plants?" called out Mandy, a friendly neighbor who lived just down the road. Her arms were laden with colorful flowers, ready to be strategically placed throughout the yard.

"Over by the front gate would be great! It'll add some charm when people walk up," Celine replied, her voice filled with excitement.

Jemima emerged from the house, wiping sweat from her brow. "Alright, I think the last coat of paint is drying in the living room. Thanks for all your help, everyone!"

"Of course, Jemima!" said another neighbor, Tom, as he cleaned off his paintbrush. "We're happy to have you both here in Fountain Springs."

As the day went on, Celine and Jemima worked alongside their friends and neighbors, painting fences, planting flowers, and grooming the property. The community's strong bond was evident in the way they rallied together to transform the space. Celine felt an overwhelming sense of gratitude for the support they had received.

"Can you believe this?" Celine whispered to Jemima as they paused for a moment, taking in the scene around them. "Our home is really coming together, thanks to everyone's help."

"I know," Jemima replied, her blue eyes filled with warmth as she looked at Celine. "All we need now is a proper celebration to thank everyone for their hard work."

"Sounds perfect," she agreed.

A week later, Celine and Jemima threw open the doors of their newly renovated home, hosting a house-warming party to express their gratitude. Laughter and music filled the air as neighbors mingled, sharing stories about life in Fountain Springs.

"Thank you all so much for helping us settle in," Celine said as she stood with Jemima in the center of the room, raising a glass in a toast. "We couldn't have done this without you, and we're so grateful to be part of such a wonderful community."

"Here's to new beginnings and lifelong friendships!" Jemima added, her voice full of sincerity.

The crowd raised their glasses in response, cheers and applause echoing through the room.

As the night wore on, Celine found herself leaning against Jemima, smiling at the sight of their friends dancing and chatting around them. She knew that this was more than just a party – it was a symbol of the love and support that surrounded them as they embarked on this new chapter in Fountain Springs.

"Thank you," she whispered softly into Jemima's ear, her heart swelling with happiness.

"For what?" Jemima asked, genuinely curious.

"For everything," Celine replied, her eyes locked onto Jemima's. "For bringing me here, for supporting my dreams, and for giving us a place to call home."

Jemima smiled warmly, pulling her close. "No need to thank me, Celine. I wouldn't want to be anywhere else but here, with you."

~

A soft, golden light filtered through the gallery windows as Celine carefully arranged her tattoo designs on display. The hum of excited chatter filled the air as people began to enter, admiring her intricate work that adorned the walls. She could feel Jemima's presence behind her, her strong hands resting gently on her shoulders as she whispered words of encouragement.

"Your work looks amazing, Celine. I'm so proud of you."

"Thank you," she replied softly, her heart swelling with gratitude. "I couldn't have done this without your support."

As the evening progressed, Celine found herself greeting guests and discussing her art with enthusiasm. Jemima, keeping a watchful eye on her throughout the night, ensured that she felt comfortable and confident in her element.

In turn, Celine accompanied Jemima to local wood-working events where she showcased her own master-pieces. They walked hand-in-hand through the bustling crowds, stopping at various booths to appreciate the craftsmanship on display. Celine marveled at Jemima's ability to create such beautiful pieces, each one reflecting her passion and dedication.

"Jemima, your work is incredible," Celine said, running her fingers along the smooth, polished surface of a wooden table she had crafted. "You've poured your heart and soul into these creations, and it shows."

Jemima smiled warmly, taking her hand. "You inspire me, Celine. Our life together in Fountain Springs has given me the motivation to pursue my dreams."

Throughout these events, they shared countless conversations about their aspirations and the future they were building together. Celine's thoughts often drifted to the day they decided to settle down in Fountain Springs, and how deeply intertwined their lives had become since then.

"Sometimes, I still can't believe we're here, doing all of this together," Celine mused aloud during one of their quiet moments together.

"Neither can I," Jemima admitted, her eyes mirroring

Celine's wonderment. "But I know that we're exactly where we're meant to be."

As they continued to support one another, Celine and Jemima found that their dreams were no longer solitary pursuits. Instead, they had become shared visions for a life filled with love, passion, and creativity.

"Promise me something," Celine asked, her eyes glistening with hope.

"Anything," Jemima replied, her voice full of conviction.

"Promise me that we'll never stop chasing our dreams, together."

"Of course," Jemima said without hesitation, pulling her close as they made a silent vow to keep pushing each other towards greatness.

And so, hand-in-hand, Celine and Jemima continued to navigate the complex world of art and craftsmanship, their love and support serving as the foundation upon which their dreams took flight.

CHAPTER 23

The celebration in Fountain Springs was nothing short of magical. As twilight settled over the town, the quaint buildings that lined the cobblestone streets seemed to shimmer with a warm glow. Twinkling lights were strung from the rooftops, casting a soft, inviting luminescence on the faces of those who passed by. Celine couldn't help but be captivated by the picturesque beauty of her surroundings, feeling as if she had stepped into a scene from a fairy tale.

"Can you believe this place?" she murmured to herself, her eyes sparkling with wonder.

As they approached the venue, the festive atmosphere grew even more enchanting. Colorful banners swayed gently in the breeze, their vibrant hues a testament to the joy and love shared by all in attendance. Fairy lights adorned the trees and fences, their delicate glow casting an ethereal aura over the entire space. The floral arrangements were a breathtaking sight, with lush bouquets of roses, hydrangeas, and peonies artfully arranged on tables and along walkways. Celine marveled at the exquisite display, struck by the sheer effort and attention to detail that had gone into creating such a romantic setting.

"Wow," Jemima breathed, echoing Celine's thoughts. "They really outdid themselves, didn't they?"

Celine nodded, too mesmerized to form words. She glanced over at Jemima, noting the way her blue eyes sparkled with appreciation. It warmed her heart to see her so captivated, sharing in her awe of the beautiful scene before them.

"Let's go in," she suggested, her voice barely above a whisper. "I don't want to miss a single moment of this."

Hand in hand, they stepped into the celebration, eager to join their friends and loved ones in the night's festivities. Surrounded by the vibrant decorations and the gentle hum of conversation, laughter, and music, Celine and Jemima couldn't help but feel a sense of serenity and contentment. In that moment, they knew that the love they shared was not only cherished by them but also celebrated by their community.

As they mingled with friends, Celine's thoughts drifted back to the journey that had led her here – the late-night conversations with Jemima, their shared dreams, and the support they had received from those around them. She took a deep breath, her heart swelling with gratitude, and she knew that this magical night would be one she would treasure forever.

~

*C*eline felt the warmth of Jemima's hand in hers as they stepped into the celebration, their fingers intertwined. She looked up at Jemima, her eyes brimming with happiness, and saw that same joy mirrored back in her blue eyes. They both radiated love and contentment, like the sun shining brightly on a clear summer day.

"Ready to dive in?" Jemima asked, giving her hand a gentle squeeze.

"Absolutely," Celine replied, her heart swelling with anticipation.

Their attire showcased their individual styles and personalities – Celine's flowing, floral dress highlighted the artist within her, with its vibrant colors and intricate patterns. Her blonde hair was swept up into an elegant bun, adorned with delicate wildflowers she had collected earlier in the day. Jemima, on the other hand, wore a crisp white silk blouse, rolled up at the sleeves, paired with dark jeans and polished shoes. Her dark hair framed her kind face, and her warm smile seemed to light up the room.

As they entered the venue, Celine and Jemima were greeted by a sea of familiar faces. Friends and family members approached them, offering warm hugs and heartfelt congratulations.

"Congratulations, you two!" Aunt Lucy exclaimed, pulling Celine into a tight embrace. "I'm so happy for you both!"

"Thank you, Aunt Lucy," Celine replied, her voice choked with emotion. "It means the world to us that you're here."

"Jemima," Uncle Frank chimed in, clapping him on the back. "You've found yourself a real gem in Celine! I always knew you two were perfect for each other."

"Thanks, Uncle Frank," Jemima responded, her cheeks flushing with pride. "I couldn't agree more."

As they continued to mingle, Celine felt a surge of gratitude for the strong bonds they had formed with their loved ones. She marveled at how effortlessly Jemima fitted into her family, and how easily her friends had welcomed her into their circle. It was as if she had always been a part of her life.

"Can you believe it?" Celine whispered to Jemima, looking around at all the people who had gathered to celebrate their love. "All these people are here for us."

Jemima leaned in, her breath warm on her ear as she replied, "I can't think of two people more deserving of such a celebration."

It was in that moment that Celine truly understood the depth of their connection – not just with each other, but with the community they had built around them. As they continued to share joyful conversations and laughter with their loved ones, she knew that this night would be etched in her heart forever.

~

*A*s the evening progressed, the atmosphere inside the quaint venue buzzed with excitement and joy. Celine and Jemima found themselves in the midst of a lively conversation with their closest friends, laughter ringing through the air as playful banter was exchanged.

"Alright, Celine," teased Laura, one of her longtime friends, "I've got to ask – who would've thought that a city girl like you would fall head over heels for our very own small-town charmer?"

Celine playfully rolled her eyes, unable to suppress a

grin. "Well, it's not every day that you meet someone as genuine and kind-hearted as Jemima, you know," she replied, giving her hand a gentle squeeze.

Jemima chuckled, joining in on the fun. "And I still can't believe that this talented artist fell for me, of all people. But hey, love works in mysterious ways, right?"

The group erupted into laughter once more, their shared sense of humor and camaraderie evident in every interaction. As they continued to jest and share stories, Celine couldn't help but marvel at the beautiful tapestry of relationships they had woven together over time.

In the midst of the laughter, the sound of a fork tapping against a glass caught everyone's attention. The room hushed as one of Celine's closest friends, Vanessa, stood up, raising her glass in preparation for a toast.

"First of all," Vanessa began, her eyes glistening with emotion, "I'd like to say how incredibly honored I am to be here tonight, celebrating the love story that is Celine and Jemima. From the moment Celine first told me about her online friend, I knew there was something special about Jemima. And when they finally met in person, it became clear that their connection was nothing short of magical."

She paused for a moment, taking a deep breath before continuing. "Through trials and tribulations, distance and doubt, their love for one another has only grown stronger. And as we stand here tonight, witnessing the union of these two beautiful souls, I can't help but feel an overwhelming sense of happiness and pride."

Celine felt her eyes brimming with tears as Vanessa's heartfelt words resonated throughout the room. She glanced at Jemima, whose own eyes were shining with emotion, and squeezed her hand tightly.

"Here's to Celine and Jemima," Vanessa concluded, raising her glass even higher. "May your life together be filled with love, laughter, and endless moments of joy. Cheers!"

The room erupted in a chorus of cheers and applause, glasses clinking together in celebration. As they took a moment to bask in the warmth of the love and support that surrounded them, Celine and Jemima knew that they had truly found something rare and precious – a love that would stand the test of time.

~

*A*s the applause and cheers began to fade, Celine gently tugged at Jemima' hand, her eyes sparkling with a sense of adventure. "Come on, let's get some fresh air," she whispered, leading her away from the bustling crowd. Their loved ones continued to celebrate around them, their laughter echoing through the charming small-town venue.

Upon stepping outside, they found themselves in a quiet corner of the cobblestone courtyard, where twinkling fairy lights illuminated the night. The cool evening breeze brushed against their skin as they leaned against an old stone wall, enjoying the serenity of the moment.

"Can you believe it, Jemima? We've come so far together," Celine murmured, her voice brimming with gratitude. She glanced up at her, her blue eyes reflecting the soft glow of the lights above.

Jemima smiled warmly, her gaze tender and full of admiration. "I can hardly believe it myself, Celine. From messaging each other online to standing here now, it feels like a dream."

"Thank you for always being there for me," she said, reaching out to touch her arm gently. "Your unwavering support has meant everything to me."

"Likewise, Celine," she replied, her hand covering hers. "You've brought so much joy and color into my life, and I couldn't be more grateful."

Just then, the sweet melody of a slow song drifted from the celebration indoors, inviting the couple to dance. Jemima extended her hand, and Celine accepted without hesitation. With a graceful twirl, she stepped into Jemima's embrace, their bodies swaying in perfect harmony.

As they danced under the starry sky, the world around them seemed to vanish. The intimate connection they shared deepened with every step, every gentle brush of their fingertips. Celine rested her head on Jemima's shoulder, her heart swelling with love and contentment. She could feel the reassuring strength in her arms, the steady rhythm of her heartbeat.

"Jemima," she whispered, her voice full of emotion. "Promise me that we'll always be there for each other, through thick and thin."

"I promise, Celine," she replied, her voice filled with conviction. "There's nothing that could ever tear us apart."

The song came to a close, but their dance continued long after the music had faded away. And as they held each other under the shimmering lights of Fountain Springs, they knew that they had found their happily ever after. A love that would stand the test of time, an unbreakable bond that would only grow stronger with each passing day.

*a*fter sharing their heartfelt promises beneath the starry sky, Celine and Jemima returned to the celebration hand in hand, their eyes shining with love and devotion. The atmosphere inside the venue was electric, the laughter and chatter of their friends and family mingling with the romantic melodies that filled the air.

"Are you ready for this?" Jemima asked, her voice tinged with excitement as they stood before the grand wedding cake.

Celine bit her lip, her heart pounding with anticipation. "I've never been more ready for anything in my life," she replied, her fingers tightening around Jemima' hand. Their connection felt more profound than ever, each beat of their hearts echoing the other's.

The cake itself was a masterpiece, a testament to Celine's artistic talents and Jemima' unwavering support. It stood tall and proud, adorned with intricate sugar flowers and delicate vines that seemed to dance around its tiers. The pale blush frosting shimmered in the candlelight, reflecting the warmth and love that enveloped the room.

Together, they grasped the knife and cut through the first layer of the cake, symbolizing their unity and shared future. The sound of joyous cheers and applause erupted from the crowd, their loved ones eager to share in this momentous occasion.

"Here's to the start of our journey together," Jemima whispered, offering Celine the first bite of cake on the tip of the knife. She opened her mouth, closing her eyes as the rich flavors danced across her tongue - a perfect blend of sweetness and depth, much like their love.

As Celine savored the taste, she couldn't help but think back to the early days of their friendship. How they had laughed and confided in each other, the spark between them growing brighter with each conversation. And now, standing beside the love of her life, she knew that they had made the right decision in pursuing a life together.

"Thank you, Jemima," she murmured, her voice choked with emotion as she met Jemima's gaze. "For believing in me, for loving me, and for making me the happiest woman alive."

"Thank you for being you, Celine," she replied, her eyes shining with love. "And for showing me what it truly means to live and love without fear."

As they fed each other another bite of cake, their friends and family gathered around them, snapping pictures and cheering them on. It was a moment that would be forever etched in their memories - the beginning of their new life together, bound by love and an unbreakable bond.

Amidst the laughter and well-wishes, Celine couldn't help but feel an overwhelming sense of gratitude for the life they had built together, and the love that continued to blossom between them. And as she looked into Jemima's eyes, she knew that this was just the beginning of their story - a tale of love, adventure, and endless possibilities.

~

The warmth of the setting sun cast a golden glow over the celebration, illuminating the faces of Celine and Jemima's nearest and dearest as they gathered around the newlyweds. The laughter and happy chatter filled the air, creating a harmonious symphony of love and support.

"Everyone, please join us in forming a circle around Celine and Jemima," urged Aunt Clara, her voice brimming with emotion. Friends and family members eagerly obliged, linking arms and holding hands as they encircled the couple. The connection between them was palpable, a physical manifestation of the unwavering love that surrounded Celine and Jemima.

Tears glistened in many eyes as they looked upon the

couple, their hearts swelling with joy at the sight of their happiness. The circle seemed to act as a protective barrier, shielding them from any negativity or doubts that may have once plagued their minds.

"Thank you all for being here with us today," Celine said, her voice warm and sincere. "We couldn't have done this without your love and support."

Jemima nodded in agreement, her hand instinctively reaching for Celine's. "You've all played an integral role in our journey, both as individuals and as a couple. We're truly grateful to have you in our lives."

As the words of gratitude hung in the air, the circle tightened ever so slightly, each person drawing nearer to the couple as if to physically embody their unyielding support. Tears streamed down cheeks, smiles broadened, and the happiness in the air reached a crescendo that threatened to sweep them all away.

Soon after, Celine and Jemima found themselves alone on the cobblestone patio, the last rays of sunlight casting a warm glow on their surroundings. They stood close together, foreheads touching and hands entwined, reveling in their newfound unity.

"Can you believe it, Jemima?" Celine whispered, her eyes locked onto hers. "We're finally here."

"Believe it?" Jemima echoed, a smile tugging at the

corners of her mouth. "I've been dreaming of this moment since the day we first met."

As they stood there, wrapped in each other's embrace, the world around them seemed to fade away. All that remained was the love that flowed between them, stronger and more vibrant than ever before.

"We did it, Celine," Jemima murmured, pressing her lips lightly against her forehead. "We found our happily ever after."

Celine's heart swelled with joy, her own sense of contentment mirrored in Jemima's beautiful blue eyes. Together, hand in hand, they had triumphed over every obstacle life had thrown their way, emerging stronger and more united than they had ever been before.

"Here's to forever, my love," she whispered, sealing their promise with a tender kiss.

~

The sun dipped below the horizon, casting a warm golden hue over the quaint town of Fountain Springs. Celine and Jemima stood hand in hand, gazing out at the picturesque scene before them while friends and family continued to celebrate inside. With laughter and joy echoing through the air, they allowed themselves a brief glimpse into their future together.

"Can you imagine it, Jemima?" Celine asked softly, her eyes filled with hope. "Our little house here in Fountain Springs, surrounded by our loved ones and the community that has embraced us both."

Jemima squeezed her hand gently, her voice full of certainty. "I can see it so clearly, Celine. You, continuing your art and bringing beauty to this town with your tattoo studio. And me, supporting you every step of the way, as we build a life that's uniquely ours."

Celine smiled, envisioning the cozy home they would create, adorned with her paintings and the memories they would forge together. She imagined the community gatherings they would host, and the friendships that would only deepen with time. The love between them, a beacon that would continue to light their path.

"Can you hear it, too?" she wondered aloud, her heart soaring with anticipation. "The laughter of our friends and neighbors stopping by to share stories and good times?"

"I can," Jemima replied, her eyes shining with love and determination. "And, if you want to have children, there are ways we could do that, and make this a family home. And I promise you, Celine, that we will make whatever you decide a reality. Together, we'll nurture our dreams, overcome any challenges, and find happiness in every moment."

As they turned back towards the celebration, the sense of hope and possibility enveloped them like a warm embrace. The cheers from their loved ones carried on the gentle breeze, lifting their spirits and filling them with an overwhelming sense of gratitude for all they had found in each other.

"Here's to our future, Celine," Jemima whispered, pressing a tender kiss to her temple. "A lifetime of love, laughter, and endless possibilities."

"Here's to us," Celine agreed, her voice full of conviction. And as they stepped back into the welcoming arms of their friends and family, the promise of a bright and beautiful future unfurled before them, waiting to be written in the stars.

~

Months had passed since the celebration, and the charming town of Fountain Springs continued to embrace the love story of Celine and Jemima. Autumn had arrived, painting the landscape in hues of gold and russet, as if reflecting the warmth and passion that permeated their lives.

"Jemima, it's perfect!" Celine exclaimed, her eyes sparkling with delight as she surveyed the cozy art studio they had built together. The room was filled with sunlight, casting a luminous glow over the easels, brushes, and vibrant paints that awaited her artistic touch.

"Your talent deserves the best space to flourish," Jemima replied, wrapping her arms around Celine. "And I'll always be here to support you, in every way."

Celine turned to face her, with a heart swelling with gratitude. "Thank you, my love. Your belief in me means everything."

"Hey, what are partners for?" she teased, pressing a soft kiss to her lips.

"Speaking of partners," Celine mused, "I heard from Anna this morning. She's organizing a charity art auction next month and wants us to contribute some pieces."

"Sounds like a great opportunity for us to give back to the community," Jemima said, excitement evident in her voice. "What do you say we start brainstorming ideas tonight?"

"Deal," Celine agreed, her mind already whirring with possibilities

As they delved into their work, laughter and light-hearted banter filled the air, testament to the deep bond they shared. They took breaks to share tender kisses and whispered words of encouragement, nurturing the love that had grown stronger with each passing day.

Later, as twilight painted the sky in shades of lavender and rose, Celine and Jemima walked hand in hand through the cobblestone streets of Fountain Springs. Their neighbors greeted them with warm smiles and friendly waves, a testament to the strong connections they had forged within the community.

"Sometimes, I still can't believe how much our lives have changed," Celine confessed, her gaze locked with Jemima's. "But every step of this journey has led us to where we are now, and I wouldn't trade it for anything."

"Neither would I," Jemima agreed, giving her hand a gentle squeeze. "We've built something truly special here, and I know that our future together will be filled with love, laughter, and countless memories."

As they strolled beneath the canopy of twinkling fairy lights, their hearts brimming with hope and contentment, it was clear that Celine and Jemima had found their happily ever after in each other's arms. And as the night deepened and the streets grew quiet, the vibrant melody of their love story continued to unfold, echoing through the quaint town of Fountain Springs.

Milton Keynes UK
Ingram Content Group UK Ltd.
UKHW041820211123
432980UK00001BB/72